**Martin reached out impulsively to pull her close. . . .**

It was a natural action on his part, a desire to console her after a harsh experience, and she knew no more than that could be read into it. But Tansy wanted to slip her arms around him and take far more than consolation from this closeness. She pulled away self-consciously, afraid she might give in to the temptation.

He immediately became self-conscious as well. "Please don't misinterpret, for I meant nothing. . . ."

"I know you didn't, and I haven't misinterpreted," she replied quickly. "It's just that I felt a rather childish urge to cling to you for comfort, and that would indeed have been open to misinterpretation." She managed to give him a quick smile. Childish was the very last thing her stifled urge had been!

The smile was reciprocated. "I'm sure I would have taken the impulse for what it was, because I am equally sure that you would never behave forwardly or improperly in any way."

*No, but I would* like *to,* she thought ruefully. When he walked into the hidden room at Tel el-Osorkon, her senses had awakened from a lifetime of slumber. One arresting glance of his dark eyes had sealed her fate, sending abandoned emotions leaping through her veins. Oh, such wonderful, spellbinding emotions. As if she had been waiting for him.

# Playing with Fire

## Sandra Heath

A SIGNET BOOK

SIGNET
Published by New American Library, a division of
Penguin Putnam Inc., 375 Hudson Street,
New York, New York 10014, U.S.A.
Penguin Books Ltd, 80 Strand,
London WC2R 0RL, England
Penguin Books Australia Ltd, Ringwood,
Victoria, Australia
Penguin Books Canada Ltd, 10 Alcorn Avenue,
Toronto, Ontario, Canada M4V 3B2
Penguin Books (N.Z.) Ltd, 182–190 Wairau Road,
Auckland 10, New Zealand

Penguin Books Ltd, Registered Offices:
Harmondsworth, Middlesex, England

First published by Signet, an imprint of New American Library,
a division of Penguin Putnam Inc.

First Printing, March 2002
10  9  8  7  6  5  4  3  2  1

PUBLISHER'S NOTE
This is a work of fiction. Names, characters, places, and incidents either
are the product of the author's imagination or are used fictitiously,
and any resemblance to actual persons, living or dead, business
establishments, events, or locales is entirely coincidental.

# 1

Sir Julian's large ginger tomcat, Ozzy—short for Ozymandias—had been curled up asleep on a fireside chair for some time, but now awoke with a low growl. The sound was quite bloodcurdling in the silence of the vaulted library at Chelworth. Sir Julian looked up from the fragment of papyrus he had been studying. Both he and his pet knew they were no longer alone, because the dark green brocade curtains moved, and then the candle flame shivered as someone stealthily opened the glass doors from the south terrace. Whoever it was did not speak or make any attempt to reveal his or her presence.

For a moment the sea could be heard crashing on the rocks down in the bay; then the draft subsided as the doors were closed again. Whoever it was had no legitimate business at the house, that much was certain. Sir Julian, middle-aged and none too strong, reached for the beautifully carved and polished alabaster beetle, called a scarab, that he used as a paperweight.

It was November, 1800, and the last chime of midnight had just faded. Coals glowed faintly in the hearth of the marble fireplace, and the candle on the desk cast only a poor light in the lofty chamber. Shadows cast gloom over the Ancient Egyptian statuary and formed a cloak over furniture of the style the French called *pharaonique*. A great deal of Egypt had found its way to the remote estate on the heath above

Chelworth Bay in Dorset. The house itself had recently been extensively improved to resemble a temple plucked from the banks of the Nile.

The golden tassel of Sir Julian's scarlet nightcap shone in the candlelight as he gazed uneasily at the drawn curtains. He was a tall, thin man of fifty-six, with an aquiline nose, kindly brown eyes, and graying hair that he always cropped very short and hid beneath a wig. He wore a floor-length blue paisley dressing robe over a nightshirt, and his bare feet were tucked into Turkish slippers, for he had been on the point of retiring when impulse had brought him to the library again. It was his great dream to be the first man to decipher hieroglyphs, and to that end he often worked well into the night; but hieroglyphs were banished from his mind as he sought to quieten Ozzy.

"Hush, you fool of a cat!" he breathed, then spoke aloud to the unseen intruder. "I know you're there; so show yourself, damn you!" No one responded; so with a shaking hand Sir Julian replaced the scarab on the desk, pulled open a drawer instead, and took out the pistol he kept there.

At last the curtain moved, and a young man of about thirty emerged. He was of the highest *ton,* as was abundantly clear from the immaculate cut of his indigo velvet coat, white silk waistcoat and breeches, to the rich lace on his shirt and the flawless sapphire pin in his starched neck cloth. No low thief he, but a gentleman to his fingertips. Strong and well proportioned, with his long fair hair tied back with a black ribbon, Randal Fenworth, sixth Earl of Sanderby, was the coldhearted, ruthless son of Sir Julian's late adversary, the fifth earl. But for all his arrogance and harshness, he was ultimately a coward, although no one in society had yet tested him to the point of finding out.

Outraged by the intruder's effrontery, Sir Julian rose to his feet. "Sanderby!"

"The same." Randal's blue eyes were cold as he swept an insolent bow.

"How dare you come here!" The pistol was leveled with a quivering hand.

Randal hesitated, but only slightly. "Richardson, if I wish to speak to you, I have no choice but to come here. Mahomet and mountains, and so on."

"I cannot imagine why you wish to speak to me, for I most certainly do not wish to speak to you." Sir Julian could not conceal his loathing for all things Fenworth.

"I am disappointed, for I expected more of you than to brand the son with the imagined sins of the father."

"There was nothing imagined about what your father did," Sir Julian answered coldly. "Besides, you have sins enough of your own." Randal's excesses were known throughout society.

"I like to enjoy myself to the full, as I rather fancy you once did. Or does it please you to forget your own dissipations?"

Dissipations? For a moment Sir Julian's mind wandered. Long ago he and Randal's father, Esmond, had been fellow antiquarians, sharing a passion for the land of the pharaohs. It was all that had brought them together, for in character they were as unalike as chalk and cheese, but solving the mysteries of hieroglyphs had united them. Their efforts had been in vain, and even today antiquarians across Europe still strove to find the key to Ancient Egypt's inscriptions. But all those years ago, he, Julian Richardson, believed he had stumbled upon the answer, or at least, the first step toward the answer. It was then that Esmond revealed his true colors, destroying all the research in a fit of jealous rage, and substituting his own unlikely theories to the Society of Antiquaries, claiming they were Julian's.

Julian had been derided as a blinkered, misguided fool, and so complete had been his humiliation that he had retreated here to Chelworth. He had seldom returned to London since then, nor had he forgiven the Society for allowing Esmond to belittle him before the entire antiquarian world. The names Fenworth and Sanderby continued to be anathema even now.

Guilt stabbed through Sir Julian, for although it had always suited him to blame Esmond's professional jealousy for all that had happened, rivalry and jealousy of a very different kind had been as much the culprits. Esmond had been a cuckolded husband thirsting for revenge upon his wife's lover—not that he was any ordinary husband, or that the lover regretted so much as a single kiss. And not that the new Lord Sanderby knew of his mother's adultery. At least, that was Sir Julian's fervent hope, although the use of the word *dissipations* was somewhat disquieting.

Randal watched the older man's face. "Well? Have you no reply?"

"Just that I wish you to leave this house."

"First I will say my piece."

"No, damn your eyes, you'll leave *now*!" cried Sir Julian, steadying the aim of the pistol with both hands. It was strange to find himself face-to-face with Felice's son after all this time. Oh, how she had treasured this boy; were she still alive, how wretched she would be to see he had turned out not in her mold, but in that of his despicable father.

The sound of Sir Julian's raised voice agitated Ozzy. Ginger fur on end and back arched, he jumped down from the chair. To Sir Julian's surprise, Randal stepped nervously back. "Keep that brute away from me, or so help me I'll wring its neck," he warned. However, it wasn't fear of being attacked that moved him, but an acute susceptibility to cat fur. His nose had begun to tickle not long after he entered the library; now his eyes had started watering. Cats always seemed to sense his affliction, and in his opinion took perverse delight in triggering it.

"Ozymandias!" Sir Julian spoke sharply, fearing that Randal was the sort of scoundrel to kick an animal. The tomcat's ears went back resentfully, but he sat down where he was and confined himself to fixing

Randal with the sort of feline glare that might well have prompted even the saint of Assisi to think twice.

Randal gave an enormous sneeze and fished a large handkerchief from his pocket. "Get him right away from me," he repeated.

"I don't know why I should tell my cat to do anything at all. He lives here and is at liberty to come and go as he pleases. You, however, have no right at all in this house."

"How very ungracious you are, to be sure," Randal said softly.

"You are surely not surprised? Your father ruined me in antiquarian circles, and set the interpretation of hieroglyphs back by years."

Randal walked toward the desk. "Who are you to criticize my father when your own conduct does not stand up to close inspection?"

Did the fellow know about the affair with Felice? Sir Julian tried not to show anything. "We have absolutely nothing to say to each other, Sanderby."

"On the contrary, I have some excellent news to impart."

"News?"

Randal had forgotten that in order to approach Sir Julian, it was necessary to go nearer to Ozzy as well. He knew his error within seconds, for his eyes began to stream all the more. Now would come the impossibility of pronouncing the letter *M*. Instead a *B* would be substituted, with unfortunately comic results. However, having advanced to confront Sir Julian at close quarters, Randal had no intention of immediately performing a craven retreat, so he stood his ground. "We bust talk, Richardson, whether you like it or not."

*Bust* talk? Sir Julian looked at him in bewilderment. What was the matter with the fellow?

Randal went on. "As you are . . . er, paterfabilias, so to speak, I ab here to seek your blessing." *Damn* that confounded feline!

Sir Julian became very still. "Paterfamilias?" he repeated cautiously

"Yes. There is good news frob Constantinople. I ab to be barried to your niece. I refer to Abanda, of course, not Tansy, for it wouldn't do to ally byself to the penurious branch of the fabily." Randal tried to maintain his dignity, even though he knew how silly he sounded. In one thing he had definitely not been silly, however, and that was his choice of bride. Of Sir Julian's two brothers, it was Franklyn not Bertram who married into wealth; therefore it was Franklyn's daughter who was the great heiress.

Sir Julian was both bemused by Randal's sudden speech impediment and dismayed by the news he imparted. "Marry Amanda? You're lying! My brother Franklyn wouldn't—"

"Oh, but he would. Your tarnished reputation as an antiquarian beans little when his daughter has the chance to be Lady Sanderby. Oh, *dab* that cat!"

Sir Julian suddenly realized that Ozzy was the cause of Randal's speech problems. The new Earl of Sanderby wasn't *afraid* of cats; he was excessively sensitive to their fur!

Randal's eyes ran with tears, which he mopped with a large handkerchief as he continued. "Abanda herself is very anxious to proceed with the batch. You see, I have been low enough to secretly correspond with her. I write a very passionate letter, very passionate indeed, and she is very spoiled, vain, and, er, gullible."

Shocked, Sir Julian gazed at the younger man in disgust. "You are base, sir, base beyond belief!"

It was water off this duck's back. "Abanda is quite a beauty," Randal said, taking an oval miniature from his pocket, and glancing down at the golden-haired lovely smiling from it.

Sir Julian was goaded. "If you think I'm going to stand by and—"

Randal interrupted. "And what? There's nothing you can do about it! I ab at liberty to barry where I please, and by bride is bore than willing." He sneezed again before putting the miniature away. Then he raised a slender finger to the barrel of the pistol and turned it safely aside. "Oh, don't think I ab barrying Abanda entirely out of spite, for I ab not. She suits because she is pretty and will bake be even bore wealthy. The fact that she is your niece is but the jewel in the crown. Dear brother Franklyn has agreed to everything. The barriage contract is signed and sealed, and when he leaves Constantinople for his new post in Australia, he is quite happy for Abanda and Tansy to sail for England in the care of a chaperone. When they arrive—always assubing they do, of course, there being such hazards as pirates, storbs, shipwrecks, and even the French—he wishes theb to reside here with you until the wedding. He is engagingly sure that your pleasure for Abanda will outweigh your personal antipathy toward by fabily. By the way, she is woefully vain and indiscreet."

"I'll see you in Hades before I let you marry my flesh and blood!" Sir Julian cried, so bitterly angry that his voice broke.

Ozzy was provoked beyond endurance. With a horrible yowl, he again leaped down from his chair to march upon the unwelcome intruder. Randal snatched the pistol from Sir Julian, turned it upon the tomcat, and squeezed the trigger.

# 2

$\mathcal{B}$ut there was only a hollow click when Randal fired the pistol at Ozymandias. It wasn't loaded! Sir Julian smiled. "An old man's foolishness, I'm afraid," he murmured.

"Dab you, Richardson!" The pistol was flung away.

"Oh, I've been damned for quite a long time now, Sanderby." *Ever since your mother decided to stay with your father, in spite of his crimes.* Sir Julian turned to Ozzy. "Come here to me, you foolish old boy," he coaxed.

The tomcat obeyed, leaping up to the desk beside Randal, who jerked back out of the way as if splashed with boiling oil. He couldn't evade the fur that floated invisibly in the air, and sneezed again anyway. Sir Julian immediately evinced concern. "Oh, dear, have you caught a cold? It's the Dorset air, you know, especially at this time of year."

"Don't bake the bistake of bocking me, Richardson!" Randal snapped, at the same time blowing his nose like a trumpet. Ozzy sat facing him, paws neatly together, ginger tail curled around them. He squeezed his big amber eyes, pleased with the effect he had.

Randal gazed at Sir Julian through a shimmer of tears. "I ab going to barry Abanda, and there is nothing you can do about it. Perhaps you should regard it as a chance to bake abends for the bonstrous accusations you hurled at by father when your idiotic theories about hieroglyphs were set before the Society of Antiquaries."

Sir Julian regarded him across the candle flame. "They were not my theories. Your father presented them as mine, after destroying all my work."

"I ab shocked that you should speak ill of the dead. Ah, but we bust not forget that the rift between you and my father concerned far bore than a bisunderstanding between brother philoaegyptians. It involved by dear baba's adventures outside the barital bed. She was your bistress, was she not, Richardson?"

Sir Julian's heart sank, but outwardly he remained composed. If it was the last thing he did, he would protect Felice's good name. "What on earth are you talking about?" he inquired, feigning complete bewilderment.

Randal smiled again. "Bethinks you know exactly what I ab talking about."

"Your mother, God rest her lovely soul, was not my mistress, nor indeed any man's mistress." Sir Julian met Randal's eyes squarely and stroked Ozzy, who began to purr.

"Liar," Randal breathed.

Sir Julian coolly changed the subject. "Sanderby, my niece Amanda may be beautiful, and an heiress, but you obviously feel nothing for her. If you had an ounce of decency, you'd withdraw from this shabby contract right now."

Randal blew his nose again, then sniffed. "And who, pray, are you to lecture be on decency? Don't think you can deflect be frob by purpose, because no abount of denial will alter the fact that by adulterous baba adorned your bed."

"You are wrong, but it is your prerogative to think as you please."

"I think a great deal where you are concerned, Richardson. You oppose by barriage to Abanda for purely personal reasons. After all, she will hardly be baking a bisalliance, will she?"

"Any alliance with the Fenworths is a misalliance."
*And never more so than if you are the bridegroom,*
came Sir Julian's added thought, which he kept to
himself.

Randal spread his hand, seeming the picture of innocence. "Why? Ab I or ab I not one of the forebost
earls in the land?" But in spite of the apparent absence of guile in his voice, his red-rimmed eyes were
fixed upon Sir Julian, watching, waiting, alert.

"Oh, I'm well aware of your lofty title and its ancient lineage; make no mistake of that! My family only
descends from a successful Bristol merchant who
flourished early last century; you, however, can name
your noble ancestors as far back as Crécy. Or so I
believe the story goes."

"Oh, the story goes, Richardson, the story goes."
Randal felt the onset of another bout of sneezing.
Dear God, why couldn't the old fool have had a dog?

Sir Julian stopped stroking Ozzy. "Look, Sanderby,
I don't know exactly what your purpose is in all this.
A note would have sufficed to tell me your so-called
good news."

"A note? Ah, yes, the power of the written word."
Randal gave a thin smile to see the mask that was Sir
Julian's face. "I can see in your eyes that it is true
about you and Baba. Oh, the ghosts that are with us
now, eh?"

Ghosts indeed, Sir Julian thought. Esmond had died
in a duel with a man he tried to cheat at cards; Felice,
so adored by her lover, so held in contempt by her
so-called husband, had died alone of influenza at
Sanderby Park in Westmorland. Sir Julian managed to
hold back his tears. "Who told you this fairy tale
about your mother and me?"

"By father left a diary, which I have only recently
discovered. It was in very poor condition, and in light
of its contents, you bay be sure I have been careful
to destroy it."

Ozzy ventured to growl again, then paused in anticipation of his master's tapping finger on the top of his

head. When none came, he continued to growl, curling his lips back to show a fine set of needle-sharp teeth.

Sir Julian gave a short laugh. "Well, I do not doubt that any journal composed by your father contained as much pure fiction as the theories he pretended were mine."

Randal's watering eyes were reptilian. "Have done with the pretence, Richardson, for I ab not gulled. She is long gone and cannot suffer now. We are alone; so what possible harb can it do to confess the truth?"

"Only someone who is not a gentleman could express such a view." But even as he spoke, Julian knew that his own gentlemanly conduct did not extend indefinitely. Felice, beloved as she was, was in fact his *second* consideration; the first was, and always would be, a young man whose whereabouts remained as much a mystery now as it had all those years ago. Did Randal also know about him?

Randal's gimlet gaze remained fixed upon him. "Well, I suppose dear Abanda bust weigh your conscience a little. It wouldn't do for society to snicker because the bride's uncle once had a passionate affair with the bridegroob's bother."

Sir Julian's dislike bubbled up. "Dear God, you are a mirror of your vile father."

"Oh, I do not deny that Papa had his bad points, but it obviously has not occurred to you that it bay have been the result of being barried to a whore. One always has to wonder which cabe first, the chicken or the egg."

A nerve twitched at Sir Julian's temple. "Get out of this house," he whispered, and Ozzy, sensing the intensifying atmosphere, spat at Randal.

The latter deemed it a prudent moment to comply. "Very well. I've had enough of these pleasantries, anyway. I cabe to test the lie of the land, and I fear you bake me very nervous, Richardson. So be rebinded of by fabily's botto, *Noli tangere igneb*." He meant to say *ignem,* but Ozzy's fur prevented that. The motto meant *Do not stir up fire.*

"Maybe your own fingers will be burned, or had that not occurred to you?"

"You are no batch for be." Randal gave a mirthless chuckle that was stopped by another drenching sneeze. He blew his nose like a trumpet, then continued. "Your lips will rebain sealed because Abanda is going to wear by ring and grace by bed. Oh, and her fortune is going to fatten by purse. It seebs a shame to leave poor Tansy out of things, but she really isn't worth having. But then again, plain and penniless febales often learn arts to bake them bore interesting between the sheets, so I bight bake her by bistress. To return your favor of the past, so to speak."

"Lay one finger upon Tansy, and I swear I will—!"

"You'll what?" Randal's glance was freezing.

Sir Julian despised the other so much that for a moment he could not even bear to look at him. Tansy was the only child of his younger brother, Bertram, who had died two years ago, and she had gone to Constantinople to live with Franklyn as company for Amanda. Franklyn was with the Foreign Office, and until recently had been appointed to assist Lord Elgin, British ambassador extraordinary to the sultan of Turkey. Now had come the new post in Australia, to which his daughter and niece were clearly no longer accompanying him.

Sir Julian had never been entirely happy about Tansy residing with Franklyn, suspecting she would be treated little better than a servant. Her father, Bertram, had been something of a ne'er-do-well, squandering his fortune and leaving his motherless daughter with nothing, so that she was reliant upon the rest of her family. Sir Julian wished she had come to Chelworth, but at the time it had not seemed suitable because he was a bachelor, and anyway, in Constantinople she and Amanda would be company for each other. He had worried about her since she left.

Randal's taunting voice broke into his thoughts.

"What is the batter, Richardson? Don't you think I ab ban enough to satisfy both your nieces?"

Ozzy couldn't bear Randal's presence any longer, and loosed a blood-chilling yowl that made Randal start with fear. "Sweet Jesu—!"

Sir Julian barely trusted himself to speak. "Just get out, Sanderby, before I let him have you. He's more ferocious than any dog."

Randal turned on his heel and hurried toward the window. Ozzy immediately leaped after him, and Sir Julian had the satisfaction of hearing Randal's frightened curse as he just managed to get out ahead of the tomcat. Ozzy was furious, and he scratched wildly at the bottom of the door until Sir Julian called him off.

Outside, the blustery night air swept over Randal, clean, sharp and tasting of salt from Chelworth Bay. He felt his eyes and nose begin to clear as he crossed the terrace and went down the wide flight of steps to the grassy, bracken-covered slope that undulated down to the sea. His steps quickened toward the woods in the narrow valley that formed the boundary of Sir Julian's Dorset estate. There, in the winding lane that led off the road between Weymouth and Wareham, his carriage was waiting.

Behind him in the library, Sir Julian sat weakly at the desk with his head in his hands. With so very much in the past, he had always dreaded a confrontation with Randal, but never had he imagined it would entail the added problem of a match with Amanda. Ozzy returned to the desk and sat beside the fragment of papyrus, regarding Sir Julian in puzzlement. After a moment he stretched out a paw to pat his master's tasseled nightcap. Sir Julian looked up. "Oh, Ozymandias, what am I going to do, eh?"

The tomcat squeezed his eyes and began to purr, which prompted Sir Julian to smile. "It is all so easy for you, isn't it? Would that my situation were as simple. I cannot allow Amanda to marry that . . . that maggot! I know he's right about one thing, however, and that is her character. She is indeed a spoiled, vain creature, and she will not take kindly to my efforts to dissuade her from the match. But I must try." The tomcat yawned, and Sir Julian raised an eyebrow. "Well might you show your boredom, sir, but it is a very great problem for me." His glance moved to the life-size statue of Isis that stood to one side of the fireplace. The god Osiris graced the other side, but it was only at the goddess that Sir Julian looked, for her headdress contained a secret compartment. In that compartment was Felice's parting letter, written when the husband she despised compelled her to stay with him. If made public, the letter would ruin Randal, as it would have ruined his father before him, but Felice had begged her lover not to tell, and he had given his word.

"Do you think Sanderby knows about the letter, Ozzy? Do you think his wretched father mentioned that too in his diary? I pray not, for he is the one person in all the world who would benefit from the letter's destruction." Sir Julian looked at the candle flame and thought again of the Fenworth family motto. *Noli tangere ignem;* Do not stir up fire. There was only one person in the world capable of prompting him to stir up this particular fire, but the likelihood of that person being found after all this time was so remote as to be almost impossible. Felice's reputation would therefore remain unharmed, and her letter a secret; but the letter would remain intact too, just in case the impossible happened. Then, and only then, would Felice's good name be sacrificed.

# 3

"Oh, Tansy, I'm never going to escape from here alive. I know I'm not! If the Mamelukes don't kill me, the French surely will!"

Amanda's selfish wail was almost lost in the wind-swept Egyptian darkness as she stood sobbing on the bank of one of the many narrow channels that fanned crookedly across the Nile delta. The Mediterranean storm howled and blustered, and the shower of hail and rain that had fallen after sundown gave the air a raw edge more worthy of the North Sea than these southern climes.

It was February, 1801, four months after the bitter confrontation between Sir Julian and Randal in the library at Chelworth, and Randal's nineteen-year-old bride-to-be was a very sorry sight. With wet blond tresses fluttering forlornly around her shoulders, mud on her face, and Nile weeds clinging to the remains of her costly cloak and sapphire satin dinner gown, she little resembled the delightful creature of the min-iature that had been sent to Randal. That gentleman could not have known how accurately he had foretold the hazards his bride might encounter before reaching England. Storms, shipwrecks, and pirates had already struck. Only the French remained.

However, although Amanda's situation was unfortu-nate to say the least, her customary disregard for oth-ers remained constant. She was devoid of concern for her two female companions, her cousin Tansy, and

Mrs. Hermione Entwhistle, the clergyman's widow engaged as the cousins' chaperone for the voyage. All three had been together since the naval sloop *Gower* weighed anchor in the Bosporus, and all three were now in the same plight, wondering if they would ever again be safe. A few yards away from where they stood among the reeds and irises on the riverbank, the felucca on which they had been abducted slid silently beneath the deep, sluggish water. There was no sign of the six pirates, who had saved themselves when the felucca first began to founder.

"Please don't cry, Amanda, for I'm sure we will be rescued." Tansy put her arms around Amanda's shaking shoulders and tried to sound heartening, even though she too was cold, wet, and frightened. She was twenty-three, with short, dark brown curls, freckles, a generous mouth, and expressive gray eyes. Her cloak was one of Amanda's castoffs, and her mustard velvet dinner gown was as plain and simple a garment as her cousin's was rich and ornate.

Amanda was too distraught to be comforted. "How can you say that? We were shipwrecked, then kidnapped by pirates. Now we've been shipwrecked again, and marooned in the middle of nowhere in a land overrun by the French!" she cried with a stamp of a foot that was always pretty, no matter what. "Sometimes, Church Mouse, I think you are stupid beyond belief!"

"Try to be optimistic, for I am convinced we will be rescued," Tansy insisted, trying not to be pricked by the unkind nickname. Even now Amanda could not miss an opportunity to remind her of her less fortunate background.

Mrs. Entwhistle came to Tansy's rescue. "Your cousin is quite right, Amanda. Of *course* we will be rescued," she declared stoutly, although the look in her thoughtful green eyes was anything but hopeful. Hermione Entwhistle was about fifty, and had been described as embonpoint. She had small hands and ankles, salt-and-pepper hair, a button nose, and was the sort of person who kept to herself. Beneath her sodden cloak she was wearing a modest wine-red velour gown that had seen faithful service over a succession of Mediterranean winters. Although she never wore black on his account, she had been very fond indeed of her late husband, who had passed on some ten years ago. The only thing her two charges could say of her with certainty was that she enjoyed crochet. Having a dry sense of humor, she once quipped that she'd set herself the target of trimming every tablecloth, cushion, and pillowcase in the Levant. Tansy saw the funny side of such a ridiculous claim; Amanda took the remark literally, and sneered about it.

Now Amanda started to sob again, so loudly that her uneasy companions feared she would be heard. The pirates might be nearby, or the French, or others who would prove no more friendly, so Mrs. Entwhistle adopted a brisk tone. "Come now, my dear. We must not let ourselves be beaten. We have survived everything so far, and are here on the shore. I am sure that if we remain of good heart—"

Amanda's foot stamped once more. "Good heart? Oh, you stupid woman!"

Tansy was aghast. "Amanda!"

Mrs. Entwhistle became flustered. She really did not know what to do with someone as willful, spoiled, and downright difficult as the prospective Lady Sanderby. For Tansy, however, she had a great deal of time, so she gave her a quick little smile. "It is of no consequence, my dear," she murmured, shivering in another gust of icy wind.

But it *was* of consequence, Tansy thought, quelling the urge to shake Amanda until her perfect white teeth rattled. An impoverished relative could hardly lay violent hands upon the heiress of the family, much as it was warranted, so she said nothing. Besides, their situation was indeed critical, for although they had reached dry land at last, far from being safe, Egypt was occupied by the French. But at least the French would probably treat captured British women with respect, which was more than could be said for the Mamelukes, Turks, and native Egyptians. All in all, it had to be conceded that chivalrous help seemed a very distant prospect indeed.

If only this horrid storm had never arisen! By now they would have been well on their way to Gibraltar, from where they would have taken passage for England on an escorted packet boat, and in a few weeks be safe at Chelworth with Uncle Julian. Instead, the northerly gale had driven all before it for several days, pushing them far south of their original course. The women had been dining with the captain when the *Gower* foundered on the notorious sandbar at the Rosetta mouth of the Nile. Rescue feluccas had put out from the shore, but while the sloop's crew was distracted by the shipwreck, pirates had snatched the women and sailed south into the Nile for the slave markets. Then the felucca struck something submerged in the water, losing her rudder, oars, and sail, and the pirates abandoned everything. Now the felucca had disappeared forever beneath the river, and there was only the lapping of water and gusting of the storm as it swept inland over the low-lying land.

Tansy tried to take her bearings. How long ago had the *Gower* met her end? How far upstream had the pirates brought them? In the darkness, and being so frightened, it was difficult to think clearly at all, let alone judge time and distance. The weakening storm racketed through the reeds, and choppy wavelets slapped the muddy banks of the river channel, which she guessed was twenty-five yards wide at this point. The land was gray and indistinct now, but in daylight it would be a place of fertile fields and rich marshes, filled with waterfowl and bright with every green imaginable. That much at least she knew about the Nile delta. Distance remained impossible to gauge, but she fixed the time at about midnight. Many hours of bleak darkness still lay ahead.

Then she noticed steps leading from the remains of a mooring place, and she turned quickly to see where it led. On a mount about fifty yards behind her was a ruined temple, above which soared the huge granite figure of a seated god or goddess that seemed to be gazing down at the three fugitives on the riverbank. The ruins were not entirely from the time of the pharaohs, for the immense stone walls had at some time been used to enclose a small Mameluke palace or summer residence, with a loggia overlooking the river, and long-deserted gardens of date palms and sycamore figs. It seemed that no one had been anywhere near here for centuries, she thought.

Suddenly the storm seemed to pause for breath, and the women heard sounds that struck them with fresh alarm. A bugle call sounded behind the temple mound; then orders were shouted in French. At the same time there were French voices on the river as well, and the approaching lights of a *canja,* one of the larger Nile vessels. Tansy gasped. "Come on. They mustn't find us! We're bound to find shelter up in the ruins!" Their wet clothes flapping unpleasantly around their legs, the women hurried up the steps to the ruins, but as they neared the loggia, a low shadow darted silently across their path.

Amanda stifled a scream, but Mrs. Entwhistle was quick to reassure her. "It's only a cat. It won't hurt you," she said as she continued toward the loggia. Tansy smiled in spite of their hazardous situation. Only a cat? Amanda hated cats, and they hated her!

Amanda shuddered, but she quelled her loathing in order to follow the chaperone. Almost immediately she trod on something hard and metallic that rolled down a sharp incline into the overgrown temple gardens. Then some of the masonry crumbled beneath her as well, and with a startled squeal, she disappeared down into the dense, wind-torn oleanders at the bottom of the loggia's retaining wall.

# 4

$\mathcal{M}$rs. Entwhistle turned in dismay as Amanda fell, and for a moment Tansy was too startled to move, but then she scrambled down the slope after her cousin. "Amanda? Are you all right?" she cried.

Amanda's tearful response was little more than a whimper, and almost lost in the storm as it buffeted through the surrounding greenery. "I think I've broken my ankle."

"Oh, no . . . !" Tansy pushed her way into the oleanders and found her cousin sitting on the ground with her knee drawn up, rubbing her ankle.

Mrs. Entwhistle called from above, trying to moderate her voice so that it was just audible above the gale. "What's happening? Is everything all right?"

"I'm afraid she's hurt her ankle," Tansy replied, kneeling to examine the injury.

The chaperone made her way gingerly down into the bushes, then knelt down next to them. She felt the ankle with deft, knowing fingers. "A slight sprain; no more," she declared.

Amanda wasn't prepared to have a slight anything. "It's broken. I *know* it is," she announced in a tone that brooked no argument.

But for once Mrs. Entwhistle was adamant. "Nonsense, my dear. It will be as right as rain in a little while."

Amanda gave her a furious look. "How would you

know whether or not I've really hurt myself? Have you ever broken your ankle?" she demanded.

"Er, no, my dear, but—"

"But nothing!" cried Amanda.

Tansy intervened hastily, keeping her voice low and level. "Look, this isn't the time or place to argue the finer points of broken ankles, least of all in raised voices that might easily be overheard by the French. We need to find somewhere to hide, preferably somewhere well protected from the weather."

Mrs. Entwhistle glanced around. "Well, we're safe where we are, for these bushes conceal us very well and keep off a lot of the wind, but if it should rain again . . ." She shook her head.

"*This* is what I slipped on," Amanda said through clenched teeth, and she brandished the object before tossing it away over her left shoulder. They all expected it to strike the solid retaining wall, but instead it flew through the air for a second or so, then rattled metallically on what sounded like a stone floor.

Curious, Tansy scrambled through the oleanders to investigate, and discovered a low entrance leading to a little chamber of some sort, small and square, with a ceiling barely six feet high. It was part of the original temple, and judging by the undisturbed foliage, it had not been used for a long time. "There's a room where we can hide!"

Mrs. Entwhistle breathed out with relief. "Thank goodness, for I'm *freezing!*"

Amanda's lower lip jutted. "How long do we have to hide? Until we die of hunger and thirst?"

"Until we think of what to do," Tansy said patiently. "Look, the French are nearby, so we *have* to be out of sight come daylight. This little room is the best chance we have."

"Oh, all right, but I wish I'd never heard of Lord Sanderby, because by now I'd be safely on the way to Australia with Papa!"

That made a change, Tansy thought wryly, for re-

cent weeks had been filled with endless bragging about
the wonderful Sanderby match. Amanda had always
assumed airs and graces because she was an heiress,
and the opposite sex appeared to find her irresistible,
but betrothal to an earl had made her quite insuffer-
able, especially toward her plain, far-from-rich cousin.
Tansy served only one purpose—providing a captive
audience to whom to boast not only of the match, but
of various indiscretions with diplomatic gentlemen.
And there were the written indiscretions as well, especially to Lord Sanderby. Not that he was any better,
Tansy thought, having been obliged to read the craftily
passionate letters he had sent to Constantinople.
Amanda was convinced of his ardor, but Tansy judged
him to be up to no good. For instance, why would he
bother with a Richardson bride? The bitter quarrel
between his father and Uncle Julian made it almost
beyond belief that the son of one should embark upon
an arranged match with the niece of the other. Uncle
Franklyn's motives had been simple enough—he
wanted the kudos of a titled daughter—but what did
Randal Fenworth gain? His coffers were already over-
flowing, so he didn't *need* Amanda's fortune as well.

Tansy did not dwell longer on the mystery of his
lordship's motives, for she and Mrs. Entwhistle had to
help Amanda into the hidden chamber, where the
floor was dusty but at least dry. There they huddled
together in a corner, feeling a false sense of warmth
simply because they were out of the wind. But they
were still in danger, for by the sounds from outside,
the French seemed to be setting up camp. Suddenly
the oleanders rustled. It wasn't the wind; something—
or someone—was out there! Mrs. Entwhistle sat forward nervously, and Amanda's breath caught as a
robed man appeared in the doorway and spoke to
them in a hoarse whisper. "Peace upon you, ladies.
Fear not, for I am your friend."

"Who are you?" the chaperone asked, for in this
part of the world it was nothing for a sworn enemy
to pretend friendship.

He entered, and by now Tansy's eyes were sufficiently accustomed to the dark to make him out in some detail. He was in his mid-thirties, and his chin was clean shaven, but he had a bristling mustache and fine side-whiskers. He wore the shirt, waistcoat, and exceedingly baggy trousers of the Mameluke, and was pale skinned instead of dark like the native Egyptians, because the Mamelukes were white slave warriors of Circassian origin. The tarboosh on his head was swathed in a turban fixed with a spray of jewels that sparkled so much they had to be diamonds. Tansy knew that Mamelukes carried all their wealth upon their persons, so that this man probably wore many other jewels among his clothes. He bowed, and then addressed them in immaculate English. "By God's grace I am called Tusun. I help the British, and it is my business to learn all there is to know about the French. I was scouting this place and saw your felucca sink. I heard you speak English." He dropped some bundles at their feet. "Food and milk, dry blankets, and robes. I stole them from the French. You must change out of your wet clothes."

Tansy gazed incredulously at the supplies. "Oh, thank you," she said gratefully.

Mrs. Entwhistle smiled at him. "Yes, thank you very much indeed, Tusun."

"It is important you stay very quiet, for there are many French here, and so far they do not know of this place."

"Long may it stay that way," Mrs. Entwhistle murmured.

"Indeed so. Tell me how you came here. European women are rare in this land."

They explained about the loss of the *Gower*, and he drew a long breath. "Ah, yes, that sandbar has claimed many a ship."

"Many of the crew must have been rescued. If you could get us to them . . . ?"

"I have another plan for your salvation, lady," he said quietly; then his glance fell upon Amanda's ankle, which was exposed because that young lady, annoyed at not being the center of attention, began to make a fuss about her injury. "You are hurt, lady?"

"I tripped on something and fell down the slope from the steps," she said, stretching out her dainty foot, even now unable to resist the urge to make a conquest.

Tusun crouched down beside her. "With your permission, let me see." Amanda displayed no maidenly modesty as she submitted to his stranger's hands. Tansy and Mrs. Entwhistle looked at each other, for neither of them was under any illusion about her. The chaperone in particular was dismayed, having seen enough of the world to know that Amanda often played with fire. At first Tusun gave no indication of what he thought. His expert fingers probed the slightly swollen ankle; then he nodded. "God is merciful, lady. There is no injury," he said, then very deliberately and pointedly pulled the hem of her gown down over her foot. Amanda flushed, for there was no mistaking the silent rebuke, but for once she said nothing.

Embarrassed, Mrs. Entwhistle sought to divert attention by telling him about Amanda's accident. "We were seeking shelter here when a cat crossed our path, and—"

Tusun stepped back as if scalded. "A cat?" he gasped, making a superstitious sign before him. "You saw a cat? *Here*?"

"Why, yes. It was just a cat. . . ."

"Oh, no lady, not *just* a cat, not if you saw it here at Tel el-Osorkon. Long ago in the time of the pharaohs, this place was dedicated to Bastet, the cat goddess. On top of the temple mound there is a statue of a cat-headed woman, Bastet herself, seated upon a throne, with cats and kittens at her feet. Once there were a thousand cats here, but now there are none. Cats will not come here because Bastet has sent them away, to show her displeasure at no longer being worshipped."

Mrs. Entwhistle was adamant. "Well, I assure you we saw one."

Tusun made another superstitious sign. "Then it is an omen," he murmured.

"Good or bad?" Tansy inquired.

He spread his hands. "That I do not know." He glanced up as more sounds came from the loggia above them. "I must go now, for I have a task to do. You are safe until I bring help, God willing."

Mrs. Entwhistle got to her feet. "Bring help from where? The crew of the *Gower?*" she asked.

"No. I am to meet the British frigate *Lucina* tonight in Aboukir Bay, to tell them what the French are doing. An officer, Lieutenant Ballard, will come ashore to consult with me. I will tell him of you, and of the *Gower,* and he will come for you."

"I see. How long will this take?"

"I will return with the lieutenant before the night is out."

Mrs. Entwhistle was relieved. "Then I wish you God speed, Tusun. *Ma'as salāma.*" *Go in safety.* She had been in the Levant long enough to have learned a little of most of its languages.

He bowed, and left them. There was a rustling in the oleanders, then nothing, except the mutter of the storm around the entrance, and the sounds of the French.

# 5

"Remember now, lads, not a word once we're close to the shore! English voices will prove our undoing!"

In Aboukir Bay, about eight miles away from Tel el-Osorkon, First Lieutenant Martin Ballard's voice was snatched by the wind as the pinnace pushed away from HMS *Lucina*. It was half an hour to midnight, the cloudy Mediterranean night was black and starless, and the muffled oars made little sound as the sailors began to pull for the shore through the wind and swell. The storm was abating quickly now, but the sea was still surly and unsettled. There were no lights on the thirty-two-gun fifth rater, for fear of alerting the French fort on the western promontory. Out of sight to the east lay the Rosetta mouth of the Nile, and the infamous sandbar where, as yet unknown to the *Lucina,* the *Gower* had met her fate.

Martin was thirty-three years old and romantically handsome, with dark curling hair, thick-lashed brown eyes, and finely chiseled lips that could as swiftly warm into a smile as press thin with anger or grim determination. His complexion was tanned from the sun and sea, and there was a ruggedness about him that rested oddly well with the grace of his movements, for he was as at home in bloody hand-to-hand action as dancing a measure at an assembly room ball. He tugged his flowing green robes around his lean, muscular body, and adjusted his turban. When he slipped ashore on these secret intelligence-gathering missions, he always wore a disguise, for to appear in naval uniform would be to sign his own death warrant. But this was his last such mission; indeed, it was his last voyage. When the *Lucina* returned to Portsmouth, he would leave the navy and start a new life in far-off America.

He checked the dagger and long curving knife thrust into the wide sash around his waist, then made sure of the pistol he carried against his heart. Only then did he gaze toward the land, where there were a few clumps of date palms, and dunes topped with waving grass. Beyond the dunes that fringed the beach there was a sandy waste that stretched to the lush fertile edge of the delta. He raked the rocky beach for any sign of activity, but all seemed deserted, just as he'd hoped. Secrecy was essential now that the British were only days from invasion to end French occupation. Information about enemy numbers and deployment was vital.

The coxswain addressed him suddenly. "Are there any further orders, sir?"

"No, it's all as before, Matthews. If I'm not there at dawn, you're to return at the same time every day until I am. If I have any urgent messages and cannot stay to deliver them in person, I will leave them in the usual place."

"Aye, aye, sir," Matthews replied. He was an experienced seaman, wiry and agile as a monkey.

The pinnace slid further from the protection of the *Lucina* and was swept forward on huge rollers. The noise of the surf grew louder, and spume flew on the air. Salt stung Martin's lips, and the lurch of the boat was almost sickening as the sailors shipped the oars and allowed the last wave to almost hurl the pinnace onto a small stretch of sand. The moment Martin was ashore, the sailors began to shove the boat back into the surf. He didn't wait to see them go, but slipped away toward the usual thicket of date palms. On reaching the trees, he ducked down among some wind-carved bushes and laid low, listening beyond the racket of the breakers for any sound than might warn of danger. The seconds passed. Out on the water the pinnace was pulling strongly back toward the indistinct silhouette of the *Lucina* out in the bay. He was alone. There was a knot in his stomach that felt as cold as ice, but the blood pumped swiftly through his veins as he took out his fob watch. Midnight. He settled back to wait for Tusun.

Time seemed to pass on leaden feet. The clouds overhead began to thin, and one by one stars appeared. Then the moon slid out of hiding, casting a cool silver light over everything. The *Lucina* was beating seaward, and come daylight no one would know she had ever been there. Suddenly there came the sound of a horse, a low whicker that was almost lost in the noise of the sea. Martin stiffened warily, and slid a hand toward the pistol inside his robe, but then a voice he knew called out quietly. "Effendi?"

"Over here, Tusun!"

Shadows moved as the Mameluke approached, leading two horses, a bay and a chestnut, exquisitely beautiful Arabian mounts of the desert. "Ah, Effendi, God has willed it that you are here safely," he declared.

Martin grinned and got up. "Have you any information?"

"Oh, indeed, Effendi. I had much to impart concerning the movements of the French, but I also have something else to tell you. Three Englishwomen need help."

"What in God's own name are Englishwomen doing here?"

"They were on a British sloop, the *Gower,* which was wrecked on the sandbar at the Rosetta mouth of the Nile."

Martin knew the *Gower,* and was acquainted with some of her officers. "You only mention the three women. What of the crew?"

"I believe they reached the shore, Effendi, but the women were taken by pirates. They came from Constantinople, and that is all I know of them. Now they hide."

"How far away are they?"

"Maybe eight miles, Effendi. It is nothing to these fine mounts." Tusun patted the horses.

"Maybe not for just you and me, but if we have three extra to bring back . . ."

Tusun gave him a wily grin. "There is a fine *canja,* Effendi. It is laden with treasure and antiquities stolen by the French."

"The French?" Martin repeated guardedly.

"Indeed so." The Mameluke shuffled his feet slightly. "You see, the place where they are hiding has become a French encampment. Most of the officers sailed from Cairo in the *canja,* but the rest—and the men—came across the desert. I was following them, so I know this."

"How many altogether?'

The Mameluke spread his hands again and shrugged. "Oh, not many, Effendi. Maybe two thousand."

"Oh, is that all? Good heavens, for a moment you had me worried," Martin replied dryly. Damn it all, why couldn't these women have stayed in Constantinople?

Tusun looked intently at him in the moonlight, then held out a pair of reins. "If we hurry, Effendi, we can accomplish all before dawn, God willing."

"Yes, but first I must leave word about the *Gower.* If there are shipwrecked British seamen ashore, they need to be saved. The *Lucina* can do that, and will be glad of the extra hands." Martin searched inside his robe for the notebook and pencil he carried everywhere. He scribbled a message about the location of the wrecked sloop and her stranded crew, and about his intention to rescue the three women if possible. Then he ripped the page from the book and hid it in a cleft in one of the date palms, where Matthews was bound to look if no one was waiting the next morning. Then he and Tusun rode swiftly away along the beach.

# 6

Tansy crept to the doorway and peered out past the oleanders. She was very tired but still couldn't relax enough to sleep. Her skin and hair were still sticky with salt and Nile mud, but at least she had been able to change into the black robes Tusun had purloined from the French. She had eaten too, just wheat cakes and milk, but she felt a good deal better than before. The storm had faded considerably now, and the reeds at the water's edge swayed occasionally. Beyond the channel the shadowy delta stretched away into a darkness that was briefly pierced by moonlight as the clouds began to break.

The *canja* was moored alongside the riverbank. It was long, low, and graceful, with a flat-topped cabin area toward the stern, and its tall mast had been lowered along the deck. She saw that it was heavily laden with antiquities, from terra-cotta jars and pieces of carved masonry, to two finely decorated caskets and a number of bronze animal figures. There were also half a dozen large crates, some of them badly packed, which soldiers were rearranging and securing with ropes. Suddenly one of the crates was dropped, and an infuriated officer bellowed from the loggia. Tansy glanced up and saw his fist brandishing in the light of a lantern. Realizing that he might see her, she drew hastily back into the room, where Amanda and Mrs. Entwhistle were asleep on the floor in Tusun's blankets. They too were now clothed in robes, and the wet garments belonging to all three women were hanging from a stone projection on the wall.

Tansy was about to join them on the floor, when more moonlight shone through the entrance onto the wall opposite. What she had previously thought was plain stonework was now revealed to be beautifully painted with a hunting scene from the time of the pharaohs. Vivid, colorful, and graceful, it showed a young man catching waterfowl among the papyrus and blue lotus of the delta marshes. Birds of every description surrounded him as he stood on a small reed boat beneath which fish swam. In one hand he held a brace of white egrets, while he held out the other to take a papyrus being brought to him not by a retriever dog but by a tabby cat! She went closer, hoping the moonlight would last long enough for her to see it properly. The cat fascinated her, not only because of its unlikely role, but also because it was painted in such exquisite detail that its fur almost invited her to stroke it.

Mrs. Entwhistle suddenly spoke from the floor behind her. "The pharaohs often used cats instead of dogs, especially here in the delta."

Tansy turned in surprise. "Really? I didn't know that."

"Oh, yes, it is quite a well-known thing." Holding the warm blanket around her, the chaperone got up and came to join her, while Amanda slept on. "Tusun said this place was called Tel el-Osorkon, and so I believe this scene depicts a myth my husband once told to me. It concerns a young nobleman named Osorkon, who lived in the delta and went hunting every day with his faithful she-cat. But the young man was really the rightful pharaoh, and his evil half brother ordered his death in order to have the throne. One day the cat brought Osorkon a papyrus that revealed his destiny; he defeated his wicked sibling, and on ascending the throne of Egypt he built a temple to his faithful cat, who became beloved of the goddess Bastet." Mrs. Entwhistle smiled. "It would be agreeable, would it not, to imagine that this place was the very temple, and that the creature we saw when we first arrived was a descendant of Osorkon's cat?''

"I had no idea you were so knowledgeable about Ancient Egypt, Mrs. Entwhistle."

"Oh, hardly knowledgeable, my dear. I only claim a little learning, gleaned from my dear late husband, who was an antiquarian of some standing."

Tansy looked fondly at her. "The Reverend Entwhistle would be very proud indeed to know how staunch and brave you've been for Amanda and me."

"You are a good girl, Tansy, and worth a thousand A—" Mrs. Entwhistle broke off awkwardly, for she had been about to say a thousand Amandas.

Neither of them spoke for a moment; then Tansy looked shyly at the older woman. "It seems rather silly for me to keep calling you Mrs. Entwhistle, when you call me Tansy. Would you mind very much if I called you Hermione?"

"No, of course not, my dear, horrid name though it is. In fact, I would like it very much if we were on more friendly terms." Hermione cleared her throat. "Now, where were we before? Ah, yes, retriever cats. It's strange, is it not? We always regard the cat as a law unto itself and quite impossible to train, yet the Ancient Egyptians seem to have managed it." She reached up to touch the hieroglyphs that also adorned the painting. "Oh, if only we could unlock this puzzle, what stories we would learn, what history would be revealed to us across the centuries. I heard that a year or so ago, the French found an inscribed stone of immense importance somewhere near here, at Rosetta, I think. It is said to be written with three different languages, one being Greek, another hieroglyphic, and I'm not sure about the third. Anyway, it is hoped that all the inscriptions are versions the same text. If so, maybe our understanding will advance at last. I was told that the British confiscated this stone, and I pray the information is correct, for we do not wish the French to have the glory of translating hieroglyphs, do we?" She smiled at Tansy.

"Certainly not. That would not do at all." Tansy smiled at her. "You have surprised me greatly to-night, Hermione."

"Ah, my dear, just because I say very little and seem inclined to regard crochet as the be-all and end-all of life, does not mean that I am a fool."

"Oh, I have never thought you *that*."

"No, my dear, maybe you haven't, but I fear your cousin has formed a very firm opinion on the matter."

Amanda sighed in her sleep and turned over, and at the same time the wind stirred the oleanders. A draft breathed in, persuading both women to return to the floor to sleep, but as Tansy began to wrap her-self as cozily as she could, she found something cold and hard caught up in her blanket. It was the object that Amanda had tripped upon earlier, and with the help of the moon Tansy saw it was a bronze figurine of a cat, about eight inches tall, with gold rings pierc-ing its ears and nose; bronze or not, it felt oddly warm to the touch. There were hieroglyphs around its neck, so she knew it was very old indeed.

"What have you found, my dear?" Hermione inquired.

"Another cat, would you believe? A little statuette this time," Tansy replied, then gasped as the cat they had seen earlier appeared at the entrance. It was a tabby, and it regarded them in that disconcerting way cats have.

Hermione saw it as well, then leaned up on an elbow to study the painted cat on the wall. "You know, they both look very alike. The fur is almost the same." The cat trotted toward Tansy and nuzzled the figurine in her hand, purring loudly. Then it kneaded the folds of the blanket for a few moments, before rather impudently making itself comfortable to go to sleep. Hermione smiled. "You have a new friend, Tansy."

"So it seems." Tansy was very fond of cats, so she stroked it gently. "Isn't it rather strange for a wild cat to come to us like this?" she said.

"Well, we don't know that it's wild, do we? I mean, come the daylight we might find that there is a village nearby. Anyway, that's enough chitter chatter for the moment, my dear. We should try to sleep while we can."

"Yes, you're right." Tansy put the figurine aside and lay down, wishing she shared the tabby cat's ability to be comfortable on a hard floor. "You do think Tusun will return for us, don't you?" she asked Hermione.

"He will do his best, I'm sure, my dear."

"It's just that if he doesn't . . ."

"If he doesn't, we'll fend for ourselves," the chaperone said stoutly.

Martin and Tusun left their horses in a thicket of young palms a few hundred yards from the temple, then slipped across a watermelon field to some heaped mud-brick remains at the base of the mound, from where they observed the French encampment. Weary men were seated around a number of flickering campfires, and someone with a fine tenor voice was singing *"Sur le Pont d'Avignon."* The soldiers were mostly infantry, with some carabineers, whose horses were tethered beneath a pomegranate tree. A number of Egyptian women were to be seen, some enveloped in black robes, others much more improper. Except for the French song, it might have been any army camp—but the British would have relaxed to "Tom, Tom, the Piper's Son." "Well, they look settled, but are the sentries alert?" Martin mused, his breath silver in the cold.

Tusun shrugged. "Who can say, Effendi? They have marched from Cairo, and are very tired. May God send a thousand scorpions to disturb their slumber, and when they set sail for France, may God send a tempest to sink them all."

Martin grinned. "Unfortunately, God's tempest sank the *Gower* instead. Anyway, take me to these Englishwomen." Tusun led him around the base of the temple mound until the channel of the Nile came into view, and with it the lantern-lit *canja*. Martin's lips pursed as he saw its cargo. "Booty for French museums," he murmured.

Tusun shrugged. "Why do they wish to have such things? Old pieces of stone and a few carvings? If they were to desire gold and jewels I could understand it, but not these ancient items that have no value."

Martin smiled. "Oh, they have value, my friend. Believe me."

But Tusun was far from convinced. He pointed toward the oleanders. "At the bottom of that wall there is a hidden room, part of the original temple of Bastet. That is where the English ladies are." He shivered, and not just with the cold.

Martin noticed. "What's wrong?"

"Oh, it is nothing, Effendi. You will say I am too superstitious."

"Well, you *are* too superstitious. What is it this time?"

"A cat, Effendi." Tusun shifted uncomfortably.

"Is that so terrible in a temple devoted to Bastet?"

Tusun gave him a look. "She banished them. There should not be a cat here at all, but the ladies said they saw one. It is an omen, Effendi."

Martin regarded him. "Omens can be good or bad," he pointed out.

"I know, but in my experience they are nearly always bad."

Martin was curious. "In your experience?"

"A great black bird perched on the balcony of my room on the night my father died. I was the firstborn, the *only* child, and I know my father meant me to have everything. Yet my uncle took it all, and I received nothing. I am thankful that I am a true Mameluke, and always carry my treasures with me, otherwise I would not even have the diamonds I wear upon my head. The great black bird was an omen, a visitation by my uncle's black soul."

"Or just a great black bird that happened to perch on your balcony," Martin said reasonably.

"No, it was an omen," Tusun insisted, then put a hand on Martin's arm as two laughing French officers strolled from the loggia and down toward the river.

Martin gave a sly grin. "They won't be laughing when we take that *canja* from under their Gallic noses. If we wait until just before dawn, when they will be less vigilant, I am sure we can slip the moorings and be away to the sea before they even know it. The *Lucina* will be lying offshore, and if the weather holds like this, we can sail out to her."

Tusun drew a deep breath. "You make it sound very simple, Effendi."

"That's because it is."

# 7

As Martin and Tusun were preparing to rescue the women from the temple, faraway in London Sir Julian's traveling carriage was passing along the ice-bound southern boundary of London's Hyde Park. Sir Julian was not alone in the vehicle, for Ozzy shared the fleecy rug over his knees.

Sir Julian looked out at the capital he had loathed since the time of the Society of Antiquaries debacle. Keeping his house in Park Lane was a pointless expense, he had decided, so he intended to sell. The proceeds would go toward providing two sphinx guardians for the pyramid folly behind Chelworth itself. The pyramid was about one-sixth the size of the Great Pyramid at Giza, and was quite a landmark from the sea.

While in London he also intended to examine a particular papyrus at the British Museum at Montagu House. He had written requesting a ticket, which should be waiting when he called. Several weeks ago it had struck him that the item at the museum was very like his own, so a viewing had become of paramount importance because he desperately wanted to be the one to solve the mystery of hieroglyphs. He had to be avenged for the lies of Esmond Fenworth, fifth Earl of Sanderby!

Sir Julian's mind turned to Amanda, from whom he had now received a letter written before she left Constantinople, in which she admitted to the intimate correspondence of which Randal had boasted. "Oh, Franklyn, Franklyn, you have been sadly remiss in your daughter's upbringing," Sir Julian murmured.

He leaned wearily back against the brown leather upholstery and gazed at the frozen trees visible above the wall of Hyde Park. The cold seeped through him even though he was well wrapped. Were winters becoming colder? he wondered. Or was it just that he was less able to keep warm? Old age crept closer all the time. He sighed as his thoughts wandered into the past, to days spent in the beautiful countryside around Paddington. Poignant memories swept back, and on impulse he lowered the window glass to call to the coachman. "Lysons, I want to see Paddington again. You know exactly where."

"Yes, sir," Lysons replied, looking back at a curricle that was keeping pace behind.

Sir Julian forgot the cold as the carriage drove out of London again and back into countryside. After a fork in the lane, Lysons reined in at the familiar gates of the elegant Queen Anne residence that had been empty and neglected since Felice decided to stay with her husband for her son's sake. Sir Julian regarded the house. When his short lease ended, possession had reverted to the landlord, the Bishop of London. Why had the Church permitted such a prime property to disintegrate? He opened the carriage door and climbed stiffly down. Ozzy jumped out and disappeared through the gates. The cat would come back when called.

For a moment Sir Julian thought he heard hooves halting along the lane behind, but when he listened there was nothing. Imagination, he thought, shaking his head ruefully. "Wait here," he said to Lysons.

"You shouldn't go in there alone, Sir Julian. You never know who might be there."

"Ghosts, Lysons, that's all."

The coachman heard something and looked back along the road. "I'm sure there's a curricle following us, sir."

"Anyone with robbery in mind could have apprehended us long before now. I will not be long. See to the horses."

"Very well, sir." Lysons climbed reluctantly down.

Sir Julian made his way between the rickety gates and along the overgrown drive to the house. *Oh, Felice, if only you'd realized what an insect your precious son would become.*

Pushing open the doors, which hung on broken hinges, he entered to find Ozzy waiting. The smell of damp and decay in the hall told how far the house had sunk from the days of its prime. Sir Julian gazed at the curving staircase, suddenly remembering Felice running down to greet him. How enchanting she had been, with her raven curls and gypsy-dark eyes. He glanced down at Ozzy. "I fear it was a mistake to come back here, my friend."

Ozzy trotted at his heels as they returned to the gates, where the tomcat suddenly disappeared into the triangular field formed where the lane had forked. Lysons was anxious to be away from this place, and had already turned the carriage. "I'm sure someone's watching us, sir," he said as he helped Sir Julian into the vehicle.

"We can't leave until Ozymandias returns."

As Lysons resumed his seat on the box, he could cheerfully have strangled all cats. However, Ozzy's decampment had a purpose. In the other fork of the lane he found the mysterious curricle waiting beneath a tree, its gentleman occupant spying upon Sir Julian's carriage through a pocket telescope. Amber eyes glinting, Ozzy climbed the tree, then moved along a sturdy branch that overhung the gentleman's head. A moment later the man began to sneeze. Sir Julian heard. There had been a time when the presence here of a Lord Sanderby would have filled him with dismay, but no longer.

Ozzy returned, and without delay Lysons drove smartly off along the lane. As the carriage bucketed back toward London, Sir Julian swept his pet into his arms. "You bad old boy," he murmured. "Fancy making his lordship sneeze like that." Ozzy looked up at him and squeezed his amber eyes.

Randal's affliction was already subsiding now that Ozymandias had gone. The existence of the lovers' house had come as no surprise, for he knew of it from his father's diary. From the same source he knew his father had purchased the property, left it to crumble, and constantly taunted his unfaithful wife with it until her death from influenza sixteen years later.

Tonight Randal had been on his way home from an assignation when he saw Sir Julian's pharaoh's-head badge on the passing carriage. He had followed, curious about the old curmudgeon's return to London. He knew Sir Julian had unsuccessfully attempted to turn Amanda from the match, so it was disquieting to find him in town again. Did it signify the playing of the trump card, the letter? Randal did not doubt the letter's existence, and  another friendly call upon Sir Julian seemed advisable. In the morning, on his way to the obligatory daily ride in Hyde Park, he would stop at Park Lane in time to put Sir Julian off his kedgeree, or deviled kidneys, or whatever.

# 8

$D$awn was still an hour away, and the moon still shone over Tel el-Osorkon as Tansy lay quietly on the floor in her blanket. The tabby cat was curled up with her, and neither of them was asleep. Amanda and Hermione were deeply asleep, but Tansy was as restless as ever, and the cat kept raising its head to look toward the doorway, as if expecting something.

Suddenly the creature gave a low growl, and Tansy heard the faint but distinct sound of earth scattering outside, then a rustling in the oleanders. She sat up swiftly, and grasped the bronze statuette, ready to hurl it with all her might. Again it was warm to the touch, when the air all around was cold.

For the second time that night a man's shadow filled the doorway; then an Englishman whispered urgently, "It's all right! I'm a friend! For heaven's sake don't throw that thing, whatever it is!"

Amanda and Hermione stirred but didn't quite awaken as Tansy lowered the missile uncertainly, "Who . . . Who are you?" she breathed, still very much on her guard.

"First Lieutenant Martin Ballard of HMS *Lucina*," Martin replied, venturing cautiously into the room.

Tansy was alarmed to see his Arab robes, for she'd expected the navy blue and white uniform of a royal naval officer. Suspicion rushed back, and once again she raised the figurine.

He hastily raised his hands in a gesture of peace. "I

really am First Lieutenant Ballard. Tusun has brought me to you. My robes are to fool the enemy. It doesn't do to wander around in King George's uniform; it rather gives one away."

The jocular tone convinced her, and once again she slowly lowered the figurine. "You'll never know how relieved I am to see you," she said, staring up at him in the faint light from the door. He was devastatingly attractive: strong, darkly handsome, and—in circumstances such as these—all that a hero should be. His Eastern robes suited him singularly well, but she could not help imagining him in his naval wear, which she considered the most dashing and attractive uniform of all. She glanced quickly away, for an unexpected warmth had entered her cheeks. It was such a strong reaction that it quite put her at sixes and sevens. She was cross with herself. What a foolish, impressionable little idiot he would think her if he knew what was passing through her mind right now!

Hermione and Amanda awoke, the latter sitting up with a frightened start, her salt-caked golden curls tumbling over the shoulders of her black robe. For a moment her beautiful face was caught clearly in the moonlight, even to the incredible cornflower blue of her eyes. As she saw his Arab robes her lips parted to scream, but Martin darted forward and clamped his hand over her mouth.

"Quiet! Unless you *wish* to become a prisoner of the French!"

Frozen with fear, Amanda stared up at him, but then the Englishness of his voice dawned upon her and she relaxed visibly. Slowly he took his hand from her mouth, but he continued to gaze down into her lovely face, as if spellbound. His lips were parted just a little, and Tansy did not need to be able to see his eyes to know they were filled with admiration, for it was a variation on a scene she had witnessed many times in the last two years. Her cousin had made another effortless conquest. Lieutenant Ballard had succumbed, as did most of his sex, because even now, with her hair in a mess and her figure concealed beneath a voluminous black robe, Amanda Richardson was memorably attractive.

Martin realized he was staring and straightened hastily, but he still looked down at Amanda. "May I know your name? Er, names?" he added quickly, glancing at Tansy and Hermione.

Amanda decided to treat him to her most beguiling smile. "I am Miss Amanda Richardson, and this is my cousin, Miss Tansy Richardson. This other lady is our chaperone, Mrs. Entwhistle." She made her voice soft and slightly breathless, as if affected by him as much as he was by her. She wasn't, of course. She was far too self-centered for that.

Martin inclined his head to them all, but his attention remained on Amanda. Tansy locked her hurt away, as she had done before when failing to compare with her dazzling cousin, but this time the hurt was greater . . . because the attraction she herself felt toward First Lieutenant Martin Ballard was greater too.

Tansy was not alone in finding Martin attractive, for the tabby cat made its liking plain as well. With a friendly *"Prrr?"* it went to him and rubbed all around his robes, making little sounds until he bent to stroke it. He was so easy and natural with the little creature that Tansy's fate was sealed. He was indeed the most perfect of men!

Tusun scrambled quietly down the slope outside and entered the room. "God's greetings," he said, and swept a dashing bow to the three women.

Hermione smiled at him. "You brought us help as you promised, Tusun, and for that we will always be in your debt."

"Do not thank me yet, lady. Do so when you are all safe aboard the *Lucina*."

Amanda glanced past him, expecting to see more men. "How many of you are there?"

"Just the two of us," Martin answered.

Amanda was aghast. "But that's not enough! The French are everywhere, and—"

Tusun interrupted. "Better too few of us than none at all," he said quietly.

It was an unmistakable rebuke, not the first the Mameluke had delivered to her, and Amanda responded with hauteur. "You clearly have no idea who I am. The Earl of Sanderby is to be my husband, and if anything should befall me he will be most displeased!"

Tansy felt uncomfortable. "Please, Amanda, these gentlemen are putting their own lives in danger to help us, so at the very least you should be civil."

Amanda's lovely eyes swung coldly toward her. "Oh, do be quiet, Church Mouse, for what would you know about gentlemen, or indeed about civility?"

Martin intervened hastily. "It is not important. After all, the circumstances are extenuating." For a moment he looked into Tansy's expressive gray gaze, but almost immediately his attention returned to Amanda.

Tansy felt his lack of interest in her very keenly. Yes, the circumstances were extenuating for Amanda, as they were for everyone, but what he did not realize was that Amanda was as disagreeable as this all the time, no matter what the circumstances. The future Countess of Sanderby was haughty, attitudinizing, and vindictive; yet men were always prepared to make excuses for her! In that respect at least, First Lieutenant Martin Ballard was no different from all the rest.

Amanda enjoyed Tansy's discomposure and rightly guessed the full reason, that the Church Mouse was drawn to their handsome rescuer! It always pleased her to make Tansy as aware as possible of being inferior, so to make her point she began to get up from the floor, extending a little white hand toward Martin, who immediately took it and assisted her. Tansy put the bronze cat down on the floor again, and got up on her own, as did Hermione.

Amanda's fingers closed trustingly over Martin's as

she made sure of his continued full attention. "How do you mean to save us, Lieutenant Ballard?" she inquired, with a skillful flutter of her long lashes.

"In a royal barge fit for Cleopatra herself," he replied.

"Really?" A spark of true interest flashed through Amanda, but Tansy was more practical.

"Do you mean the vessel moored outside, Lieutenant?" she asked.

He nodded, and Amanda's face fell immediately. "Oh."

By now Tusun had seen enough of Miss Amanda Richardson to take a dislike to her. "The lady should be pleased, for it is a very fine *canja.*"

"Yes, I'm sure you think it is," Amanda murmured in a crushing tone that was meant to take the insolent Mameluke down a peg or two.

Tusun merely looked at her, managing to make it quite clear that although Martin might be taken in by her arts, he, Tusun, was not. Tansy found herself warming to the Mameluke. It did not often happen that anyone of the masculine gender proved immune to Amanda's magic, and when it did, the moment was to be savored. It was a pity that Lieutenant Ballard numbered among the foolish majority, because Amanda would treat him badly. She always did.

Tusun noticed the cat at last. "God have mercy! There *is* a cat here!" he gasped, stepping swiftly backward and making the same superstitious sign he had earlier.

"Oh, yes, there's one here all right," said Martin, gathering the tabby from the floor and holding it in his arms. "And quite the little flirt she is too!"

Amanda's nose wrinkled with distaste. "Ugh, horrid furry thing," she muttered, and the tabby put its ears back and spat at her.

Tusun was most perplexed. "I tell you all, there is not supposed to be a cat at Tel el-Osorkon. It is an omen. Something bad is to happen."

"Or something good," Martin reminded him.

"I remember the great black bird," Tusun answered solemnly, not convinced that the cat augured well for anything.

Amanda was a little alarmed. "What great black bird?" she asked.

"It is nothing, Miss Richardson," Martin replied firmly, then gave Tusun a meaningful look.

Hermione changed the subject completely. "Lieutenant Ballard, I don't suppose you happen to have a tinderbox, do you?"

"A tinderbox? Why, yes, I do, for lighting campfires. Why do you ask?"

"There is a wall painting here that I would dearly like to see properly before we leave," she explained. "I have a candle in my reticule. I always needed one on the *Gower* to find my way around in the dark. All those hatchways and so on." She took the candle out to show him.

Tansy was eager too. "Oh, yes, Lieutenant. Please light the candle."

Amanda looked at them as if they were mad. "A wall painting? How very boring," she declared disdainfully.

Martin made to give the cat to Amanda, but she recoiled with a shudder of absolute horror. "Don't bring it near me. I hate cats! Give it to Tansy; after all, cats like mice."

Tansy felt humiliated color warming her cheeks as she took the cat from his arms. Why, oh why, couldn't Amanda be amiable for once? Why did she *always* have to be so unpleasant?

If Martin noticed anything, he gave no sign of it. As soon as his arms were free, he searched in his robes for the tinderbox. "Only light the candle for a few moments," he said, "in case the glow is visible from outside. I don't think it will be, because of the oleanders, but it won't do to test the point for too long."

Seconds later the candle flame swayed as Hermione held it up to the wall. They all gazed at the painting.

Amanda wasn't impressed by the ancient work of art. "It's not even very good. The man is looking sideways, yet his eye is looking straight at us. And whoever heard of a retriever cat? It's stupid."

"The Ancient Egyptians always painted eyes like that," Hermione said. "And the scene is from a myth that involves just such a cat."

Tansy smiled. "And even if you don't like it, Amanda, I certainly do."

"You would. It's just the sort of dull thing I'd expect would impress you," Amanda answered ungraciously.

Hermione extinguished the candle, and Martin went to the entrance to look down at the river. Then he nodded at Tusun. "I fancy the time is right to set about our act of piracy."

"I think so too, Effendi."

Martin turned to the women. "I want you to wait until you hear the sound of an owl calling. Three notes—two short, one long. The moment you hear it, you are to leave here and go down the steps to the *canja*. Keep your heads covered, for you must appear to be Egyptian women from the camp. Don't wait, don't dither, just board the *canja*. Tusun and I will deal with anyone who tries to stop you." He smiled. "We'll soon have you safe," he said, then stroked the tabby's head one last time before going out, Tusun at his heels.

# 9

*M*artin and Tusun moved secretly along the river-bank under cover of the thick reeds; then without a sound they entered the chilly water upstream of the *canja*. Their robes tugged in the current as they floated downstream to cling to the vessel's stern by some trailing ropes. Their breath was silvery in the bitterly cold air as they listened carefully for any sounds from the cabins or deck. Ashore there were lamps on the loggia, but not a soul moved; nor was there any sound from the encampment. The statue of Bastet gazed serenely from the summit of the temple mound, her stone surfaces seeming almost silver in the moonlight.

The two men pulled themselves aboard, then crouched low between the tiller and the super-structure. A single infantryman was seated on a piece of granite column among the looted antiquities. His rifle was at his side as he dozed. Tusun caught Martin's arm, and they moved silently toward the hapless sentry. A blow from Tusun's fist laid him unconscious on the deck, and Tusun immediately purloined his uniform to replace his own dripping clothes. He was very careful to transfer all his jewels, even to putting the spray of jewels from his turban in the sentry's shako.

Martin checked the cabins, and there was no one there. They were packed with more stolen antiquities, and behind a door he found some some robes. When he too had changed, he rejoined Tusun on the deck, and together they checked all the mooring ropes. It was a large vessel for only two men, but the current was favorable, and once they had slipped away from the temple, perhaps they could hoist the sails. First, however, they had to get the women aboard. They unfastened all ropes, except one at the stern, and the *canja* rocked slightly as the flow of the river sucked at her, but she remained close to the bank. Only then did Martin put his hands to his mouth and make the owl signal.

Tansy was waiting at the entrance, with the bronze cat in her hand and the tabby at her feet. As soon as she heard the signal, she nodded at the others and they all pulled the hoods of their robes over their heads, then picked up the bundles containing their European clothes. One by one they moved out to the oleanders, and Tansy was dismayed to see the tabby slip away into the shadows, for she had secretly hoped it would come with them.

The loggia remained silent and deserted, so Hermione led Amanda up the steep slope to the steps. Tansy lingered a moment in the doorway. She still held the figurine, which suddenly became much warmer. Something made her turn to look back at the wall painting. In the uncertain light she thought the retriever cat was more faded than before, as if several centuries of sunlight had shone upon it in the last half hour. She closed her eyes, and when she opened them again the cat had disappeared.

Hermione's anxious whisper drifted down from the steps. "Tansy? Is something wrong?"

"No . . . I'm all right." Tansy looked back at the wall for a last time. The retriever cat was no more, and the bronze cat now felt quite cold. Imagination and a trick of the light? Yes, for what else could it be? Gathering her skirts, she started up the slope, aware as she did so that a little tabby shadow was at her heels.

Hermione and Amanda waited nervously, and as Tansy joined them she knew how very exposed and visible they all were. They would be seen by anyone who happened to come out onto the loggia. Quickly they went down toward the river, but saw a French sentry standing on the *canja's* deck. Their progress faltered and came to a disconcerted halt. Maybe the owl had been a real one, not the signal! Maybe Martin and Tusun weren't ready for them yet! Then a Frenchman shouted from the loggia. "*Istanna!* Wait! Who goes there?"

Amanda panicked, and she would have run on had not Tansy caught her wrist and forced her to stay. Hermione rose to the occasion, having noticed from the corner of her eye that the sentry was suspiciously like Tusun in appearance. She turned to look coolly up at the officer who had challenged them, and said good morning to him in a calm, clear tone. "*SabāH an-nūr, Effendi.*"

"Where do you think you are going?" he demanded in the same language.

"Why, to see what business we can do with your sentry," she replied.

He spat roundly on the floor. "*Bedowé!*" he said. *Peasants!*

Hermione was admirably unruffled. "*Ma'as salāma,*" she replied. *Go in safety.*

The officer scowled down at them, but to their relief he went back into the residence, and all was quiet again, except for Tusun's harsh whisper from the *canja.* "God's grace is with us, ladies. Come quickly!"

They hurried onto the plank of wood that led from the bank to the deck, and Tansy was overjoyed to see the tabby dash aboard as well, but Tusun wasn't so pleased. He made a sign to ward off the evil eye as the cat disappeared among the crates; then he drew the plank onto the vessel and laid it quietly on the deck. Martin waited at the stern, and the moment the women were aboard, he cast off the remaining rope and took the tiller.

Time seemed to stand still for a long moment. The *canja* did not move, and Tansy feared it was caught fast among the reeds, but then, gradually, the bow inched away from the bank. The reeds rustled as the vessel nosed through them toward the open water in the middle of the channel. Everything remained quiet behind them, although at any second Tansy expected to hear shouts. But none came. Tusun appeared at her side, looking very odd in his stolen French uniform. "God is merciful, is he not, lady?" he whispered.

"It would seem so, Tusun," she replied softly.

He glanced at the bronze cat in her hand. "You have no fear of such things, lady?"

"Fear? No. I love cats, whatever and wherever they are." She put the bronze cat to her lips and kissed it, for if this particular cat had not tripped Amanda, they would have taken refuge in the residence itself, and by now would be prisoners of the French.

Tusun's eyes glittered as much as his diamonds in the moonlight. "Lady, in a moment I will see that your companions go into the cabins, where they will be safely out of the way. But for you I have a task."

"Task?"

He smiled. "The lieutenant needs your assistance, I think."

"In what way?"

"He cannot look ahead and behind at the same time, and I have other things to do if this vessel is to reach the sea intact. So, lady, use the opportunity. Without your cousin's false smiles to blind him, maybe he will judge for himself which pretty face is more worthy."

Tansy felt embarrassment rush into her cheeks. Had she been *that* obvious?

"I am very observant, lady, and consider myself a just man. It would not be right for the lieutenant to fall prey to such as your cousin. So take the help I offer you. Go to him. Make him see the worthiness in your eyes."

Before she could say anything more, he stepped lightly away toward Hermione and Amanda, who were standing nervously together forward of the cabins. After glancing back toward the still-silent riverbank, he ushered them inside. Tansy hesitated about going to help Martin, but then thought again. It would be craven indeed to draw back and not only do nothing to help her own cause, but at the same time allow heartless Amanda to toy with him for the sheer spite of it. Even Church Mouse could fight. So she made her way to the stern.

Martin smiled as she approached. "This is almost too smooth a getaway, is it not?" he breathed, following Tusun's example by glancing warily over his shoulder at the shore, where all remained miraculously calm.

"May it stay that way," she whispered back. "Lieutenant, I'm here because Tusun said you needed help. Two sets of eyes being better than one, or some such thing?"

"He's right. You keep a watch astern."

She did as he instructed. The temple mound rose darkly against the predawn sky, but the statue of Bastet now caught the first rays of the rising sun. As the *canja* slid slowly downstream she saw some of the campfires for the first time, but just as the escape seemed to have succeeded without detection, someone raised the alarm. Suddenly there was pandemonium as French soldiers poured toward the riverbank, firing at random so that shots whined all around. Martin shoved Tansy down on the deck so roughly that for a moment she lost her grip on the figurine. As she grabbed it, she became aware of the frightened tabby pressing against her.

Further along the deck Tusun took aim with his rifle and began to return the fire. Martin bent low at the tiller, trying to present as small a target as possible as he guided the *canja*. The current seemed so slow that he could almost have sworn the Nile had ceased to flow, but gradually, oh, so gradually, the vessel glided on. The French ran along the bank, still firing. Frightened birds rose from the reeds and palms, their cries vying with the gunfire, and throughout it all Tansy pressed so flat against the deck that she almost became part of it. Only once did she dare to raise her head, to see that the *canja* was moving toward an area of wild marshland, with reeds and dense bushes. On the far shore, away from the French, there were a number of small channels that offered hiding for even a large vessel.

Martin swung the tiller toward a narrow neck of water that disappeared beyond clumps of date palms and sycamore figs. The furious French fired indiscriminately after the *canja,* and some of the shots struck the timbers, sending splinters flying. There was a rustle of foliage as the vessel nosed into the channel. Tansy stared behind, watching the rifle flashes through the dawn gloom; then reeds and branches closed like curtains, and the stolen vessel vanished into the oblivion of the marsh.

# 10

As the *canja* slid further from the French, Tansy got to her feet again. She shook out her robes and tried to compose herself, only too aware of having just been shot at. The tabby was aware too, and it ran back to its hiding place among the crates.

Martin straightened and reached out impulsively to pull Tansy close. "It's all right now; we're safe." It was a natural action on his part, a desire to console her after a harsh experience, and she knew no more than that could be read into it. But she wanted to rest her head against his shoulders and close her eyes, wanted to slip her arms around him and take far more than consolation from his closeness. She pulled away self-consciously, afraid she might give in to the temptation. He immediately became self-conscious as well. "Please don't misinterpret, for I meant nothing. . . ."

"I know you didn't, and I haven't misinterpreted," she replied quickly. "It's just that I felt a rather childish urge to cling to you for comfort, and that would indeed have been open to misinterpretation." She managed to give him a quick smile, but she felt dreadful. Childish was the very last thing her stifled urge had been!

The smile was reciprocated. "I'm sure I would have taken the impulse for what it was, because I am equally sure that you would never behave forwardly or improperly in any way."

*No, but I would like to,* she thought ruefully. When

he walked into the hidden room at Tel el-Osorkon, her senses had awakened from a lifetime of slumber. One arresting glance of his dark eyes had sealed her fate, sending abandoned emotions leaping through her veins that still coursed through them now. Oh, such wonderful, spellbinding emotions. As if she had been waiting for him. Just for him . . .

The *canja* glided on into the depths of the marsh, finding a way through rich foliage that sometimes brushed audibly along the deck. Tel el-Osorkon slipped further and further behind, and with it the sense of danger. Tusun went quietly about his tasks, tightening a rope here, loosing one there, making sure everything was secure. To the east the sun rose steadily, sending blinding flashes of light through the leaves and branches. A flight of waterfowl flew high against the early morning sky, and Tansy gazed around, thinking how romantic it was. But Martin's next words were a douse of cold water on thoughts of romance.

"Lord Sanderby is very fortunate to be marrying a bride as beautiful as your cousin. Has she known him long?"

"She does not know him at all. It is an arranged match."

Martin watched her. "Am I to understand your cousin doesn't want the match?"

Tansy realized she had misled him. "Oh, no! Please don't think she is being forced into something against her will. Amanda is very pleased indeed to have secured so advantageous a contract."

"Arranged marriages can be successful, I know, but I would not care for one myself. I hope I will one day make a love match."

Tansy found a smile. "A sentiment I share, Lieutenant, but then I will never aspire to an aristocratic husband. Who knows how I might feel if faced with the chance of becoming a countess?"

"You say that as if it were so far into the realms of fantasy as to be utterly impossible."

"So it is," she replied emphatically.

"You do both yourself and the aristocracy a grave injustice."

"You, sir, know too well how to flatter." But although he complimented her, his words showed how little chance she stood with him. Amanda was the one to have caught his interest.

He laughed. "Flattery is part of naval training."

"So I perceive."

They smiled at each other, and she fell even further under his spell, if that were possible. But once again he brought her down to earth with a bump. "When is your cousin's wedding to take place?"

"This summer. Amanda's father—my Uncle Franklyn—was until recently on diplomatic duty in Constantinople, and we were with him. He has now been posted on to Australia, but arranged Amanda's match before he left. She and I are on our way back to England, under Hermione's . . . I mean Mrs. Entwhistle's wing. We are to live with our remaining uncle, Sir Julian Richardson, at his estate of Chelworth in Dorset."

"Chelworth? I know it. Well, perhaps it would be more accurate to say I have used it as a landmark. It stands on the slope above a bay, about halfway between Portland Bill and St. Aldhelm's Head. The house looks more like something from this part of the world than rural Dorset, and there is a pyramid folly on the hilltop behind it."

"Uncle Julian is quite devoted to the study of Ancient Egypt. Actually, he and the late Lord Sanderby—" She broke off, thinking that perhaps it would be indiscreet to mention the great quarrel.

"Do go on," Martin prompted, ducking as an overhanging branch swept along the cabin roof toward him.

"I'm sure you don't want to hear about the terrible professional jealousy that Lord Sanderby's father displayed toward Uncle Julian."

"You cannot tantalize me with such a statement, and then decline to elaborate. It would be too cruel."

"Very well, I will bore you with all the details." She told him all she knew about those long-ago events.

Martin's brows drew together as he listened, and when she finished he pulled a puzzled face. "You know, it all sounds strangely familiar. I'm sure I've heard the story before, and yet I cannot think where. Although . . ." He thought for a moment. "Actually, I think I overheard my mother telling my father. I was a child at the time."

"I believe it was quite a cause célèbre for a while. Poor Uncle Julian is still very upset about it all even now, which may be . . ." She didn't finish.

"Which may be why he doesn't approve of your cousin's match?"

Tansy nodded a little awkwardly, feeling she had elaborated a little too much. She shouldn't have told him all she had.

Martin smiled. "Please do not look so worried, for I assure you that I know when to keep a confidence. Nothing you have said will ever pass my lips."

Tusun came to join them, having accomplished his tasks for the time being. "The other ladies wish to stay in the cabins, Effendi," he said. "Well, the young lady wishes to stay there, and the older one feels she must remain with her. There are many tears, you see."

Amanda making a fuss again, Tansy thought, far from displeased that her cousin was going to stay out of the way.

Tusun leaned back against the cabin superstructure and gave them a smile of some satisfaction. "We have done it, eh, Effendi? We have rescued the ladies, stolen this fine *canja,* and escaped the French. All we need now is that God remains with us."

Martin grinned. "He will, Tusun."

"For that we must pray." Tusun glanced at Tansy. "So, Effendi," he went on to Martin, "you have another helper."

"And she's far prettier than you, my friend," Martin replied.

"This I do not dispute." The Mameluke gave Tansy

a broad wink, then looked astern, where all that could be seen was an undisturbed forest of every lush green in creation. The dense cloak of delta vegetation hid even the great statue of Bastet, so tall on the summit of the temple mound. "The French will not give us trouble now; so we must plan what to do next, Effendi."

"I'm not so sure that we've seen the last of them. That officer was not the sort to give up his booty without a fight." Martin grew pensive. "It's my guess that he'll anticipate us rejoining the main Rosetta channel. I have a feeling he'll set an ambush somewhere close to Rosetta itself. At least, that's my instinct."

"Then we must not use the Rosetta channel," Tusun replied logically. "If we keep to watercourses that take us east, to one of the other main channels . . ."

"The Rosetta is closer, and will take us more directly to the *Lucina*. Besides, the current is taking us without any need to hoist the sails, and I would rather follow the flow and lie low like this, than risk hoisting the sails to cross the delta against the water."

"So what can we do about the French, Effendi? If we must rejoin the main channel, then we must join it, and risk any ambush that may be set." The Mameluke spread his hands.

Martin nodded. "Yes, but we do not need to enter the Rosetta channel in daylight, do we? We can find a hiding place somewhere in all this damned vegetation, wait until night falls again, then make a run for the sea, and the *Lucina*."

Tusun regarded the marsh. "Are you are sure you can find your way out of here again, Effendi?" he inquired a little impishly.

"Are you questioning my navigating talents, you rogue? I'll have you know that every officer in His Majesty's navy can find his way out of any backwater, even one such as this."

The tabby cat meowed as it came to rub around Tansy's skirts again. She picked it up to cuddle, and

Tusun scowled. "Cats are bad luck on a boat," he declared, almost predictably.

Martin shook his head. "On the contrary, every vessel should have a cat; they keep the rats at bay."

Tansy cuddled the animal close. "I shall have to give you a name," she whispered to it.

Tusun shrugged. "My mother was foolish enough to like cats. She had one she called Miw. It is the name the pharaohs gave to all cats."

But Tansy had already decided. "I shall call her Cleopatra," she said. "Cleo for short." The tabby immediately looked up at her and began to purr.

# 11

Sir Julian was taking breakfast in his house in Park Lane. He wore his dressing gown over his shirt and breeches, and there was an embroidered skullcap on his head. The morning sun flooded into the dining room, which looked onto the gardens behind the house. Snowdrops and crocuses flowered on the pocket-handkerchief lawn, where the overnight frost had now melted. It was, Sir Julian reflected a little sadly, the last time he would see them in bloom here. But he wasn't sad enough to want to change his mind about selling.

A coal fire flickered in the hearth, its flames pale and almost transparent in the bright light from the window, where Ozzy was taking the sun on the sill. The tomcat had enjoyed a feast of crisp bacon fat, which had been neatly cut up for him on his special plate on the table, Sir Julian being no stickler for etiquette. Now a cheeky robin fluttered to the ground just on the other side of the window, which annoyed Ozzy very much. His tail lashed, and he began to make angry clicking noises with his jaws.

"Oh, do stop that, you foolish creature," Sir Julian muttered, picking up his newspaper and attempting to read. But Randal kept intruding upon his thoughts. At last the newspaper was set aside, another cup of thick black coffee was poured, and proper consideration was given to the man who threatened to stir up so much mud from the bottom of the lake. How very alarmed Randal must have been when he discovered the scandalous family secret that could conceivably rob him of everything. Was that the real reason for the match with Amanda? The security her fortune would provide if he did lose all because of the secret? Yes, of course . . .

Sir Julian's eyes cleared as he began to unravel Randal's motives. Of all the likely heiresses, how clever to choose her, for once she was Lady Sanderby, the letter's revelations would ruin her life too. Randal was taking the calculated risk that her uncle would not be able to bring himself to do that to his own flesh and blood. He was also relying on the fact that Felice's doting lover would continue to protect her son and her good name, as he had for all these long years. Sir Julian could imagine Randal's apoplectic fury at finding his future so completely in the hands of a man he loathed, and who loathed him.

It would be no less than justice if it were to come out at last, but there were degrees of justice, and Felice had been desperate to bury it all so that it never saw the light of day. Sir Julian reached into his dressing gown pocket for the battered leather pouch that never left his side. There, in a double lining, he kept a folded theater handbill, dog-eared now and fragile, but still legible. It was for David Garrick's farewell performance at the Theatre Royal, Drury Lane on Monday, June 10, 1775. But it wasn't the handbill itself that Sir Julian studied now, for in the margin was the message Felice had sent to him by the box keeper.

*My adored J,*
*My heart is filled with love as I sit here opposite your box. I see only you, not great Garrick's last glory. You are so near and yet so far, but soon we will be together forever. My decision is made. I will slip away from E directly after the performance is ended. There will be no going back.*

*F.*

Tears shimmered in Sir Julian's eyes. That night had seen the last moments of reckless hope, the last sighs of foolish abandonment, for as the final curtain came down upon the stage, her husband took cruel delight in revealing that he knew of her illicit love affair. Esmond then told her the shocking truth that changed everything. So few words were needed, just the plain, unpalatable facts, and as the audience rose to cheer Garrick's parting speech, Felice, Countess of Sanderby, had fallen in a faint from which it took much sal volatile to bring her around. From that moment on she had been bound to her despised husband as surely as if with iron chains. Only one person in the world did she place before herself, before even the lover she had so nearly gone to, and that was her child. Randal Fenworth, so mean hearted and despicable, did not deserve such a mother, but even he would have ceased to be of such importance if—

Someone coughed. "Begging your pardon, Sir Julian, but Lord Sanderby has called."

"Eh?" Sir Julian hadn't heard the footman enter.

"Lord Sanderby has called, sir."

What now? Sir Julian composed himself as he replaced the handbill in the pouch.

"His lordship respectfully requests a few moments to speak with you about arrangements for his forthcoming marriage to Miss Amanda," the footman explained.

"Very well, show him in. But if he should still be here in ten minutes, be sure to remind me it is time to prepare for my very important appointment in the city."

"Yes, sir." The footman began to withdraw, but then he remembered something else the caller had requested. "Begging your pardon again, Sir Julian, but his lordship trusts the cat will not be present."

"Does he, be damned? Well, he can trust away, for Ozymandias stays."

"Yes, sir." The footman bowed and went out.

Sir Julian tossed his napkin on the table, rose from

his chair, and addressed the cat on the windowsill. "Ozzy, there is more bacon fat for you if you make yourself useful while this fellow is here."

The door opened again, and Randal was shown in, his gilt spurs clinking on the marble floor. He was dressed to ride in Hyde Park, in a dark green coat, dull golden waistcoat, and white breeches, although riding was one of his least favorite pastimes. His fair hair was tied back with a ribbon that matched his waistcoat, and his starched neck cloth was an intricate work of art. An indifferent horseman at the best of times, he was nevertheless prepared to obey the rules of fashion by being the peacock in Rotten Row. To this end he was so perfectly turned out that a hair out of place would have ruined the effect. What would also have ruined the effect would be a horse that showed any sign at all of blood or spirit. However, in the bay gelding now attended at the front entrance by one of Sir Julian's grooms, he had found a mount that pranced a lot, but was actually quite docile.

He waited until the door was closed behind him, then sketched a stylish bow. "Good morning, Sir Julian. I trust you had a good journey from the coast?" he greeted, his eyes and nose initially quite unaffected by Ozzy's close proximity.

"I think you already know how my journey went, seeing you followed me for a while," Sir Julian replied, going to the fireplace and standing with his hands clasped behind him.

"Followed you?" Randal was all innocence. "If you were followed, it was not by me." Ozzy chose that moment to jump up onto the table. Ginger fur floated invisibly, and Randal's nose immediately began to react, and he reached hastily for his handkerchief. "Dab it all, Richardson. I bade it clear I wanted no cats!"

"This is my house, not yours, and it pleases me to keep Ozymandias with me. Now then, what brings you here, Sanderby?"

Randal had been on the point of advancing to a

more dominant position in the center of the room, but now he kept well back by the door. "It is a while since our beeting at Chelworth, so I thought I would pay you a friendly call."

"Only a fool would believe *that;* so get to the real point, whatever it is."

"In good tibe, Richardson, in good tibe. A few social niceties first, eh?" Ozzy bestowed a baleful look on the visitor and growled low in his throat. Randal eyed the tomcat uneasily, then blew his nose again and continued stoically. "Have you heard when Abanda will reach England?" he asked Sir Julian.

"If she has any sense, she'll still follow her father to Australia."

"Ah, how droll you are, to be sure," Randal murmured, watching Ozzy, whose amber eyes did not waver from him.

"Drollness has nothing to do with it, Sanderby, for I mean every word."

"I ab sure you do, but your opinion bakes no difference to be. What *does* bake a difference, however, is the knowledge that as a child I cabe within an inch of being deserted in favor of you."

*That isn't really what matters to you now,* Sir Julian thought, in his mind's eye seeing Felice's all-important letter in the statue's secret compartment at Chelworth. Ozzy was acutely conscious of the atmosphere between the two men, and he ventured to the edge of the table closest to Randal, then spat as threateningly as he could. Sir Julian could barely conceal his admiration for his pet's noble efforts. Ozymandias was past master of delivering feline invective. There would *definitely* be another plate of bacon after this, as deliciously light and crisp as the cook could manage.

Admiration was the very last thing Randal felt for the bristling ginger quadruped. He furiously regarded Ozzy, and then sneezed again. Handkerchief flapping at his nose, he spoke again. "Sir Julian, I suggest we stop beating about the bush. Your affair with by dear Baba is really neither here nor there, is it? What really batters is what happened five years before you and she exchanged so much as a glance, let alone stole a clandestine kiss."

Sir Julian contrived to look puzzled. "What in God's own name are you getting at?" he demanded. "I know nothing of anything that might have gone on five years before I met her."

"You are playing with fire again, Sir Julian. I know frob by father's diary that she wrote you a long and exceedingly delicate letter."

Sir Julian's heart missed a beat. Until this moment, Randal's knowledge of the letter had just been guesswork, unconfirmed and therefore not to be entirely believed. Now it was confirmed.

Randal went on. "She detailed her exact reasons for not seeing you anybore. Naturally enough, given the circubstances, by father tried to prevent the letter frob reaching you. He failed, but then you already know that, because you have the letter. Don't you." The last two words were a statement, not a question.

"I really don't know what you're talking about," Sir Julian replied, determined to protect the letter at all costs, but he could see by Randal's eyes that the denial failed to convince.

"Oh, I think we both know there was a letter, Sir Julian." Randal blew his nose. "That's why you're here in London, isn't it? To see how great a ripple you can cause in the pool?"

So that was what had prompted the visit. "You're wrong . . . about everything. I'm here in London to attend to the sale of this house and to visit the British Museum in order to examine a papyrus. And I tell you again that I know nothing of any letter from your mother."

"Why do you persist in speaking to be as if I were a boron? The letter is fact, you know it and I know it, so will you *please* stop this dabbed pretence?" Randal's eyes were now very red and bloodshot, and he looked quite dreadful, but his voice remained cold and level.

"There is no letter," Sir Julian insisted. "Believe me, don't believe me, I really could not care less."

"On the contrary, I think you care very buch. You still have the letter, and the only reason you haven't used it is because it would hurt by Baba. You don't give a dab about be; in fact, I would have been sacrificed long since if it weren't for her. And I still will be if you were to find a certain other party; isn't that so?" The last words were uttered quietly, reasonably, as if remarking upon the fine weather outside.

"Certain other party? Heavens above, man, will you please stop speaking in riddles?"

The moments hung so silently in the room that the crackle of the fire seemed suddenly very loud. Ozzy growled again, and he shuffled up and down the edge of the table, as if gauging whether or not he could leap upon Randal.

Randal tried to ignore the animal. "You know, Sir Julian, the fellow bust be dead and buried. Don't you think by father bade it his business to search? But there was no trace." His face hardened. "I warn you, Richardson, bake trouble for be and I will see you are dead and buried too."

Sir Julian raised his chin. "I've had enough of this arrant nonsense, Sanderby. How dare you enter my house and presume to threaten me! If and when you are married to Amanda, I suppose I will have to tolerate you somehow, but in the meantime, if you ever cross my threshold uninvited again, I will have you thrown out like the cur you are. Now get out!"

There was a tap at the door, and the footman entered. "Begging your pardon, Sir Julian, but your carriage will soon be ready to take you to your appointment."

"Ah, yes. Lord Sanderby was just leaving."

"Sir." The footman lingered attentively at the door.

"This isn't the last of it, Richardson, not by a very long chalk."

Sir Julian gave him a beaming smile. "Enjoy your ride in the park, Sanderby. Take care not to fall."

Randal glowered at him, then turned to leave; but as he reached the door, Ozzy decided to go out with him. The tomcat leaped from the table and darted between Randal's ankles in such a way as to unbalance him. It looked almost deliberate on the cat's part, Sir Julian thought, as his visitor's modish spurs tangled and Randal went sprawling. The dismayed footman bent to attend to him, and Ozzy, well pleased with himself, dashed away toward the kitchens, tail in the air, ears pricked.

Sir Julian made a mental note to add a dish of the very best cream to the plate of bacon fat.

# 12

*I*t was midmorning in the delta, and a palm dove was fluting in the tamarisks. The temperature had risen pleasantly with the dominance of the sun, and the wind had dwindled to the occasional zephyr that stirred the tall reeds where the *canja* lay concealed. When darkness fell, the gauntlet of the Rosetta channel would be run.

Leaving Amanda and Hermione still slumbering, Tansy slipped out of the cabin after several hours of much-needed sleep. She still wore the black robes, and her short dark curls were in a terrible tangle because she had no comb or brush. Amanda's hair, however, was once again a smooth stream of molten gold flowing over her shoulders. This could only be because the sly madam had discovered a comb somewhere, but she denied this most vehemently in order to deny the others the chance to make themselves presentable in front of the two men.

Such pettiness was proof positive of Amanda's true colors, but Tansy guessed that even so Martin only saw how beautiful she was. To make matters worse, Amanda flirted with him at every opportunity, and he seemed taken in. It seemed to Tansy that if the future Countess of Sanderby fell in a midden, she would emerge smelling of spring flowers!

In spite of her earlier resolve to put up a fight, Tansy's lack of confidence was already showing, for if there was one thing she had learned about her cousin, it was that what Amanda set out to have, Amanda always got. At the moment it amused that lady to toy with Martin Ballard's affections, so nothing the Church Mouse of the family said or did would make any difference.

At the moment Martin was asleep on the deck, wrapped in a blanket, his head on a bundle of sacks, but Tusun was on guard at the stern. The Mameluke put a warning finger to his lips as Tansy made her way to the bow of the *canja*. There she lay down on her stomach and stretched forward to part the reeds in order to look across a clear expanse of water toward the mud-brick village they now realized was on the opposite shore. When the *canja* hid among the reeds during the night, at a time when the moon had again gone behind clouds, it was thought to be a deserted part of the delta. How wrong the assumption was. Still, the reeds were very thick and tall, and no one at the village knew the *canja* and its passengers were there. Beyond the village there were fields of crops and groves of palms and sycamore figs; in the distance, just visible through the haze of sunshine that now bathed the delta, sails glided on the main Rosetta channel.

Tansy watched the villagers going about their business. A donkey cart rattled along a low causeway, chased by a noisy sand-colored dog. Two black-robed women walked gracefully in the opposite direction, balancing bundles and pots on their covered heads. Some older children were tending buffaloes and camels ten times their own size, while some smaller ones delved in the mud for catfish. A small boat rocked only yards from the *canja*, as a loin-clothed man stood in it to toss a net into the water. He was the reason for Tusun's warning finger.

Cleopatra rubbed beside Tansy, who automatically began to stroke her. "Hello, Cleo," she whispered, falling easily into the affectionate diminutive, but then her smile faded as the cat saw a white egret probing a nearby matting of dead reeds. The bird was temptingly within reach as far as any self-respecting cat was concerned.

Tansy tapped Cleo's nose. "No," she whispered sternly, but then the barking of the village dog grew much louder, and her attention was drawn back across the water. Hooves drummed on the causeway, and half a dozen French carabineers rode into view, led by an officer who looked ominously like the one from Tel el-Osorkon. Tansy turned to beckon urgently to Tusun, but it was Martin who came to lie quickly at her side.

"What is it? What have you seen?" he breathed.

"The French are here," she whispered back, and pointed through the reeds. "Isn't that the officer from Tel el-Osorkon? I know we didn't have a good view of him, but even so . . ."

The Frenchmen halted to question the children tending the buffaloes and camels, and snatches of their voices carried across the water. "Yes, it's him all right," Martin murmured, "and by the sound of it, he's looking for us."

"Do you really think so?"

He gave a ghost of a smile. "I really think so."

Tansy had quite forgotten Cleo, until suddenly the cat leaped at the tantalizing egret, which set up a panic-stricken racket that could not help but draw attention to the reeds. The fisherman's small boat wobbled alarmingly as he jerked around to see what was happening. The party of Frenchmen turned as well, and most of the village emerged, wondering what the noise was about. So many eyes were suddenly directed toward the *canja*'s hiding place that Martin slid an arm around Tansy and drew her down flat against the deck. Hearts thundering, they pressed together and prayed no one would come to investigate more closely.

Tusun had slipped into the cabin the moment the disturbance began. He knew Hermione would have the sense not to make a sound, but no such faith could be placed in Amanda. To his relief, she too remained silent, although her cornflower eyes were wide and frightened. Stealthily the Mameluke opened the cabin window and aimed his rifle at the unfortunate fisherman, ready to shoot if necessary. Amanda's eyes widened still further, and Hermione went to quickly take her hand.

Cleo, the unknowing cause of all the sudden tension, continued to set about the unfortunate egret, but the bird was not easy prey. Its white feathers scattered in all directions as it fought for its life, and to its shrieking was added the clamor of other birds all around. Martin raised his head slightly. There was a small piece of wooden plank lying within reach, and he tossed it toward the cat, not intending to hurt her, just make her loosen her grip. It worked, and the screeching egret flew off, shedding more feathers as it went. Cleo yowled with rage.

The moment the cat was heard, the fisherman began to roar with laughter. Then he shouted to the shore, and everyone, including the carabineers, laughed. Attention moved away again, and the immediate danger passed. The fisherman poled his boat a little further on, then set about his nets again, and the other villagers resumed their business as well. Tansy and Martin risked stretching up to observe the French officer ply the children with more questions, but shaking heads were the only answer he received. After a while the officer gave up, and he and his men rode back along the causeway.

Tansy breathed out with relief. "Thank goodness."

Martin rolled onto his back. "Blast that cat!" he muttered, as Cleo crept back on the deck, belly low, and disappeared guiltily among the crates.

Tansy felt guilty too. "I'm sorry."

"Why? It wasn't your fault," Martin replied, his eyes crinkling with amusement.

"But she's my cat."

He put his hand to her cheek suddenly. "And cats will be cats. It really wasn't your fault," he said again.

His touch warmed her to the very heart, like a draft of mulled wine after a walk in the snow, or her first-

ever sip of champagne. She gazed down at him. It
would be so easy to lower her lips to his, so easy to
lie down with him again, hold him in her arms, and
use the seductive arts that were every woman's by
right. . . . Horrified by the path her thoughts were
taking, she scrambled to her feet. Her cheeks were
aflame with embarrassment, and she turned away,
making much of shaking out her robes and straightening them.

He got up as well. "Forgive me. I seem to have
transgressed yet again."

"You didn't transgress before, and you haven't now.
I . . . I'm just a little upset by Cleo's antics. She might
so easily have given us away," she managed to say,
just as Amanda emerged from the cabin, followed by
Hermione and Tusun.

Later, when all was so peaceful again that the incident with the egret seemed almost never to have happened, Tansy sat with her bare feet dangling over the
side of the *canja*. Her toes were well above the water,
where fish played in the sunlight. She watched them
darting and flashing, and was reminded of the wall
painting at Tel el-Osorkon, in which brilliantly colored
fish were depicted beneath the young pharaoh's reed
boat. Her thoughts wandered on to the moment she
left the hidden room and had looked back to think
the retriever cat had gone. Could it really have happened? Well, she supposed it was no less likely than
the changing temperature of the bronze figurine.

Tusun came to sit with her. "All is now tranquil
again, is it not, lady?" he murmured, leaning forward
to look at himself in the water.

"Yes, thank goodness."

"And, I believe, you make progress with the
lieutenant?"

She went a little pink. "Oh, I don't think so, Tusun.
He likes my cousin."

"You are wrong. Believe me, for I know these
things." He drew a long breath, then added, "I have

had to learn to read the minds of others, for I suffered a very bitter lesson."

"What do you mean?"

"I have an uncle, a devious man of no heart, who stole the land that should have been mine. I trusted him, placed my faith in him, and he betrayed me. Now he enjoys my birthright, and has risen high in the service of the French."

"Is that why you help the British?"

The Mameluke smiled. "Maybe so."

"I hope you get back what is yours."

"For that I thank you, lady," he said, and he took her fingers to raise them dashingly to his lips. Then he scrambled to his feet again and left to do some task or other near the bow of the *canja*.

Tansy remained where she was, and after a while she heard a step behind her again. Thinking Tusun had returned, she looked around with a smile, but it was Martin. Her smile vanished as she immediately thought there must be something wrong.

He smiled at the expression on her face. "Don't look so anxious; all is well," he said, sitting down at her side as Tusun had.

"I thought there must be a problem," she confessed, noticing he had a rolled papyrus in his hand.

"Why? Just because I have come to sit with you?"

She had to look away. "Yes, I suppose so," she admitted, feeling certain that Amanda was the one he would have preferred to sit with, but the countess-to-be had retreated to the cabin again, complaining that she was sure she perceived a freckle on her nose. A freckle? Amanda could count herself fortunate, Tansy thought, only too aware of her own defects in that respect.

"You really should not think so little of yourself, Miss Richardson, for to be sure I find you all that is agreeable."

Agreeable? Oh, how a single word could damn!

"And I believe Tusun must think so too, otherwise

he would not have joined you a few minutes ago. Anyway, I have something to show you." He glanced at the papyrus in his hand "When Tusun and I first climbed aboard the *canja,* I noticed that the French had not packed their crates of stolen booty with care. This papyrus was sticking out of one, and just now I went to push it in properly, for it seemed to me that a gust of wind might blow it away. Imagine my surprise when I examined it first, and saw this." He unrolled it and held it up for her to see.

She gasped, for it was decorated with a scene exactly like the one at Tel el-Osorkon. "What a very odd coincidence!"

He studied it again; then his face changed. Tansy saw, and regarded him curiously. "What's wrong?"

"Well, you will probably think me very fanciful, but when I first took it from the crate and examined it, I'm sure there wasn't a cat. But there is, and it's very prominent. See?" A shiver ran over Tansy, for the cat was certainly there now—a tabby just like Cleo. Martin ran his hand ruefully through his hair. "My imagination is clearly running away with me," he murmured.

She had to say something. "Lieutenant, if your imagination is doing that, then so, I fear, is mine. I would be less than honest if I did not confess to a similar experience, although in my case the cat disappeared." She told him what had happened as she left Tel el-Osorkon.

He listened with growing astonishment, and when she finished he gave a slight laugh. "One such occurrence is strange enough and can easily be put down to a trick of the light, but *two* . . . ? Well, that verges on the uncanny."

Tansy studied the cat on the parchment. Things that appeared and disappeared? A bronze figurine that became hot or cold in one's hand? The word *magic* came into her unwilling mind. "Do you believe in magic, Lieutenant?"

"Let us just say that as with fairies and ghosts, without proof one way or the other, I cannot entirely *dis-*

*believe.* The Ancient Egyptians certainly believed in it."

"And right now, I am finding it difficult not to follow suit," she murmured. Then she forced such thoughts away and gave a bright smile. "Let's look at the rest of the treasure," she said, and swung her legs back onto the deck.

He helped her to get up, and they went to examine the crates. Almost immediately Tansy saw something that so seized her attention that the mystery of the appearing/disappearing cat temporarily ceased to matter. Propped between two crates was a slab of black basalt, and the sun fell obliquely across it, revealing lines of inscriptions on its polished surface. Curious, she crouched to look more closely, and her breath caught as she realized the writing was in three sections—hieroglyphic, Greek, and another she did not know.

Hermione's words echoed through her. *I heard that a year or so ago, the French found an inscribed stone of immense importance somewhere near here, at Rosetta, I think. It is said to be written with three different languages, one being Greek, another hieroglyphic, and I'm not sure about the third. Anyway, it is hoped that all the inscriptions are versions of the same text. If so, maybe our understanding will advance at last. I was told that the British confiscated this stone, and I pray the information is correct, for we do not wish the French to have the glory of translating hieroglyphs, do we?* Tansy gazed at it excitedly. What if this was another such stone? What if the words in Greek were an exact translation of the hieroglyphs?

Martin saw the sudden light in her eyes. "What have you found?" he asked.

She straightened. "I . . . I don't know. It may be nothing. I'll have to bring Hermione." Catching up her skirts, she hurried to the cabins, her bare feet making hardly a sound.

Moments later everyone gathered to examine the intriguing slab. Hermione was all interest; indeed her eyes shone. "I do believe you may be right, Tansy," she declared, trying to keep her voice down, for they were all still aware of the close proximity of the village.

Amanda pouted. "I really don't understand why you are all so silly about an old piece of stone. What on earth does it matter what it says?"

Tusun looked at her. "God wills it that we have minds with which to reason."

She flushed. "Really? I am surprised that you should presume to know God's will," she said coldly; then with a toss of her lovely head she stalked away to the stern, where she draped herself prettily against the tiller and gazed at the swaying greenery.

Tusun scowled after her and said something beneath his breath that Tansy felt certain was anything but complimentary.

Hermione drew Tansy closer in order to point out the finer details of the slab, and when Tansy looked around a few minutes later, she saw that Martin had gone to join Amanda by the tiller. Amanda was at her most kittenish and bewitching, placing a teasing hand upon his arm and giving him flirtatious glances that verged on the sensuous because of her long lashes. They might have been at a fashionable London assembly instead of the deck of a stolen *canja* in the furthest reaches of the Nile delta.

Tansy couldn't look away, and Hermione's voice faded into oblivion. Amanda knew the Church Mouse was watching, and it was just what she wanted. She thought it was fine sport to hurt Tansy by conquering Martin. For a split second the cousins looked at each other; then Amanda, ever shallow and heartless, gave a toss of her lovely head and moved her position a little, so that Martin had to turn his back completely on Tansy.

An invisible door closed upon the Church Mouse, as surely as if it had been paneled with wood and secured with lock and key.

# 13

The sun was high in London too, as Sir Julian drove
back to Park Lane after visiting the British Museum and keeping an appointment with his lawyer.
Arrangements for the sale of his London house were
now in hand, and so, rather shamefully, was the museum's papyrus! Sir Julian hung his head a little, for he
was guilty of theft. The moment he'd seen the papyrus
again, lying in the display case amid a collection of
scarabs, jeweled pectorals, offering trays, and bronze
daggers, it had reminded him so much of the papyrus
at Chelworth that he was sure they were both from
the same original. He recalled corresponding with a
reverend gentleman named Endpipe, or Bluntwhistle,
or some such name, who had been very knowledgeable on the topic of retriever cats. Mention had been
made of the story of King Osorkon, and Sir Julian felt
certain that was what both papyri depicted. The only
way to be certain was to place them together. Hence
the act of base theft. However, he assuaged his conscience by vowing to return the stolen papyrus as soon
as possible.

The route back to Park Lane took him through
Grosvenor Square, where the observation of a traveling carriage outside Randal's house abruptly banished
the papyrus from his mind. It was Randal's carriage,
for it had his badge on the door—a hand brandishing
a lighted torch, in honor of his family motto. Luggage
was being carried out, signifying a departure from

town, but Sir Julian's initial relief was soon replaced by suspicion. All well and good if Randal's destination was his country seat in Westmorland, but what if it was Dorset? What if he had the theft of the letter in mind? As Lysons drove around the corner into South Audley Street, Sir Julian hastily lowered the glass. "Lysons! I must speak with you!"

The coachman maneuvered the team to the curb, clambered down, and came to the door. "Sir?"

"I want you to walk back to the square, to number sixteen-B. I need to know where Lord Sanderby is going. Be discreet now, for it won't do for them to know who your master is." Lysons touched his hat and hurried back along the pavement. Minutes passed, but at last he returned. "Well?" Sir Julian demanded impatiently.

"Lord Sanderby is leaving for Dorset, Sir Julian. He has taken a house called Bothenbury somewhere close to Weymouth, in order to be nearby when Miss Amanda arrives."

Sir Julian's mind raced. Yes, being near Amanda was plausible, but was it the whole truth? More likely the letter was Sanderby's true objective. He drew back into the carriage and sat down once more. It wouldn't do to remain here in town a moment longer. He'd send a man ahead on horseback to warn the servants at Chelworth; then he'd set off for Dorset himself first thing in the morning. The letter had to be protected, for it was the only evidence he had—mayhap all the evidence that remained.

Not realizing his plans had been discovered, Randal emerged from his front door to commence his journey. He paused on the threshold for a moment, tugging on his tight kid gloves. His tall hat was at a jaunty angle, but he did not feel jaunty. He ached from head to toe, having been thrown from his horse in Hyde Park in front of everyone, and the prospect of a long bumpy journey did not please him at all.

But he needed to destroy that letter, and what better time to search Chelworth than when the old curmudgeon was here in town? Every other scrap of evidence had been burned, from the relevant parish register, to the *coucheur*'s records. The clergyman had proved impossible to trace, but must surely have gone to his Maker by now, for if he were still alive he would be damned nigh a hundred. The others involved must be dead too, so completely had they vanished from the face of the earth. The letter was all that remained, but it was a potent weapon in the wrong hands.

He walked toward the waiting carriage. Plague take Richardson for residing in so bucolic a county. Still, there would be some compensation. A pretty little *belle de nuit* was accompanying him. After all, a fellow's nights should never be spent alone. One of the footmen stepped quickly forward. "My lord?"

"Yes? What is it?"

"I think you should know that someone came to inquire where you were going, and Arnold told him." The man glanced at his fellow footman, who kept his eyes fixed guiltily to the pavement.

Randal's attention sharpened. "Who was it?" he demanded.

"I don't know, sir, but I'm pretty sure he was a coachman. A carriage drove past shortly before he came, and I feel certain he was on the box."

"Describe the carriage," Randal ordered. The footman obliged, and as chance would have it recalled the pharaoh's-head emblem on the door. Randal's eyes darkened. "Richardson!" he breathed.

Still, it was unlikely the old fool would set off before tomorrow, which still left a little time to search Chelworth for the letter.

# 14

The Egyptian twilight was very brief. The sky changed from turquoise to viridian, then to mauve and gold. At the village some small boys coaxed a reluctant buffalo out of the river and led it away. Birdsong was piercing, and a breeze crept up to ripple the surface of the water. Gradually all became quiet. Darkness seemed to descend suddenly, and the birds ceased their noise.

The matter of poling the *canja* out of the reeds commenced almost immediately. It was a very slow business, even with Tansy and Hermione assisting the two men. Amanda, naturally enough, had such delicate wrists that she could not even hold the oars strongly, let alone use them for something as strenuous as poling. As soon as the stern projected into open water, Tansy and Hermione were sent to join Amanda in the safety of the cabins, while Martin and Tusun continued the work alone.

The women waited nervously. Tansy was by a window, with Cleo curled up on her lap. She felt the vessel rock slightly as the current washed by, and looked out to see the reeds begin to slip slowly behind. Suddenly there were no reeds, and she held her breath as she had done when they left Tel el-Osorkon. On that occasion there had been shouts as the alarm was raised, but this time there was nothing. No one in the village saw the vessel as the lazy Nile flow carried it past the cluster of mud-brick buildings. Not so much as a barking dog signaled its passage, and soon everything was far behind as the *canja* made for the main channel, where her sails would be hoisted to catch the breeze, which providence now decreed should blow from the south. There was a hint of the desert from that direction, a promise of the baking hot summer that was to come.

Amanda's taunting voice suddenly fell into the silent cabin. "I rather think our gallant lieutenant is my adoring slave. Don't you agree, Tansy?"

Hermione's angry glance would have withered anyone else on the spot, but Amanda was impervious to such things. Her beautiful cornflower eyes glittered in the darkness, and her gloating smile was cruel. Tansy answered unwillingly. "He certainly admires you greatly."

"It will be amusing to break his heart."

Hermione could not hide her contempt. "Your notion of amusement leaves a lot to be desired, Amanda."

Tansy was startled by the chaperone's bluntness, but Amanda was outraged. "How *dare* you speak to me like that!" she cried, her raised voice awakening Cleo on Tansy's lap. The tabby growled, put her ears back, and swished her tail.

Hermione wasn't apologetic. "Amanda, I was employed to take care of you and Tansy, and see you both safely into Sir Julian's custody. My terms of reference are that I am to watch over you both and see that nothing damages your reputations. It seems to me that if you were to repeat such words elsewhere, they would reflect very badly indeed upon your character."

Amanda jumped to her feet. "Silence! I *will* not be spoken to in such a way!"

"I will not be silent, my dear, for you must mend your ways if you are not to be regarded as an arrogant strumpet!"

Amanda quivered with fury. "Arrogant strumpet . . . ?" she repeated, barely able to speak.

"That is what I said," Hermione repeated, without

flinching at all in the face of her charge's ominous reaction. "You are a very unlikable person, Amanda—rude, opinionated, vain, hurtful; indeed, you are without redeeming feature as far as I can tell. Everyone is pleased for you that you have secured such an enviable match, but no one wants to feel obliged to flatter you at every turn. You never miss an opportunity to remind us all that you are to be the grand Countess of Sanderby, to boast and brag about it until everyone else is sick of the word Sanderby."

"How . . . dare . . . you . . . !" breathed Amanda, her fists clenched until, had there been light, they would have been seen to be quite white.

Hermione was past caring. "You are playing with fire, you know. Do you *honestly* think Lord Sanderby would be impressed if he heard your crowing about Lieutenant Ballard? Do you think he would be pleased were he to learn how you have flirted with such a handsome naval officer?" Hermione rose calmly to her feet as Amanda stepped furiously forward, a hand raised to strike her for her effrontery. "Hit me, and I will not hesitate to retaliate." Tansy was transfixed. How could such a tigress ever have been mistaken for a meek nobody, capable only of crochet?

Amanda had second thoughts too, and slowly lowered her hand, but she remained incandescent with rage. "You're going to regret this, Hermione Entwhistle, for when we reach Chelworth I will make sure Sir Julian is told the full extent of your transgressions, and—! Ouch!" Her words ended on a cry of pain, not because Hermione had struck her anyway, but because Cleo had jumped down from Tansy's lap and was proceeding to sharpen her needle claws on the future Lady Sanderby's left knee. The black robes, voluminous as they were, presented no obstacle to such a determined feline exercise, and there was no doubt that Amanda felt every sharp pinprick. Hermione could have applauded the tabby's intervention. What excellent creatures cats were, to be sure, she thought, making no move to fuss around Amanda. The arrogant strumpet could attend to her own knee.

Amanda dashed the cat aside. "Oh, you horrid, horrid creature!" she cried, tears springing to her eyes. Cleo did not care to be dashed anywhere, and spat resentfully, but then retreated judiciously beneath a bed, for fear that Amanda's foot might take a part in the proceedings.

Just then the cabin door opened and Martin looked urgently in. "Be quiet in here! We're close to the main channel and there are other vessels around!"

To his startlement, Amanda ran sobbing into his arms. "I thought there was a snake! A most horrible thing, and I-I feared it would bite me!"

Martin hesitated, then looked inquiringly at Hermione, who shook her head. "No, Lieutenant, there is no snake. Amanda was asleep and must have had a nightmare."

"I see." He held Amanda a little awkwardly. "I'm sure it seemed very real, Miss Richardson, but there really isn't a snake in here," he murmured.

"Oh, I wasn't dreaming. I know I wasn't!" Amanda cried, clinging to him as the maiden in distress must surely have clung to St. George.

Hermione intervened. "Nonsense, Amanda. I fear you are letting your imagination run away with you," she said, at the same time surveying Martin in a way that made him release Amanda as if burned.

"I, er, must return on deck," he said, and hurried away.

The moment the door closed behind him, Amanda turned triumphantly to the others. "Oh, dear, it really is too simple," she said.

"Pride comes before a fall, my dear," Mrs. Entwhistle said quietly.

"And mayhap you should have looked before you leaped," Amanda snapped back. "You'll pay for presuming to criticize me!"

"Threaten me all you will, Amanda. It is of no consequence. My duties will be discharged the moment I give you into your uncle's care, and believe me, I shall not be sad when that moment arrives." Hermione went to the cabin door and paused with her hand on the knob. "I sincerely hope you are happy in your marriage, Amanda, but I fear you will not be. Nothing will ever satisfy you, for I do not doubt that when you are a countess, you will long to be a duchess. And if you become a duchess, you will want to be a princess. Dissatisfaction will beset your existence forever and a day."

"Since you never amounted to being more than the wife of a dreary clergyman, when you speak of dissatisfaction you clearly know what you're talking about," Amanda retorted.

Hermione flushed. "I was never dissatisfied with my marriage, which brought me nothing but love. That blessed emotion will always be denied the likes of you, Amanda." She went out, and closed the door softly behind her.

Amanda turned to start upon Tansy again, but that young lady had no intention of being at her cousin's mercy a moment more than absolutely necessary, so she too opened the door. "I think I'll go out as well. I prefer being in the fresh air. Cleo? Come on." A tabby streak shot from beneath the bed and out through the door. Behind them all, Amanda's fury centered on a hapless pillow, which she proceeded to tear to shreds.

The moon emerged just as Tansy went out onto the deck, casting a pale light over the wide expanse of the Nile's Rosetta channel, which was half a mile or more across. Overhead the sails billowed as the *canja* made good headway downstream, Tusun attending to the rigging, Martin once more at the tiller. Other boats plied the great river, the nearest being a small one-masted *jerm,* to which the *canja* was catching up quite quickly. Another was a one-hundred-foot *dahabeah,* which was so luxuriously gilded that it clearly belonged to an important Turkish official.

The lights of Rosetta glimmered on the western

bank ahead, and high overhead the moon now hung in a canopy of stars. Martin skillfully maneuvered the *canja* to quieter waters, where she would attract the least attention. Cleo ran over to him and rubbed busily around his legs. "Hello, Cleo," he said, and bent briefly to stroke the little creature. Then he saw Tansy. "I hope I did not cause offense a moment ago?"

Tansy had been hesitating about joining him at the tiller, for fear of appearing obvious, but now she had an excuse. "Offense? In what way?"

"By my presumptuousness in holding your cousin?"

Tansy cleared her throat. "I rather think it was my cousin who ran to you, Lieutenant."

He smiled. "Well, snakes are to be feared, even when only imagined," he murmured.

"Yes." Tansy longed to point out the truth to him, and prevent him from falling further into Amanda's clutches, but the hand of jealousy would surely be perceived in such a revelation. She picked up Cleo, and the cat settled purring in her arms.

"Have you thought any more about the curious incidents with the retriever cat?" he asked with a sudden change of topic.

"Yes, quite a lot. I really can't believe a painted cat can simply appear or disappear. I know it's what we *think* happened, but nevertheless . . ." She didn't finish the sentence, knowing full well that she sounded as if she were trying to convince herself. Besides, there was the added mystery of the bronze cat.

Martin nodded. "I know how you feel, for I feel it too. I've looked at the papyrus several more times since, and now I can't see how I ever missed the cat in the first place. It's brightly illustrated and very prominent indeed, yet I could swear in a court of law that it wasn't there initially."

She gave a slightly nervous laugh. "Thoughts of magic keep recurring, do they not? Maybe this is indeed a remnant of sorcery or some other supernatural thing left over from the time of the pharaohs."

Cleo suddenly growled in Tansy's arms and

stretched her neck alertly to gaze astern, as if she knew there was danger there. They both turned to look back as well, but saw nothing in particular. There were other vessels, including another *canja*. It was following about two hundred yards behind, its lanterns and white sails clear in the darkness.

"Can you see anything?" Martin asked.

Tansy shook her head. "I don't think so, but then they do say that cats see things we do not."

"Are we back to the supernatural, perchance?" Martin murmured drolly, and she laughed.

The *canja* moved serenely on downstream, the Nile lapping gently against her sides. The lights of Rosetta were brighter now, reflecting occasionally on the dark water. There was no sign at all of the expected French ambush. *Long may it stay that way,* Tansy thought as she spoke to Martin again. "Have you been in the navy for long, Lieutenant?"

"Ten years. Before that I was employed by a London city merchant, and had charge of the company's business affairs in St. Petersburg."

"Really?" Tansy's eyes were alight with interest. "How did you come to do that?"

"Because I am fluent in a number of languages. I am fortunate that such things come easily to me. Perhaps I should explain that I was brought up in Minorca, where I learned French, Italian, and Arabic almost as well as I learned English. I picked up a little Russian from an old friend of my parents. Obviously I absorbed a great deal more when I went to St. Petersburg."

"Whatever made you give it all up for the navy?"

"My talent for languages, and, er, intelligence gathering, were recognized at the Admiralty. I agreed to serve for a set period. This is actually my last mission, for I will be discharged when the *Lucina* returns to Portsmouth."

"What will you do then?"

"It is my intention to go to America."

So far away? She had to hide her dismay. "How was it that you were brought up in Minorca?" she asked.

"My parents went to live there for my mother's health. She suffered greatly with infections of the lungs. The Mediterranean air helped for a while, but she died when I was five. My father died when I was sixteen, and I hied myself to London. Then came the city merchant, and the rest you know."

They were passing Rosetta now, the lights of which now shone brightly on the dark water. They could hear Arab music drifting on the night air from one of the many buildings along the crowded waterfront. The French were still nowhere to be seen as Martin looked at Tansy. "Well, I have answered all your questions, Miss Richardson, so perhaps it is now your turn to answer mine."

"I cannot imagine what there is to tell about me. I have already explained how I came to be in Constantinople. I am the less fortunate of Sir Julian's two nieces, and will most probably suffer a future as a lady's companion, or some such dull thing."

Cleo growled again, and craned still further to look astern. The other *canja* was closer, having hoisted more sail, but there still seemed nothing that would cause the cat to behave in such a way. Suddenly she leaped from Tansy's arms and dashed away along the deck to her hiding place between the crates. Tansy watched her uneasily. "How very strange. What do you think is the matter?"

Martin laughed. "Have you ever heard of spooks, Miss Richardson?"

"Of what? No. What are they?"

"They are two things. The first is an undercover agent, which I have to say applies to me. The second is a ghost. So mayhap Cleo has seen both, hmm? First me, then a Nile specter."

Tansy gave him a look. "I think you are teasing me, Lieutenant. Spook is too silly a word to be either of those things."

"Silly it may be, but I am telling you the absolute truth."

Hardly had he spoken than rifles were fired from the following *canja*. Tansy gasped and whirled about. The other vessel was close enough to see in detail now, and she saw French uniforms and recognized the officer from Tel el-Osorkon. Another round of shots rang out. She heard something whine through the air; then Martin gave a grunt of pain as it glanced off his temple.

She screamed as he slumped to the deck.

# 15

Onboard the *Lucina* a week later, when it was still not known if Martin would survive his injury, Tansy kept vigil beside him as he lay unconscious in his cabin. He wore a shirt and legwear, his head was bandaged, his face was the color of parchment, and he had only come around for a few seconds since being shot. That had been when he was being transferred from the *canja* to the frigate. He had been lucid enough to make Tansy promise to tell Captain Castleton not to send him ashore at Gibraltar. If he was going to die, he wished it to be in England.

Oblivion had claimed him since then. He felt cold to the touch, yet his entire body was damp with perspiration, and the soft dark hair at the nape of his neck clung to his skin, as did the gold chain and locket Tansy now knew he always wore. The locket was oval and beautifully chased, although whether it was empty or contained a memento of some sort, she did not know.

She recalled the terrible minutes when the French had continued to bear down on the fleeing *canja*. Shots had seemed to fly constantly through the air, but somehow in all the confusion, Tusun managed to sail the *canja* to safety in the darkness where the Nile emptied into the sea. The French hadn't followed. Maybe they knew the *Lucina* was nearby. The *canja* waited for the dawn light in order to sail around the hazardous sandbar into Aboukir Bay, but then the

*Lucina* came, having arranged to rescue the stranded crew of the *Gower*. The frigate had received the message Martin left in the date palm, and over the following hour or so had taken on board the shipwrecked seamen and the passengers and antiquities from the *canja*. She was even stowing the three women's sea trunks, which had also survived the shipwreck. So at least some fresh clothes were to be had. Thus Tansy was now no longer clad in black robes or a torn mustard merino gown, but in long-sleeved lemon fustian that felt very clean, fresh, and good after the horrors of Egypt.

Tusun had remained on the *canja,* and the last Tansy saw of him, he had been waving from the tiller as he swung the empty vessel back into the mouth of the Nile. As he slid from view, his voice could still be heard wishing them well. "*Ma'as salāma.* Go in safety!" Tansy had continued to wave even after he had disappeared, and she hoped with all her heart that one day the Mameluke would regain all that his treacherous uncle had stolen from him.

Martin's cabin on the *Lucina* was eight feet square, with just over five feet of headroom, and like all cabins allotted to first lieutenants on frigates, it was situated at the stern, on the starboard side of the gun deck. The floor was covered with black-and-white-checked canvas, and the oak-framed bed was narrow and hard, with red cloth curtains tied back with thick string. The only other furniture was Martin's sea chest, the wooden chair upon which Tansy sat, and a table suspended on ropes from the deck beams. His uniforms, dress and ordinary, were on hooks on the wall, protected by muslin bags. Also on the wall was a gimbal-mounted lamp that was only to be lit when absolutely necessary, because flames of any kind were used with caution onboard ship.

The *Lucina* being a large frigate, the cabin enjoyed—if that was the word—the advantage of a gun port through which fresh air could be admitted, although the disadvantage of this was the presence of the gun, a thirty-two-pound carronade capable of inflicting awesome damage upon an enemy vessel. The cabin also possessed its own washroom and seat-of-ease, which greatly improved it upon the cabins provided for the rest of the ship's senior officers, excepting Captain Castleton, of course, who had a much grander accommodation on the upper deck.

It was in the captain's quarters that the three women were taking passage, officially as Captain Castleton's guests. Makeshift cots had been erected in the light and airy great cabin, which stretched across the entire stern of the vessel. It enjoyed a fine view through a row of handsome glazed windows that also stretched the entire width of the stern. The captain, who was something of a martinet with his crew, but a more than gallant gentleman where the fair sex was concerned, had decided he had little choice but to keep his own private bed cabin for himself.

It was all that he kept for himself, having sacrificed the rest of his quarters to the ladies, but even this left Amanda dissatisfied. She felt *she* ought to have the best bed on the frigate, and created quite a scene about it until Hermione pointed out that Captain Castleton had to have somewhere to sleep. Amanda was on very frosty terms with Hermione and had no intention of forgiving her the things that were said on the *canja,* but the point made about Lord Sanderby's reaction to his bride's conduct had not gone unheeded.

It would be wrong to say that Amanda's behavior had improved considerably, for such a leopard could not possibly change its spots to that extent, but there had indeed been an improvement of sorts. Thus, when the chaperone made it very plain that the alternative to Captain Castleton being permitted his own separate bed, would be for him to use the great cabin with his other two lady passengers, Amanda knew that such an arrangement was out of the question. She did not like having it pointed out to her, however, and remained at daggers drawn with Hermione. So Captain Castleton kept his own bed, but Amanda still managed to make it seem as if he were being far less than a gentleman. There was no doubt that hers was a generally disruptive presence onboard, but—as always—the eyes of all beholders saw only her astonishing beauty, not her meanness of spirit.

That meanness had never been more apparent than at the moment Martin had been shot. Tansy had worked desperately to staunch the flow of blood from his temple, all the time screaming to the others for help. Hermione rushed to assist, while Tusun took the tiller, but Amanda, having a horror of blood, had remained in the cabin. Since then she claimed that as there were already two women fussing over Martin, a third was quite unnecessary, and as for helping Tusun with the *canja,* well, she knew nothing about sailing and would therefore be no use at all. Besides, she had such delicate wrists that all in all it was surely better all around if she remained out of the way.

Tansy glanced around the cabin as she sat, hoping Martin would awaken. She had looked around it a thousand times or more since coming aboard, for she and Hermione shared the task of watching over him. It went without saying that Amanda did not bother with him at all while he was unconscious. Cleo was curled up on the bed, having now firmly established herself as Tansy's pet, but the cat awoke with a little mew as there came sounds of new activity on the deck overhead. The frigate was lying in Gibraltar's Rosia Bay, and was on the point of weighing anchor for the two-week voyage to Portsmouth. Whistles blew, orders were shouted, and bare feet ran across the ceiling as preparations quickened toward the moment of departure.

Captain Castleton had received new orders that

would take his ship out of the Mediterranean for the first time in over a year, and the crew, strengthened by the men rescued from the *Gower,* had been initially delighted at the prospect of going home again. However, their pleasure had been short-lived when they learned that on arriving in Portsmouth the vessel would take on military supplies for a regiment in Canada, to which dominion she would also convey a minor, unnamed royal personage. There was much resentment among both officers and men, who felt that at time of war, the brave *Lucina* was demeaned by becoming little more than a mixture of army supply vessel and waterborne hackney coach for one of King George's petty relatives.

The disturbance overhead penetrated Martin's private world, and he stirred, muttering something unintelligible. His eyelids fluttered, and for a split second she saw his eyes, but then they closed again. Hope sprang through her, and she quickly got up to hurry into the washroom. There she dipped a cloth into the bowl of water that was kept there, then hurried back to dab it gently to his forehead. She was only too aware that his life was hanging by a thread, and she was desperately afraid he would cease the struggle long before England's shores were reached.

The ship's surgeon, Mr. Cathcart, a man hardened by many a sea battle, held out little hope, even going so far as to declare that it would be kinder to let the injured man fade away. But Tansy would not hear of such a terrible thing. Nothing would persuade her to give up on Martin, and she remained at his side as much as possible, often going without sleep herself because she was so distraught about him. So this was love, she thought as she gazed down at him. The emotions kindled that first moment at Tel el-Osorkon had strengthened inexorably, binding her to him more and more until now there was no going back to the innocent, uncomplicated Tansy Richardson who had set out from Constantinople.

This man had captured her heart completely, and while it was in his possession she was no longer her own woman. Tears stung her eyes as she continued to pat the cool cloth to his skin.

There was a tap at the cabin door. "Yes?"

"It's Mr. Pettigrew, Miss Tansy. I'm due on deck in five minutes, but I thought you'd like a mug of hot, sweet tea."

She smiled, having quickly come to like the *Lucina*'s boatswain. "Please come in, Mr. Pettigrew."

The door opened, and he stepped inside with the mug. He was a craggy man of about fifty, with great bushy eyebrows and a bulbous nose that was as red from navy rum as the blast of wind off the sea. "It may not be the finest Pekoe, miss, but it will do you good," he declared as he pressed the mug into her hands. "How is the lieutenant?" he asked then, taking the cloth from her to apply it to Martin's forehead with a surprisingly gentle touch.

"I thought he was going to come around a few moments ago, but there is no real change, I fear," she replied, sipping the tea gratefully. She did not as a rule enjoy sweet tea, but right now it had an agreeably restorative effect.

"Just like the Frenchies to shoot a brave English fellow from behind," the boatswain muttered.

"I think they were very angry that we stole their antiquities."

"Which they stole from someone else in the first place," he pointed out.

"True."

Mr. Pettigrew looked at her. "You really should get some sleep, miss. Mrs. Entwhistle will gladly take your place; she said I was to tell you so." It was noticeable that he made no mention of Amanda. That young lady was at the moment getting in the way on deck, but received no chastisement because she fluttered her eyelashes at the ship's officers. Even strict Captain Castleton was inclined to indulge her.

"Mrs. Entwhistle is kind, but I'd rather stay here," Tansy said.

The weathered sailor looked shrewdly at her. "Well, the lieutenant is a handsome devil, is he not?" he said kindly. "Don't look so embarrassed, Miss Tansy. I have daughters of my own, and I have been around long enough to observe such things. Lieutenant Ballard is more to you than just an injured man who needs nursing. And on that account he is very fortunate." He bent to stroke Cleo, who got to her feet and nuzzled his hand. "Do not fear that my tongue will clack to all and sundry, for Uriah Pettigrew knows when to keep his mouth shut."

Tansy smiled. "I'm sure he does, sir."

"The lieutenant is a strange one. This is his last voyage, and he'll be a great loss to the navy, for there's no better intelligence-gathering officer. He's a very popular fellow, and no mistake, yet at the same time he's what might be termed an outsider."

Tansy looked at him in puzzlement. "What do you mean?"

"Well, he's not one of the others. You'd never find him drinking and laughing with his fellow officers in the gun room. While they are socializing, and most likely imbibing too much, he'll be out on deck gazing at the horizon, or in here reading some foreign book or other. A man of many tongues is Lieutenant Ballard."

"Yes, that I do know about him."

"You do? Then he's confided more to you than to most. I'm just about the only man on the *Lucina* who knows anything about him, yet for all his reticence, he's very well liked. You won't come across his name at any fancy London gathering, almost as if his background's too lowly for that, yet no one looks down his nose at him. The likes of Admiral Nelson and Sir Sidney Smith will happily sit down to dine with him. He's a mystery, and no mistake." The boatswain dabbed Martin's forehead again, assisted by Cleo, who continued to rub against his arm.

Tansy gazed at Martin's face, and the bandage that was once again slightly stained with blood. "He told me he was brought up on Minorca," she said.

"Did he now? Well, I didn't know that. There's no fellow on this earth I'd rather have at my side in battle. I'd trust him with my life, as would every man jack onboard this ship. I cannot speak too highly of our first lieutenant, and if he dies from a bullet fired from behind, it will be a great crime the French have committed."

Tansy swallowed. "Mr. Pettigrew, do . . . Do you think he will survive?"

He put a quick hand on her shoulder, then hastily removed it again. "I don't know, Miss Tansy. If there's any justice, then he will."

"Mr. Cathcart doesn't think so."

"Mr. Cathcart is as hard as nails. He's had to be. These are bad times, miss, and when a ship is on active service, the surgeon can't allow sentiment to come before expediency. It's no good having a hold full of badly wounded men who'll be an age—if ever—recuperating. They're a liability."

"Is Lieutenant Ballard regarded as a liability?" she asked.

The boatswain smiled and shook his head. "No, miss, for he has you to look after him. If you're strong on his behalf, I think he'll see England safely."

"I suppose there is a naval hospital of some sort at Portsmouth?"

"Yes, across the harbor at Haslar, miss, although Portsmouth is no longer the lieutenant's destination. Didn't you know?"

"Know what?"

"That Mrs. Entwhistle suggested to the captain that when we sight England, it might be better for the lieutenant if you and he are put ashore at Chelworth, which we will reach before Portsmouth. She believes, and Captain Castleton is in complete agreement, that the quiet of a country estate would be more beneficial than the noise and undoubted crush of a large and busy hospital such as Haslar.''

Tansy stared at him. "Am I to understand that just the lieutenant and I are to land at Chelworth?"

"Yes, miss."

"But . . . why?" What of Amanda and Hermione?

The boatswain cleared his throat. "Well, miss, it seems that your cousin wishes to go on to Portsmouth; in fact she is insisting upon it. Mrs. Entwhistle tried to reason her out of it, but then said that she too would continue to Portsmouth, in order to be your cousin's chaperone. It was felt that once you were at Chelworth, you would be safe under your uncle's protection."

Tansy could have hugged the boatswain for imparting such news, but most of all she could have hugged Hermione for suggesting the stop at Chelworth. She would see more of Martin after all! And for a while at least, there would be no Amanda, who was determined to go to Portsmouth simply to meet the royal personage who was to board the frigate for the voyage to Canada. Until now Tansy had resigned herself to parting from Martin at the hospital in Portsmouth. Of course, it was all assuming he survived the voyage from Gibraltar anyway. . . .

Mr. Pettigrew was thinking about Amanda, and after a moment simply had to speak his mind. "Begging your pardon for saying this, Miss Tansy, but your cousin is a hard young woman, full of herself and no one else. She created a great scene when she heard of the suggestion about stopping first at Chelworth. You see, she thought she would have to go ashore too, and that did not suit her at all. She began to insist that the lieutenant belonged at Haslar, until Mrs. Entwhistle declared that she would go on to Portsmouth too. I know I should not express an opinion, Miss Tansy, but Miss Amanda is the most unamiable creature it has ever been my misfortune to meet. She looks like an angel, but she has the character of a gargoyle."

The frank criticism came so out of the blue that Tansy found herself choking back her first laugh since Martin's wounding. "Mr. Pettigrew, you are full of surprises!" A gargoyle? Yes, that was indeed a good description of Amanda!

There was more noise overhead, and the boatswain gave a gasp. "I should be up there now! Captain Castleton will nail my hide to the mainmast!" He scooped a rather surprised Cleo from the bed. "Come on, cat, you can earn your keep. No ship is without rats, four legged *and* human." With that he left to return to his duties.

Tansy finished the tea, then set the mug aside. Martin continued to be disturbed now and then by the ever-increasing noise overhead, but just as a chantey rang out for the hauling of the anchors, he lay very still indeed. Too still. Tansy leaned forward anxiously. "Martin?" Oh, how easily his first name slipped from her lips at a time like this; were he to open his eyes and know her, she would call him Lieutenant Ballard. . . .

Suddenly his eyes did open, but they were sadly changed from the bright, penetrating brown gaze of before; now they were dull and almost lifeless, seeming to see and yet not see at the same time. A frown creased his forehead as he tried to focus. "Amanda . . . ?" he whispered.

She tried not to show her hurt. "No, it's Tansy."

His gaze became more aware. "Ah, yes . . ."

In the midst of her joy that he was sentient again, Tansy's heart was wrenched at his palpable disappointment on realizing it was the Church Mouse in attendance. "How are you?" she asked.

The ghost of a smile reached his lips. "I have no idea."

Quickly she went to pour him a glass of water from the jug in the washroom, then supported his head with her arm and put the glass to his parched lips. "Here, drink if you can," she said.

He struggled to do as she asked, but sipped only a

little before giving up. He grimaced with pain and
tried to put a hand to the bandage, but she prevented
him. "Don't. You've been wounded."

He tried to remember, but couldn't. He looked
around. "Am . . . Am I on the *Lucina*?" he asked
then.

"Yes. We're about to leave Gibraltar for England."

He grimaced again. "Dear God above, my
head . . ."

"Mr. Cathcart says he will give you laudanum for
the pain. I'll find him now, for he was most insistent
that he was to be summoned the moment you came
around." She hurried out to find the surgeon, but as
she hastened past the red-coated marine the captain
had placed on guard at the cabin door, she almost
cannoned into Amanda, whose lovely face immediately assumed a cross expression.

"Oh, good heavens, Tansy, *must* you gallop around
like a horse?" she snapped.

"I'm sorry, Amanda, it's just that the lieutenant has
awoken, and I must find Mr. Cathcart!" Without pausing to say more, Tansy ran through the gun room to
the hatchway that led to the upper deck.

A sly glint slid into Amanda's eyes, and as soon as
Tansy had gone, she flicked her skirts aside to pass
the marine into Martin's cabin. She closed the door
carefully behind her, then went to the chair by the
bed.

Martin's eyes were closed as she took Tansy's place,
then enclosed one of his hands in both hers. "Lieutenant Ballard? Martin . . . ?" she whispered. He looked
at her, recognition lightening his gaze, and she gave
him one of her most bewitching smiles. "Oh, I'm *so*
glad you know me. I've been sitting here beside you
day and night. . . ."

"You have?"

"Can you doubt it?"

"But, I . . . I thought your cousin . . ."

"Oh, Tansy came in for a short while. I've sent her
to bring Mr. Cathcart." Skillful tears filled Amanda's

wonderful cornflower eyes. "Oh, I've been so distraught about you. You'll never know how deeply I . . ."

"Yes?"

"How deeply I feel for you." She stretched forward to put her cool lips to his, but drew back just as footsteps sounded outside the door.

# 16

*I*t was sunset, and the *Lucina* was making excellent speed before a brisk wind. In spite of the cold of the February air, Tansy was out on deck with Cleo in her arms. The men on duty had much to attend to, so no one took any notice of her as she stood between the signal-flag lockers at the stern, gazing past the fluttering ensign at the frigate's foaming wake. Another rhythmic chantey was being sung as more sail was hoisted, and sailors ran along the deck as Mr. Pettigrew's whistle blew for the next watch.

Cleo nestled cozily beneath Tansy's cloak and peeped out nervously from time to time as the frigate forged through the white-topped waves. The sun was sinking in a glorious blaze of crimson and gold, there was spray in the air, and the sails cracked and strained overhead. It was a blessed relief from dinner in Captain Castleton's dining room, where all the ship's officers had joined the ladies. Amanda's brittle laughter, coy attitudes, and slyly manipulative conversation had become a little too much for Tansy to stomach, so she had come outside.

She drew a long breath. Amanda was truly awful in every way, yet fate had seen fit to bestow a glowing future upon her. What future lay in wait for Tansy Richardson? "What's to become of me, Cleo?" Tansy murmured. It all depended on Uncle Julian. Would he offer his penniless niece a roof over her head? If he didn't, if he found such a prospect quite abhorrent—which as a bachelor might well prove the case—what then? Becoming a lady's companion was all very well, provided the lady was a lady, but what if she were another Amanda?

Another Amanda? Surely there could not be two such horrid creatures? Tansy blinked back tears, recalling the moment she had taken Mr. Cathcart back to Martin's cabin, only to find her lovely cousin leaning affectionately over the bed. Amanda had drawn swiftly back, her cheeks flushed and her sweet lips parted on a silent gasp, as if she had been caught in an indiscretion. But there had been a calculating light in her cornflower eyes and something very artful in the way she'd released Martin's hand, unlinking her fingers just slowly enough to be sure the Church Mouse was under no illusion about the interrupted intimacy. Amanda had been reasserting her spell over him, and she must have been most gratified that he had been gazing up at her as Tansy entered.

Mr. Cathcart promptly banished the two women while he attended to his patient, and later told Tansy that he had administered rum and laudanum, as well as a dash of lime juice. He was confident that the return to consciousness had marked a change for the better, and that from now on Martin would start to improve. "But it will be some time before he is a well man again, Miss Richardson, and it is too early yet to see how he has been affected by the wound. It is my experience that the memory is often damaged by such wounds to the temple, and sometimes even the personality itself is harmed. However, it is to be hoped that in the lieutenant's case, all will be restored to its previous state. The fact that he has rallied at all makes me optimistic." Tansy prayed so. Oh, how she prayed so.

There was a step behind her, and Hermione joined her. "Amanda has gone to her bed to rest for a while, having expended all her energy being the doxy to every officer onboard. Her foolishness astounds me. I thought she had seen the error of her ways, but still she plays with fire. If Lord Sanderby were to find out even a quarter of the things his bride gets up to, he would call off the match immediately. She is wearing me so ragged that I now need copious amounts of fresh air to recover." The chaperone tickled Cleo's ear.

"Amanda has that effect on me too. I know I should not say it, but my heart sinks whenever I see her coming. I cannot bear being with her."

"It is hardly surprising, for she treats you abominably. She will fall from grace one day, you mark my words. Beauty and a bewitching smile are all very well, but in her case they are on the surface only. What lies underneath is very different."

*What lies beneath is a gargoyle,* Tansy added silently, thinking of Mr. Pettigrew.

"I fear that unless she turns over a completely new leaf on arriving in England, she will quickly ruin her match. Not that I think his lordship is to be greatly admired either."

"Oh?" Tansy wondered what the chaperone meant, for she knew she was the only person in whom Amanda had confided about the imprudent letters she and Lord Sanderby had been exchanging.

Hermione gave her a querying look that soon dissolved into a knowing smile. "I can see from your face that you know of the correspondence. Oh, she didn't tell me about it; far from it. As guardian of her well-being during this journey, I made it my business to know what she is up to. Her portable escritoire, er, met with a slight mishap on the *Gower,* and I happened to glimpse the missives he sent to her at Constantinople. From their content, I can only imagine that hers to him were in a similar less-than-circumspect vein. I fear she is quite convinced of her own infallibility, and I have had enough of her. The sooner she is in Sir Julian's hands, the sooner I will be done with my responsibilities."

Tansy had not really thought that the end of the voyage would also mean the end of their association. "Where will you go then?"

"Well, I have a small income, sufficient to purchase myself a little house or cottage somewhere." Hermione chuckled. "I shall end my days sitting in a comfortable chair with my crochet. Mayhap with a plump cat on my lap." She fondled Cleo's ear again, and the tabby rubbed against her fingers.

Tansy could not imagine Hermione Entwhistle leading such a mundane existence. "You are far too intelligent to simply do *that*. What of your knowledge of Ancient Egypt, and other such places? I believe that you should write a book, Hermione."

"Oh, my dear, you flatter me, I fancy."

"No, I don't. Just think of the basalt slab with the inscriptions. I am certain that if you applied yourself, you could decipher them."

At that, Hermione went into peals of laughter. "My dearest Tansy, now you are definitely in the realms of fantasy. There any number of learned gentlemen all over the world striving to interpret hieroglyphs. If you imagine that I, a mere woman, could come along and defeat them all on such an important matter . . ." She didn't finish, but chuckled again, shaking her head.

"I don't think that being 'a mere woman' has anything to do with it. Women are just as capable as men; more so, probably. So admit it—you at least have a theory about how to interpret hieroglyphs." Cleo jumped lightly down to the deck, and trotted off toward the hatchway that led down to the gun deck. Presumably to find somewhere warm to sleep, Tansy thought.

Hermione continued. "A theory about hieroglyphs?" she mused. "Well, as it happens I do, although I should qualify that by saying the theory did not originate with me. Actually, it is your uncle's—Sir Julian's, that is."

"Really?"

"Yes. My dear late husband regarded him as the

finest antiquarian in all England, and corresponded with him for a short while. Their letters touched upon the riddle of hieroglyphs, and Sir Julian confided his thoughts on the subject. My husband was in full agreement with his reasoning. But then, of course, there was that terrible business with Lord Sanderby's father, and the correspondence ceased."

Tansy gazed at the wake stretching away behind the frigate. "Don't you think it strange that the earl has chosen Amanda as his bride? I mean, his father and Sir Julian fell out most acrimoniously, and my father believed the hieroglyph business was not the only thing they fell out about." There were rumors of a further quarrel over an affair one or other of them had. Tansy's father heard a garbled whisper one night at his club, but no one knew anything for sure. Certainly no one knew who the woman was.

"Oh, Tansy, my dear, who are we to question the whys and wherefors of the aristocracy?" Hermione smiled. "You know, I believe I shall give some consideration to your suggestion about a book. I shall give myself a pseudonym like Algernon Scrimblestitch, and set the cat among the pigeons by resurrecting Sir Julian's theories. I have sufficient funds to publish a volume myself, you know."

"Well, Mr. Scrimblestitch, if you require a humble clerk to write out your text, I will gladly be of assistance."

Hermione regarded her. "If you are available, then I shall take you up on that, my dear, but I do not think you will be."

"Oh? Whatever makes you say that? The Church Mouse is *bound* to be available; just ask Amanda," Tansy replied wryly.

"There is Lieutenant Ballard to consider," the chaperone said quietly.

Tansy was glad of the glowing light of the sunset, because it hid the embarrassed color that again warmed her face. Had she been so obvious about her feelings that *everyone* knew? First Amanda, then

Tusun, then Mr. Pettigrew, and now Hermione. She prayed Martin himself did not realize as well, for that would be too awful. "Hermione, the lieutenant and I are acquaintances, that is all."

"Ah." The chaperone uttered the word enigmatically.

"Don't say 'Ah' like that, for it is the truth. If he is enamored of anyone, it is Amanda."

"I'm not so sure. There is more to our handsome lieutenant than meets the eye, and if he is taken with your obnoxious cousin, my name really is Algernon Scrimblestitch."

Tansy smiled, but then became serious again. "I shall miss you dreadfully when we reach England. You will write to me at Chelworth, won't you? I mean, I'm bound to be there for a while at least, until I know whether or not Sir Julian will let me stay for good. . . ."

"Oh, he will, my dear, I'm sure of it. I cannot imagine that he is the sort of gentleman who would oblige his unfortunate niece to make her own precarious way in life when he could offer her a home. Besides, there will not be any need for me to write to you at Chelworth, since I will be there myself."

"You will? But, I thought you and Amanda were going on to Portsmouth."

Hermione gave another of her wicked chuckles. "Well, we were. Amanda was all agog for the opportunity to meet royalty . . . until she found out a little more about the personage in question."

"What do you mean?"

"The personage is a very fine billy goat that King George has graciously given to a regiment in Canada, to have as its mascot."

Tansy stared. "A . . . a goat?"

"Baa-a-a-a-a . . ."

Tansy almost collapsed with laughter, Hermione soon joined in, and in a moment they were both helpless. Members of the crew looked at them in surprise, then grinned, for the women's amusement was infectious, and their friendship only too evident. It was good to see, and it made everyone feel lighter.

Shortly before the laughter broke out on deck, Martin had awoken from his daze of laudanum to find Cleo seated on his pillow, washing her front paws. She halted the exercise to look down into his pain-filled brown eyes; then she patted his face gently, as if to test if he was truly conscious. Slowly he drew a hand from beneath the bedclothes to touch the cat's fur, and she began to purr.

He heard the low murmur of female voices carry on a swirl of air through the gun port, which was slightly open, and knew the voices belonged to Tansy and Hermione, but couldn't make out what they were saying. Then they began to laugh, and Cleo jumped down to trot toward the cabin door, where she paused to look back at him, as if to say, "Aren't you coming with me?"

Through the veil of laudanum, Martin knew she was going to the women on deck, and a spark of something fired through him, urging him to go too. The cabin seemed to revolve as he pulled himself into an upright position. His whole body ached and he felt quite ridiculously weak, but if it was the last thing he did, he would go up on deck. With a huge effort he made himself stand. His legs shook, and the throbbing pain in his head was so intense that it seemed to pulse through him. A red haze blurred his vision, but something still urged him onward. He managed to pull on a cloak that hung behind the cabin door; then with Cleo leading the way, he staggered through the empty gun room, where for once there wasn't a marine on duty.

All sound was exaggerated, and the red haze made everything seem unreal as he climbed the hatchway. He felt as if he were in a nightmare, except that the pain was too agonizing to be imagined. No one saw as he came out into the open air, where the wind seemed to strike his skin like needles of ice. The men at the double wheel were too preoccupied with their task, the duty officer was bawling orders to a midshipman on the lower deck, and Mr. Pettigrew was blowing his whistle fit to burst as men at the masthead took too long about their work.

But Martin could still hear the two women's laughter, clearer now, and so enticing that he had to go toward it. He saw Tansy in the light from the setting sun, her dark curls and cloak blowing in the sea breeze. Cleo ran ahead of him and brushed around the women's hems. Hermione bent to stroke the cat, but something made Tansy turn sharply to look directly at him.

Her smile dissolved into alarm, and she hurried to him. "Lieutenant? Whatever are you thinking of? You shouldn't be out here!" she cried, not hesitating to put an arm around his waist as she saw him sway.

He gazed at her in a dream, drawn by the generosity of her lips, the expressiveness of her big gray eyes, and the sheer honesty of her concern. Everything about her reached through his pain and fever, brushing restraint aside and exposing emotions he would otherwise have stifled into submission. He reached out to touch her cheek, and when she did not pull away with shock, his fingers slid into her hair, then to the nape of her neck, where all was warm and sensuous. He drew her mouth toward his and kissed her tenderly, lovingly, his lips clinging in a way that ached through him like the sweetest of memories.

Tansy's whole body keened with love. He kissed her as if she meant everything in the world to him. Her mouth trembled beneath his, and she did not have the will to draw away, only the will to stay. She knew it was the laudanum that ruled him, that he probably did not even know who she was, but for these few wonderful moments she did not care. She held him to her, savoring the joy of his body cleaving to hers, and she returned the kiss in a way no proper young lady should.

But all too soon his strength faded and he began to sag to the deck. Hermione, until that moment too stunned to do anything but stand and stare, ran to help Tansy.

Later, as the last of the sun sank beyond the horizon, Cleo sat on Tansy's cot in the great cabin, carefully licking her paws and washing her face. If ever a cat looked pleased, that cat was Cleopatra, for she had the sleek expression of one whose plan had gone well. Her expression became sleeker than ever as she got up to go to Tansy's pillow, which she pulled aside with deft claws.

Beneath it lay the bronze cat from Tel el-Osorkon. Tansy kept it there, for no good reason other than that she liked to look at it just before she went to sleep. The tabby began to purr and knead the blanket; then she curled up against the figurine and closed her eyes.

# 17

Randal was standing at the edge of the woods below Chelworth. Sunset was drawing to a close, and seagulls called loudly as they swooped above the bay, where the waves crashed and foamed ashore. By his feet the grass was covered in snowdrops that trembled in the raw wind, and on the hillside above him the lights of the house were bright against the heath. The cursed place had never seemed more like an Egyptian temple, he thought sourly, studying the display of Nile grandeur set so incongruously in the Dorset landscape.

He hunched deeper into his greatcoat, stamped his feet to stay warm, and tugged his tall hat lower over his forehead. His temper, not good at the best of times, had been very frayed since he returned to this back-of-nowhere county. Not only had Richardson left London hot on his heels, leaving him very little time to find the letter, but the one search he had been able to achieve had proved completely fruitless. Aided and abetted by two Chelworth footmen, whom he paid well for their betrayal of trust, he'd turned the library upside down for dear Mama's scribble. To no avail whatsoever. He'd been so certain the library would be the place, but it seemed not. The old boy had the vital script hidden *somewhere* in that damned mausoleum, and sooner or later it was going to come to light—preferably sooner, because he, Randal Fenworth, would not—*dared* not—rest until he had destroyed it.

So even though Richardson was in residence, he was

about to try again. It would be a risky business, but it had to be done, and when the last of the sunset had gone, the same footmen would admit him once more. Tonight was as good a night as any, better than most, because nearly all the servants had time off to attend a nearby wedding. The house would be virtually empty, and Randal would be let in by way of the billiard room. Billiards? What a note of discord in a shrine to the pharaohs. He could not imagine Ramses the Great amusing himself in such a way. The deflowering of Nubian slave girls maybe, or the worship of Apis bulls, or even the hunting of crocodiles in the delta, but not *billiards!*

"Why have we come here again tonight, Dandypoo?" asked a petulant female voice behind him.

"Don't call me that!" he snapped.

The St. James's light skirt he had brought with him came closer, slipped her arms around his waist, and rested her head against his back. Barely out of her teens, she was a full-bosomed redhead who liked to place a heart-shaped patch at the corner of her mouth. Her name was Liza Lawrence, and she was always overrouged and underdressed, which was what Randal looked for in such women. Beneath her cloak she wore a new black fur scarf to protect her bare throat, her yellow satin gown being such a flimsy garment that it could be said to be neither here nor there. She knew how he hated fur, but it was so cold that she simply had not been able to bring herself to sally forth without it. "I can think of *much* nicer things to do than wait around in this damp old wood," she said seductively, as she slipped her fingertips between the buttons of his waistcoat.

"There will be time enough for that when we return to Bothenbury," he replied, clamping a firm hand over the questing fingers.

Liza's hands withdrew, and she came around to look at him from the front. "Oh, *please* . . ." she wheedled, untying the front of her cloak to tempt him with a glimpse of her décolletage. Of course, she forgot that the fur scarf concealed almost everything he might find alluring; indeed, she forgot the scarf altogether.

Randal's pale eyes swung from the house to her face. "We'll return when I'm ready, not before," he said in a tone that should have warned her not to pester him.

But she flung her arms around his neck and twiddled the ribbon tying back his hair. "Dandypoo, I—!" Her voice broke off in shock as he suddenly flung her away so violently that she stumbled backward and landed on her rump among the snowdrops.

"I told you not to call me that!" he cried. "And I also told you we'll go when *I* say so!"

She stared up at him. "Yes, Dandyp—I . . . I mean, my lord," she said warily. He was a strange one, and no mistake. There were gents and there were gents, and she understood most of them, but not this one. Just when she thought she had his measure, he'd do something that reminded her how dangerous her profession could be. This rum cove might have paid her well for her services, but right now she wished she'd never left the safety of Mother Clancy's nunnery in St. James's Street. It wasn't even as if he was much use between the sheets, because he thought only of himself. Well, if that was how he wanted it, she would suit herself too. She knew many a fine trick when it came to pleasuring men, but she didn't use one of them on *him!* Instead she lay there like a lump and thought about other things.

Randal made no move to assist her to her feet again. She was only a whore, not even a particularly good one, and did not warrant courteous treatment. Besides, his eyes had begun to water and his nose tickled in that familiar way. Damn it, Richardson's mangy ginger tom must be nearby! He glanced swiftly around, expecting to see the gleam of feline eyes in the shadows, but there was nothing.

Liza looked around too. "What is it? Do you hear something?" she asked nervously.

"No. I just thought . . . Oh, it doesn't batter." He

reached hastily for his handkerchief as a huge sneeze erupted.

Liza looked curiously at him. Batter? What was he talking about?

"There's a cat here subwhere. Cat fur bakes me sneeze." Randal wiped his eyes and nose, then sniffed.

"A cat?" Still not thinking of her scarf, Liza glanced around again. She started to tie her cloak, for the sea breeze really was chilly, and if he wasn't interested in her, she might at least be warm.

But just before the cloak was fully closed, Randal at last glimpsed the scarf. He wrenched the cloak open again. "What's this? Cat?" he demanded in horror.

"No, it most certainly is not!" She drew herself up crossly. The scarf had cost her a good deal, and the fellow who sold it to her promised it was the best wild *chattie* from Russia. She'd asked what *chattie* was, and the man swore it was sable. Mother Clancy had since told her that sable was weasel fur, which was obviously not true, for who would wear weasel?

Randal seized some of the fur between his finger and thumb, and tested it. "It *is* cat, dab it!"

"It's not, it's Russian *chattie!* A sort of sable, the man said."

*"Chattie?"* Randal stared at her, then his watering, bloodshot eyes hardened. "You bindless jade! *Chat* is French for cat! It's a dabbed Tiddles! Get rid of it!"

"But it's *freezing* out here!" Liza protested, moving defensively away and tying her cloak over the scarf, as if hiding it would make everything all right again.

Randal was livid. "Don't bake be angry, Liza. That dabbed rag has to go. Do I bake byself clear?"

"Will you buy me something else?"

"Yes, I'll buy you whatever you want, just get that thing away frob be!"

Mollified, she removed the scarf and threw it away, then turned to go back to the carriage. Once inside, she huddled in the cloak. Her neck felt cold now, and she was resentful in spite of Randal's promise to replace the scarf. It was the most expensive accessory

she had ever purchased, and it didn't really matter if
it was *chattie,* cat, weasel, or rat; it was *hers.* She glared
out at the leafless trees. Then she bit her lip to prevent
herself from snickering, for he really did sound silly
with his nose all blocked.

Unaware he was an object of amusement to her,
Randal again directed his attention toward Chelworth.
Now that Liza's damned scarf had been thrown away,
his eyes and nose had swiftly returned to normal
again. Moments ticked by; then at last he saw a swaying light at the far end of the house. The lantern signal
from the billiard room! Without glancing back at Liza,
he left the shelter of the trees and began to make his
way up the grassy clearings between the thick patches
of winter-brown bracken.

Sir Julian was in the library, poring intently over the
two fragments of papyrus. There were several lighted
candles on the desk, to give a better light, and he was
feeling pleasantly replete after an excellent roast beef
dinner. A glass of brandy—not the first of the evening—was by his right hand, and he had settled down
to enjoy a few hours' work. Ozzy was curled up asleep
on his favorite chair by the fire, having shared his
master's roast beef dinner, even to a helping of York-
shire pudding.

Sir Julian now knew he had been right about the
papyri. They *were* from the same original, and but for
a few missing pieces, they fit together most satisfy-
ingly. Since his return, he had spent every moment
studying them, and although he had not yet proved
anything for certain, he was becoming more and more
sure that the work he had done years ago, which had
been destroyed by Esmond Fenworth, had been on
the right line. Instinct told him he was getting somewhere at last, yet at the same time he felt as if he
were floundering! Oh, if only there was someone he
could discuss it all with, someone who thought as he
did; someone who knew what he was talking about!

The Reverend Endpipe . . . er, Bluntwhistle . . . whatever the fellow's name was . . . would have been ideal.

Exasperated, Sir Julian reached for his glass of brandy. As he swirled it and took a sip, his gaze stole back to the papyrus he'd purloined from the British Museum. Was it his imagination, or was the entire thing much brighter and clearer now? Why, it almost looked as if it had been professionally restored. He put down his glass and pulled the two pieces of papyrus apart. For a moment they resisted, as if joined in some way. He stared down at the two edges. They were as fresh and clean as if he had simply ripped a single papyrus in two! And the line of the break wasn't the same as before either! Good God, he thought, he must have had one brandy too many. He pushed the glass away, vowing to restrict himself in the future.

Ozzy awoke and stretched, then jumped down from the chair and padded to the French door. There he sat down again and fixed a meaningful stare upon Sir Julian, who grumbled at him but got up to do the honors. The cold air from the sea wafted into the library as the ginger tomcat slipped outside. Sir Julian returned to the desk and resumed his studies.

Randal had almost reached the terrace, but then halted in dismay at the foot of the steps, for Ozzy was seated at the top, his amber eyes shining in the very last vestiges of the dying sun.

One of the footmen came hurrying to see what was the matter. "My lord?" he said softly.

"Get rid of that damned cat!" Randal hissed.

"Eh?" The man, whose name was Joseph, looked at Ozzy, who calmly began to wash his face and whiskers.

"Get rid of it, I say!" Randal repeated.

Joseph reached hesitantly toward the tomcat, but Ozzie wasn't a feline to tangle with. He paused in his washing to utter one of his horrible growls. The footman flinched, but then reached out again. Ozzy emitted a vile spitting sound, and his tail began to sweep to and fro on the stone flags.

Randal was beside himself. "For God's sake, it's only a cat!" he cried, forgetting to keep his voice lowered, and forgetting too that as far as he himself was concerned, there was no such thing as "only a cat."

Joseph swallowed. If it was *only* a cat, he thought, why didn't this tricky swell remove it himself? Ozzy's growls drowned the sound of the library windows being opened, and neither the footman nor Randal knew Sir Julian had come out onto the terrace to see what was going on, and he had his pistol with him.

The footman was anxious to get Randal inside. "My lord, if you don't come inside now, we may be caught!"

"You already have been." Sir Julian cocked the pistol. Joseph whirled guiltily about, but Randal was too resigned to be dismayed. He exhaled wearily. Not the empty pistol trick again! This damned exercise was going from bad to worse!

Sir Julian glanced at Ozzy, who was still growling. "That's enough, Ozymandias," he said calmly. The tomcat immediately fell silent and resumed the washing of his face and whiskers. Sir Julian turned to the footman. "Well, I've had my suspicions about you, Joseph, and now it seems I was right. You are dismissed. I want you out of Chelworth within the hour. No, don't attempt to plead with me. I have no doubt that you have been well paid for your treachery. Now get out!" He waved the pistol, and Joseph took to his heels along the terrace, where his companion-in-disloyalty, named James, was very careful to keep well out of sight.

Then it was Randal's turn to have the pistol pointed at him. "Well, Sanderby, this is becoming something of a habit, is it not? I warned you not to trespass on my property, but you seem set on ignoring my wishes. I presume this latest visit concerns the letter you seem convinced I have in my possession?"

"The letter I *know* you have in your possession," Randal corrected.

"Exactly what do you imagine it says, assuming it exists?" Sir Julian inquired, interested to hear the answer, but Randal shook his head.

"I don't play games, Richardson. You and I are both fully aware of the letter's contents."

Sir Julian raised an eyebrow. "I fear you are wrong, sir. However, if there were indeed such a missive, do you honestly imagine I would leave it somewhere you could find? You may count upon it that I would use a hiding place so cunning you would never locate it even if you searched Chelworth for a month of Sundays! Now then, be a good fellow and turn around to go back the way you came." The pistol waggled.

Randal loathed his mocking adversary enough to choke him on the spot. In fact, a little violence suddenly seemed a very tempting—and possibly rewarding—notion! Would the aging casanova be quite so triumphant with a pair of strong hands around his throat? Would the letter's whereabouts remain quite such a secret if suitable pressure were applied to the old fool's windpipe? Of a mind to test the theory, Randal began to advance up the steps.

Sir Julian stiffened, and directed the pistol at Randal's heart. "That's far enough," he warned.

"Ah, but you don't keep it loaded, remember?" Randal murmured.

"That was then. Now is different."

"Really?"

"Yes, really." To prove it, Sir Julian aimed the pistol skyward and squeezed the trigger. The shot went off like a thunderclap, reverberating along the house as if to split it asunder.

Randal was so startled that he staggered backward, missed his footing on the steps, and went flying among the dead bracken. Then, utterly enraged, he began to leap to his feet again. The pistol was certainly empty now, and once he got ahold of Richardson's throat, he'd tear the very life out of him! But in his fury, he overlooked Ozzy. The tomcat was delighted to see his adversary at such a disadvantage on the ground, and launched himself at Randal, hitting him with such force that he fell back to the grass again. As he sprawled a second time among the bracken, Ozzy sat on Randal's chest, put his whiskered, furry face close, and growled most evilly.

Such close proximity had the inevitable result, and a moment later the tomcat was obliged to leap away again or be blasted by a succession of monumentally loud sneezes. Sir Julian descended the steps, the pistol once more at the ready. "Now then, Sanderby, I trust you will not repeat your folly, for although I may have been naive enough to fire unnecessarily a moment ago, you may count upon it that I have reloaded again now. You may also count upon it that unless you leave immediately, I will not hesitate to fire directly at you. Well, at a certain part of you, anyway." The pistol muzzle moved toward Randal's groin. Alarmed, that gentleman scrambled to his feet, and without another word fled down the hillside, his manhood intact.

As he disappeared into the gloaming, Sir Julian winked at Ozzy. "Phew, that was close, eh, old chap? Reload in this light with my eyesight? Pigs will fly first. Come on, you are due some more cream for that truly splendid display of feline fortitude. Most impressive. Most impressive indeed."

He turned to go back into the library, preceded by a highly delighted Ozzy, who knew the word *cream* when he heard it.

# 18

Fourteen days later, on a March morning suddenly darkened by fog, the *Lucina* inched toward Chelworth. Torches flared and smoked, and the sea was as smooth as a millpond as the ship's boats hauled the frigate into the bay. At last the anchor was dropped, and preparations began to put ashore her injured officer and lady passengers, and their sea trunks and antiquities. Not forgetting one small tabby cat.

Further out to sea, the booming of warning guns could be heard from other vessels caught up in the sudden fog. The atmosphere was rather eerie, and not at all what Tansy would have wished for her arrival back in England. She shivered as she stood on deck with Amanda and Hermione. Cleo was in her arms, and a carrying box made by the ship's carpenter was on the deck by her feet. It was complete with a sturdy handle and a lid that could be closed with hooks and eyes, so the cat couldn't leap out from the launch and fall in the sea. For the moment, however, Tansy just wanted to cuddle her much-loved pet. The cat figurine from Tel el-Osorkon was in the inside pocket of her cloak. It was heavy and felt a little uncomfortable, but she had forgotten to pack it with her other things; indeed, she had almost forgotten it altogether, and had been obliged to hurry back to the great cabin for it.

In these chilly northern climes the three women were very well wrapped indeed. The cold of England was different from that of the Mediterranean, for it seemed to seep through to one's very marrow. Nevertheless, she was glad to be home again—if Dorset could be termed home. Tansy had never been to the county before, having spent all her childhood and early youth in Northamptonshire. Uncle Julian had always paid visits to her, never the other way around, so Chelworth was unknown to her. Would it soon feel like home? "Oh, how I wish I knew the answer to that," she whispered, raising Cleo to rest her cheek against the cat's soft fur.

Another question to which she would have liked an answer was why she had to be so unfortunate as to fall in love with Martin, for whom that wonderful kiss was not even a memory. He had lost consciousness in her arms and had been carried back to his cabin. When next he awoke, Amanda's name had again been first on his lips. The Church Mouse was of so little consequence that he didn't seem to know she had remained at his bedside since boarding the *Lucina*; instead it was Amanda he credited with having nursed him. Of course, that artful madam now went out of her way to prove the point by spending as much time with him as she could. It really was second nature for her to inflict hurt upon Tansy, and she gleaned a great deal of spiteful delight from the knowledge that the Church Mouse cried about it in secret.

Tansy did all she could to hide her feelings, thinking it would help to bring the heartbreak more quickly to an end. She tried to tell herself that any man foolish enough to fall for Amanda was simply not worth bothering about, but it was one thing to think this, quite another to act upon it. First Lieutenant Martin Ballard *was* worth it. He was worth everything, everything in the world. . . .

She was determined not to think about him as she gazed at the swirling vapor that now enveloped everything. The land was lost from view, but visibility had been good until the bank of fog rolled in so suddenly. Sir Julian's Egyptian-style house overlooking the bay had reminded her so forcibly of Tel el-Osorkon that

she felt an almost childish urge to rub her eyes and
pinch herself to be sure of not dreaming. On the hilltop behind the house, piercing the skyline like a huge
arrowhead, was the pyramid Martin had mentioned.
It was a very dramatic sight. Everything about Chelworth was dramatic, and very, very beautiful.

Two teams of seamen had been alerted to lower the
ship's launch, which had been loaded with the sea
chests and the first consignment of antiquities, including the intriguing slab of basalt. Martin was to be
placed aboard on a stretcher before the launch was
swung overboard, because he was far too frail to manage the rope ladder that everyone else would use.

Tansy heard voices and footsteps coming on deck
from the wardroom, and turned to see two men carefully carrying Martin up from his cabin on the
stretcher. His face was ashen and sculptured, seeming
almost beautiful in its fragility, and his eyes were
sunken and set in shadows. There was still a bandage
around his forehead, he remained desperately weak,
and he was much thinner, but at least he no longer
slipped in and out of consciousness. He wore his uniform beneath a heavy naval greatcoat that hung
against his body because he had lost so much weight.
His tricorn hat rested beside him.

The launch still wasn't quite ready, so the stretcher
was laid carefully on the deck. Tansy saw how his
hands trembled just from the effort of having been
dressed. She wanted to go to him and put her arms
around him, to make him believe he would get better,
but she knew that was not possible. Besides, Amanda
was ever vigilant.

In a rustle of costly cloak, her golden hair shining
in the peculiar morning light, Tansy's spiteful cousin
rushed to kneel beside the stretcher. Her lovely face
was so saintly with concern as she clasped his hand
and gazed down into his eyes, that Tansy had to look
away. Please let him see how false it all was!

Cleo stirred suddenly in Tansy's arms. The cat had
been staring toward the land, her ears pricked and

alert as she heard a sound that was too faint for humans. A cat was calling, an uncanny, wavering cry that gradually became louder until everyone on the frigate could hear. The crew exchanged uneasy, superstitious glances, and even Tansy shuddered, but then Cleo responded. The tabby threw back her head and gave vent to an earsplitting yowl that made everyone start, especially Amanda, who jumped so much that with a squeal she lost her balance and toppled backward on the newly scrubbed deck. Her legs and petticoats were revealed to all and sundry, and the two sailors looking after Martin stepped hastily forward to assist her up again. It was all very undignified, and it quite ruined the image Amanda had conjured a moment or so before. Her face flushed crimson with mortification as she angrily shook herself from the sailors' attentive hands and then made a silly fuss about straightening her clothes.

Tansy was secretly overjoyed and had to keep her head bowed to hide the broad grin that now lit her face. There was some justice after all! She could sense Hermione's concealed mirth, although the chaperone was careful to keep her back toward her difficult charge. What Martin thought was anyone's guess, for his face gave nothing away at all, but Tansy imagined he was filled with heartfelt sympathy for poor, sweet, kind, adorable Amanda.

Mr. Pettigrew deemed the launch to be ready and Martin's stretcher was lifted into it. As soon as this had been accomplished, the order was given for the teams of seamen to haul upon their ropes. Another chantey was required as they slowly winched the heavy boat over the frigate's gunwales, and then down to the smooth, gleaming water. The oarsmen swarmed down the rope ladder to take their places.

Tansy bent to put Cleo in the box, then closed the lid securely before allowing another seaman to take it down to the launch. Then she followed Amanda and Hermione to the ladder. Amanda, of course, made a great noise about having to clamber down something so precarious, nor did she like it that a common rating was assigned to assist her. She thought she should have had an officer at the very least, so she demanded to know why she too could not have gone in the launch. In vain did Mr. Pettigrew point out that it was always a risky business to have people in a boat that was being launched, and Captain Castleton was very set against it unless in exceptional circumstances. Martin's injuries necessitated special consideration, but when the sea was as flat as a baby's bath, a rope ladder was perfectly safe for every one else, including ladies.

Amanda was not best pleased by the insultingly patient manner the boatswain adopted for his explanation, and she would have complained to the captain, except she knew Mr. Pettigrew had been too subtle for her to harbor any real hope of having him punished. As she stood in the swaying launch, debating whether or not to say anything more, her annoyance was heightened when the boatswain made a point of personally assisting Tansy and Hermione. How dared the others receive help from him, while the future Lady Sanderby only warranted the lowest ranking seaman of all!

So, just to be difficult, she sat down in the first available place in the launch, thus obliging Tansy and Hermione to clamber around her. Only when it was too late did she realize that this display of petulance meant that Tansy was able to sit next to Martin. So Amanda seethed silently, her back straight as a ramrod, her chin raised.

Martin smiled at Tansy. "I trust you will forgive me if I do not get up to greet you, as a gentleman should?"

"Of course I forgive you, Lieutenant," she replied, then shifted awkwardly as the figurine dug into her a little.

"Is something wrong?" Martin asked.

"No, just uncomfortable," she answered, taking out the figurine to show him.

"Is it part of the booty?"

"No, it's what Amanda tripped on." She told him about the incident. "I rather like it, so I've kept it ever since," she finished.

He reached up to touch the cold bronze, and then they both gasped as a searing heat seemed to pass through it. Tansy's fingers burned so much she almost dropped it, but then the heat seemed to settle to a comforting warmth. At least, it did to Martin; to Tansy the bronze was suddenly quite cold again, as she observed to him. "I really don't understand why the bronze gets hot and then cold. It's very odd."

"Cold?" He touched it again, and felt its warmth stream into his fingers.

"Yes." She regarded him. "Well, it's cold now, isn't it?"

"No, it's very pleasantly warm; in fact it feels good. Almost restorative."

"Really?" Quickly she pressed it into his hands. "Then you must have it. No, I insist, Lieutenant. Please keep it."

Nothing more was said as the ropes were cast off and the launch pushed away from the ship. Soon the only sound was the gentle splash of the water and the rumble of the oarlocks. But as the launch glided through the fog toward the shore, Martin felt noticeably stronger than he had only minutes before. The heat from the figurine seemed to fill him, and the tiredness he felt now was more a comfortable need to sleep than the enervating lack of strength that had beset him before. And he had the most uncanny feeling that the figurine was vibrating slightly, for all the world as if it were purring. . . .

When Ozzy first started to call out on the terrace, the noise brought Sir Julian quickly out to see what was wrong. He found Ozzy again seated at the top of the steps, staring toward the fog-swathed bay. The tomcat had taken to sitting there recently, gazing out to sea as if waiting for something.

"What is it, old chap?" Sir Julian murmured, bending to stroke his pet. Then he straightened sharply as Cleo's loud answering yowl carried up through the fog, closely followed by a woman's squeal. Little realizing that the last was only Amanda sprawling unbecomingly on the deck of the *Lucina,* Sir Julian gasped. "Good heavens, is murder being done?"

Ozzy's ears twitched, and he looked up at his master as if to chide him for being so foolish.

Sir Julian gazed down the hillside, and then thought he heard something. Yes, he could hear men singing as they lowered a boat from a larger vessel. Alarmed, he wondered if some particularly impudent smugglers were making use of the fog, or worse, if the French invasion had commenced at last! But then he realized that the chantey was not only very British, but was one associated with the Royal Navy. Curiosity got the better of him. "Come on, Ozymandias, let's go down to investigate!" he declared, and set off down the steps.

Ozzy got up to stretch, then yawned and followed.

# 19

Sir Julian could hear the steady rhythm of oars as he reached the beach, and he strained to see through the fog. Ozzy sat at his side, his ears pricked attentively. At last a ghostly silhouette emerged, at first a pale indistinct gray, but gradually becoming more clear until both Sir Julian and the cat could see every detail of the naval launch as it glided toward them.

The man standing at the stern saw the figure on the beach and called a challenge. "This is Uriah Pettigrew, boatswain of His Majesty's frigate *Lucina*. Identify yourself!" he called.

Sir Julian was taken aback. Identify himself on his own property? He'd be damned if he would!

"Your name, sir?" Mr. Pettigrew prompted.

"Sir Julian Richardson, owner of this land!" Sir Julian replied irritably.

Amanda stood up and waved excitedly, making the launch roll from side to side. "Uncle Julian? Oh, Uncle, it's me, Amanda!" she cried.

"Amanda?" Sir Julian's jaw dropped, for he had been awaiting word of his nieces' whereabouts, and had expected to send his traveling carriage to collect them from one of the ports. Instead the navy had brought them to his very door! And they seemed to have sufficient baggage with them to provide for half a dozen women, he thought, observing the crates that were piled on the boat.

The seamen shipped the oars as the launch slid onto the sand; then some of them leaped out to haul the craft clear of the water. As they then prepared to help the three women, Mr. Pettigrew jumped down and strode toward Sir Julian. He was passed in the other direction by Ozzy, who rushed toward the launch with almost indecent haste. The tomcat was mewing excitedly, and his calls were being answered with equal excitement from Tansy's box.

The boatswain reached Sir Julian. "Good morning to you, sir. This is indeed a happy coincidence, for you are the very gentleman we seek."

"So it would seem. So it would seem," Sir Julian murmured, looking past him at the launch, where Tansy and her box were now on dry land again. Amanda was being lifted out to join her, and then a third woman, older, and presumably the chaperone Franklyn mentioned in his letter.

Sir Julian could not help noticing how akin Tansy's cloak was to the chaperone's. Both garments were practical, plain, and clearly not expensive, whereas Amanda's was richly decorated and had clearly cost a considerable sum. He could not help reflecting that his fears about the place Tansy would occupy in Franklyn's household had been justified. Tansy was, and had no doubt been made to feel, the poor relation, but the shy smile she directed toward him now was a world away from the sulky pout on Amanda's lips. Sir Julian knew which niece he was drawn to, and it certainly was not the countess-to-be!

But then his attention was snatched by the very odd sight of Ozzy scuttling up and down beside Tansy's box like a thing demented. What in the world was the matter with the old ginger fool? The answer was forthcoming almost immediately, as another loud meow issued from the box. Ah, thought Sir Julian sagely, spring was in the air, and female feline company to hand.

Mr. Pettigrew spoke again. "I have an injured officer who is to be put ashore here, sir. He was shot while rescuing your nieces, and they wish him to recuperate at Chelworth instead of Portsmouth."

"Injured officer? Rescuing my nieces?" The import of the words was borne in on Sir Julian. "*Rescuing* them? Oh, good heavens . . . What happened?"

"They will no doubt tell you all about it, sir. Suffice it that they are now safe, thanks to First Lieutenant Martin Ballard."

"Well, if he saved my nieces, then of course he is more than welcome at Chelworth."

"Thank you, sir. Thank you kindly." Mr. Pettigrew saw that Sir Julian's attention kept wandering past him, and he turned to look as well. Ozzy was hardly able to wait for Tansy to open the tantalizing box. He danced around on tiptoe, ears pricked, tail so high a flag could have been hoisted upon it. The boatswain watched in surprise. "Well, will you look at that. He's ready to make Miss Tansy's tabby more than welcome!"

"So it would seem, Mr. Pettigrew. It's most out of character. Where strange cats are concerned, Ozymandias is—"

"Ozy-what, sir?"

"Ozymandias. It's another name for Ramses the Great, an Egyptian king."

"Oh, I see, sir." Mr. Pettigrew thought it a ridiculous name for an ordinary ginger tomcat.

"Ozzy is usually at the ready to see strangers off his territory; this time, however, he's clearly delighted," Sir Julian went on.

"Well, Cleo is as shipshape a little she-cat as I've ever come across. By the way, Cleo is short for Cleopatra, the—"

"Egyptian queen? Yes, I did know that," Sir Julian replied, watching as Tansy at last opened the box. Cleo looked out cautiously, saw Ozzy, and jumped out to him. They touched noses and rubbed around each other like old friends; then they dashed away up the hillside and were soon lost in the fog.

Tansy looked earnestly at Hermione. "Oh, you do

think Cleo will come back, don't you? There hasn't been time to put butter on her paws, and—''

"My dear, I don't think you need to worry. She has attached herself to you and will not go far."

Amanda was cutting. "Oh, for heaven's sake. I don't know why you're bothered. It's just a horrid common feline!"

No one responded.

Sir Julian had watched Tansy with approval. He had always liked her, but now that he knew she loved cats, he approved more than ever. Amanda, however, had sunk further in his opinion. He already frowned upon her because of the letters she had exchanged with Randal; now it seemed she had no respect for cats.

Amanda chose that moment to run to him. "Uncle Julian? Oh, Uncle Julian, I have had a simply terrible time! Truly I have! I don't know how I have coped!"

From being coldly contemptuous a few moments before, she was now all choked sobs and feminine weakness, but it did not fool her uncle at all. To his horror she burst into noisy tears, obliging him to press a handkerchief upon her. "Good heavens, child," he murmured, observing the telling glances that passed between Tansy and the chaperone. So this was nothing new to them, he thought.

His response exasperated Amanda. "You don't understand, Uncle! I was shipwrecked, kidnapped by pirates, almost drowned in the Nile, shot at, and—Oh, it was quite terrible!" She hid her face in her hands and dissolved into hysterical sobs.

Tansy and Hermione shared another look. Poor, dear Amanda must have suffered quite terribly when she was enduring such horrendous trials all on her own, they were both thinking.

Sir Julian, however, was shaken by Amanda's revelations. He had realized from Mr. Pettigrew's remarks that his nieces' voyage had been hazardous, but he hadn't for a second envisaged such a catalog of horrors. He looked askance at the boatswain, who nodded.

"It's all true, Sir Julian, except that the two other ladies were there as well."

"Yes, I rather imagined they were."

Amanda sniffed, her face still hidden in her hands. "The leader of the pirates was going to sell me for the highest price he could. Because of my golden hair and beauty."

Such modesty too, Sir Julian thought, but then felt a little guilty for his lack of charity. After all, she really had suffered all she claimed, albeit in a little less isolation than she liked to admit. So he patted her shoulder kindly. "There, there, my dear. You are quite safe now."

She lowered her hands to look accusingly at him. "I do not think I will ever recover. No bride should have to cope with such adversities. What dear Lord Sanderby will say I cannot begin to imagine." With that she resumed her whimpering.

Sanderby would not care less, Sir Julian thought. The bride and her fortune had survived, and that was all her fine husband would be interested in. But Sir Julian remained kindly as he conducted Amanda to a conveniently flat rock and bade her sit down to rest; then he went to speak to Tansy and the chaperone.

"Ah, Tansy, my dear, I'm so glad you are unharmed," he declared, pulling her close and giving her a warm hug.

"I'm glad too," she replied wryly, then smiled at him. "And I'm glad to see you again, Uncle."

"And I you, my dear, and I you."

"Please let me introduce Mrs. Entwhistle, who has been our excellent chaperone from Constantinople." She presented Hermione, then excused herself to go to the launch, where she could see that some of the seamen were about to carry Martin ashore.

Behind her, Hermione smiled shyly at Sir Julian. "I am honored to meet you, sir."

"And I you, madam."

"My late husband was the Reverend Henry Entwhistle, with whom you may recall being in correspondence?"

Sir Julian gaped at her. So it hadn't been Endpipe or Bluntwhistle! "Entwhistle is not a common name, madam, so I must wonder if your husband was by any chance an antiquarian with particular interest in Ancient Egypt?"

"He was, sir."

Amanda's whimpering grew louder as she perceived she was being forgotten, but Sir Julian took no notice as he beamed at Hermione. "Oh, your husband was an excellent fellow, madam, a truly excellent fellow. I do indeed recall corresponding with him."

She returned the smile. "He was always full of praise for you too, sir. He especially agreed with your theories about hieroglyphs."

"Hmm, then he must have been the only soul in creation who did," Sir Julian muttered.

"Not quite, sir, for I also agreed with them."

"Did you indeed?" She had his undivided attention. "Are you interested in Ancient Egypt, Mrs. Entwhistle?"

Amanda sobbed dramatically on her rock, but was ignored by everyone.

Hermione continued. "I am greatly interested in the land of the pharaohs, Sir Julian, and therefore trust that when you examine the antiquities we have brought with us, you will not exclude ladies from the proceedings?"

Sir Julian's eyes lit up. "Antiquities?"

"We purloined them from the French. At least, Lieutenant Ballard did. The first of them have already been put ashore." She indicated the launch, from which the crates were being lifted by the seamen.

Sir Julian was enthralled. "So *that's* what the crates contain! I thought it was all your baggage," he breathed. "Antiquities, eh? By the saints, fog or not, this is set to be a grand day! Of course ladies will not be excluded, madam. I would not dream of such an ungallant thing!"

Tansy waited by the launch as the stretcher was lifted ashore. "How are you, Lieutenant?"

"Well enough under the circumstances," Martin replied.

For a moment she thought there was something in his eyes, a transient warmth that touched her like a caress. No, she was foolish to imagine such a thing. "It will not be long before you are in a proper bed, with a proper doctor to examine you," she said, trying to show just sufficient concern to be correct.

"I think I am already on the path to recovery," he murmured, indicating the figurine, which he still held firmly. "Your bronze cat has a very beneficial effect. Quite magical . . ."

Hermione and Sir Julian came over to them, and Hermione drew Tansy away so that Sir Julian could bend over the stretcher. "Lieutenant Ballard?"

"Sir."

"Sir Julian Richardson, your grateful servant, sir. How are you?"

"Overdue for a proper recovery."

Sir Julian nodded. "Well, sir, you shall have the very best care possible here at Chelworth, for I am in your debt. I gather you single-handedly saved my nieces from certain death?"

"Not single-handedly, sir."

"Whatever the circumstances, I am grateful to you. Chelworth is at your disposal for as long as necessary, and we will get you to the house without further shilly-shally." Sir Julian straightened and went to Mr. Petti-grew. "Please instruct your men to convey the lieuten-ant up to the house without further ado."

"Sir Julian."

Within a minute the stretcher had been lifted again, but as everyone began to follow Sir Julian from the beach, Amanda got to her feet in dismay. "You mean we have to *walk* up that hill?"

"Yes, I fear so, my dear," Sir Julian replied.

"Oh, but I cannot possibly do that! I'm too weak

from all my trials. There will have to be a pony and trap at the very least."

"Shank's mare is all that can be provided, unless of course, you think Lieutenant Ballard should surrender his stretcher to you?"

Amanda flushed and said nothing more. His tone was an indication that she had done herself no favors since stepping ashore. Tansy, on the other hand, appeared to shine in his eyes. As, for some reason, did the odious Mrs. Entwhistle, with whom dear Tansy was now wont to speak on first-name terms. And they had *all*—including Martin—ignored her, Amanda, as she sat sobbing and distressed on the rock. Well they would pay for inflicting such a snub on the soon-to-be Countess of Sanderby. She would show them!

# 20

The fog did not last beyond midday, at which hour the March sunshine broke through and dispersed the gloom to leave a beautiful early spring afternoon. A lone horseman rode along the summit of the hill behind Chelworth and reined in beside the pyramid, around which the sea breeze sang quite pleasantly.

Randal would have much preferred the comfort of a carriage, but today had seen Liza driving off in style to Weymouth, to purchase a folderol to replace the so-called *chattie* scarf by which she set such ridiculous store. He had tried to wriggle out of his obligation, but she had moaned on and on about the damned thing until he could not bear it a moment longer. However, he drew the line at actually accompanying her. Be seen in fashionable Weymouth with a common whore on his arm? She was mad if she expected *that!* So he had given her a purse and told her to get on with it on her own.

Taking out his pocket telescope, he trained it upon the bay, where the *Lucina* was just setting sail. There was only one reason he could think of why a naval frigate would anchor at Chelworth, and that was to put something or someone ashore. Randal smiled as he closed the telescope again and replaced it inside his coat. If he was not mistaken, his bride had arrived, and the sooner he sought a private word with her, the better. It was as much in her interest to find the letter as it was in his.

He did not doubt that Amanda would be his willing accomplice, for he had more than gained her measure from the things she'd written. The lady was the sort who would stoop to anything, and in that respect at least she was a woman after his heart. Not that any woman was truly after his heart; there wasn't another living creature worthy of such a place in his estimation.

Randal's pale eyes were thoughtful. He had an uneasy feeling about all this, the sort of feeling that required every loose end to be taken care of *pronto,* as the Spanish said. First the disposal of the letter, then—as quickly as could be managed—the marriage. He had taken the precaution of securing the promised services of a crooked clergyman at the nearby market town of Wareham, who would not ask awkward questions about the haste and irregularity of the ceremony. He also had the absolute promise of the necessary special license, backdated with all the necessary details, there being an unfortunate fellow in the relevant church office with so much to hide that he did not dare refuse.

So before old Richardson could even blink, his niece was going to be deflowered in her marriage bed, and her considerable fortune made safe in her new husband's grasp. Then, even if the worst came to the worst, and he lost his title and fortune, at least *her* inheritance would be secured. A nerve fluttered at Randal's temple, and his lips grew pale as he pressed them together. But that would be at the very worst, for if he had his way, everything would be his.

He looked down at the rear of the house, where gardens and outbuildings were as formal and tidy as the land at the front was wild and bare. Daffodils nodded in flowerbeds, topiary bushes—sphinxes, of course—were precise and regimented, and there were paths, steps, ornamental pools, dovecotes, and a summerhouse that was modeled on the roofed and columned court of a small Nile palace. Randal supposed that the entire place was either beautiful, or breathtakingly hideous, depending upon one's point of view. He leaned toward the latter, having encountered nothing but difficulty to everything he had tried to accomplish there. All he was doing was defending what he regarded as rightfully his, and the likes of Sir Julian Richardson had no business standing in his way.

He closed the telescope and prepared to ride away again, but as he turned the horse he suddenly found himself looking at something he hadn't noticed before—the entrance to the pyramid. It was set below ground level and was reached down a flight of stone steps that were covered with dead leaves and other debris from the heath, across which the winter winds often howled with a vengeance. No one could have been inside since at least the previous autumn.

Curiosity got the better of him, and he dismounted to descend the steps and test the door. To his surprise it wasn't locked, so he was able to push it open. The hinges groaned and complained as they swung back to let the sunlight fall upon a low-ceilinged room that was completely empty. It wasn't unadorned, however, for the wall opposite was painted with a beautiful Nile hunting scene, complete with waterfowl, fish, and lush stands of stylized reeds and willows. There was also a boat upon which stood a young king with two egrets in his hand. The other hand was extended to take a papyrus from the mouth of a . . . a *cat*?

Randal looked contemptuously at the painting. What a ridiculous premise! No one in their right minds hunted with cats. For one thing, the damned things were impossible to train. . . . As he looked at the tabby that had been so meticulously painted, it seemed to him that it was meeting his gaze. There was a crafty look in its green eyes, a willful, designing gleam that made him suddenly want to shiver. Then he was sure he heard it spitting at him! A cold finger ran down his spine, and he withdrew swiftly, pulling the door closed behind him. He almost ran up the steps to his horse, but once in the sunshine he felt foolish for having been so impressionable.

He paused with a hand on the saddle, his head bowed to compose himself; then he remounted and glanced back at Chelworth again. A solitary figure was hurrying across the garden toward a postern in a corner of the high ivy-covered surrounding wall. Recognizing James, the footman he'd hired with the now-dismissed Joseph, Randal set his horse down the steep, awkward slope toward him, wincing with every jolting, lurching yard of the descent.

James waited nervously outside the postern, where the wild heath began again and there wasn't another soul to be seen. Nevertheless he glanced around, only too aware of taking a considerable risk by slipping out in daylight like this. He didn't want to suffer the same fate as Joseph, but neither did he want to forgo the fine purse promised by Lord Sanderby. "My lord?" he said as Randal reached him at last. "I saw you up by the pyramid. I . . . I was just about to send a boy to Bothenbury with a message."

"To tell me Miss Richardson has arrived?"

"Yes, sir."

"Where is she now?" Randal inquired, gazing through the slightly open gate toward the house.

"All the ladies are taking tea with Sir Julian in the drawing room."

"*All* the ladies?"

"Sir Julian's nieces are accompanied by a chaperone," James explained. "And they brought an injured naval officer with them, so are awaiting Dr. Chivenor from Weymouth."

"I see." Randal searched in his pocket and took out a piece of paper and a pencil. He scribbled a few words on it and handed it to James, whom he already knew could not read. "Give this to Miss Amanda as quickly as possible. And don't be obvious about it. Just slip it to her secretly. She will come to you, and I want you to bring her here. I will wait."

"Yes, sir."

James hurried away, closing the postern carefully behind him, and Randal slowly dismounted. He

stretched and rubbed his sore back, but in spite of his
discomfort, there was a faint smile of anticipation on
his lips. Soon he would find out if his assessment of
his bride was accurate or not. Not that he doubted it.

He took a deep breath of the pleasing spring air,
then flicked his riding crop against the back of his
boots. He would make sure of her at this first meeting.
Charm and gentleness would mark his conduct now,
with no awkward facts that might frighten her off.
Selected tidbits would be divulged at their second
meeting, which he fully intended would be tonight.


Amanda was seated a little apart from the others
in the huge green-and-gold drawing room, which had
a ceiling so high that she wondered if any light
reached it at all. The room was like a necropolis, or
some such place, she decided, glancing around at the
lines of animal statues that stood guard along the walls
like weird zoological exhibits. She particularly disliked
the hippopotamus, which reared on its hind legs in a
most unlikely way, and was so fat that it reminded her
of a satirical cartoon of the Prince of Wales.

She hated everything about this house, she decided,
still seething about the treatment she had received on
the beach. Even now the others were all talking together, sipping tea and exchanging ancedotes about
the voyage while they waited for Dr. Chivenor to hie
himself from Weymouth to examine Martin. Amanda
Richardson might as well not exist, for all the attention she had received! How dared they, oh, how dared
they! She was more important than any of them, as
they would all be reminded by the time she was done!

She glowered at them as they sat near the fire, the
coals of which glowed palely in the full stream of sunlight from the nearby window. The sunlight also
flooded over a faience figure of a demon that stood
on a small table. Amanda was beginning to feel as if
it were staring at her, fixing her with its evil glittering
eyes. She tried not to think of it as she watched the

three people she now regarded as her foes. Uncle Julian and Hermione Entwhistle were clearly birds of a feather, chattering about Ancient Egypt as if it were the only interesting topic in the world. Tansy was listening and adding a remark now and then, but she clearly did not understand half of what they were talking about.

Most of the conversation centered upon the wretched antiquities, now stored in the stables. Of especial interest was that stupid slab of black basalt, about which Uncle Julian seemed even more dizzy and nonsensical than the chaperone, if such a thing were possible. He had gone on and on about how sure he was that his studies of hieroglyphs were on the correct course, and that he had two pieces of papyrus that were somehow important. He seemed convinced that the basalt would provide a vital missing piece in the jigsaw. Or some such thing.

Amanda sighed crossly, for she really didn't care whether hieroglyphs were solved or remained a closed book forever more. Oh, it really was so *boring* here! If only fashionable Weymouth were just outside the door, instead of four miles or so away by road, at least there would be society worthy of her. She had tried to ask Uncle Julian about Lord Sanderby, but he had *prevaricated.* Yes, that was the word, prevaricated. Clearly he was still set against her becoming Lady Sanderby. He had muttered something about getting around to such things later, when everyone had settled in, and she rather gained the impression that her bridegroom was in London, so presumably it would be a positive *age* before she came face-to-face with him at last.

The door opened and a footman entered. He looked a little out of breath, she thought, and was then surprised at the way in which his glance moved meaningfully toward her before he bowed to Sir Julian.

"Begging your pardon, sir, but would you like more tea?"

"No, James, we have drunk our fill, I fancy."

"Sir."

James bowed again, then pretended to notice something amiss with the curtain by Amanda's chair. He went to straighten the folds, and as he did so he dropped Randal's note into her lap. Then he withdrew from the room again.

Amanda was startled, and for a second or so she simply looked at the folded piece of paper as if it had no business soiling her lap with its presence, but then she glanced around at the others. No one had noticed anything, so she quickly read the note. *My beloved, I await you outside. James will bring you to me. Come to my arms. R.*

She recognized the writing from Randal's letters. Her breath caught, and her fingers closed excitedly over the paper. He was outside now? Not in London? Well, she didn't give two figs what dear Uncle Julian thought about her or her magnificent match, for he certainly wasn't going to keep her from the man she was to marry. If Lord Sanderby wanted her to go to his arms right now, then go she would! She got up. "Er, if you will all excuse me, I . . . I have a headache and need to lie down for a while."

"As you wish, my dear," Sir Julian replied, trying to remain equable, for he found her a considerable trial. He was completely unaccustomed to tantrums and tears, and was of the opinion that portmanteaus and sea chests were not the only baggage to come from Constantinople!

Hermione began to get up in concern, but Amanda gathered her skirts and left the room, trying hard not to break into a run. James was in the atrium that formed the heart of the house. He lurked by the potted ferns that had been arranged around the base of a huge statue of a pharaoh that stood in the center of the black-and-white-tiled floor. The statue's head was on a level with the gallery landing that encircled the second floor above, and looked as if it were keeping watch on what happened up there, where sunlight flooded through an array of skylights.

James had brought Amanda's cloak, and he hurriedly placed it around her shoulders before leading her past the staircase toward the billiard room, which had French doors to both the front and rear of the house. Unknown to them, Ozzy and Cleo emerged from the ferns around the statue to follow. Stealthy paws padded softly behind as James conducted Amanda past the daffodils and ornamental pools, past the summerhouse and the leafy sphinxes, to the postern tucked away in the furthest corner.

"His lordship's waiting out there, miss," he said, then withdrew to a discreet distance. He heard the ivy rustling further along the garden wall and saw the two cats scrambling up to sit on the top. Tails swishing idly, they sat with their backs to him, gazing over the other side of the wall at Randal, who as yet knew nothing of their presence.

Amanda's hand shook as she opened the postern. Randal turned, a quick smile on his lips, admiration warming his eyes as he regarded her swiftly from head to toe, before fully meeting her cornflower eyes. "How beautiful you are," he breathed, coming to take her hand and raise it to his lips.

Her heart thundered. This illicit assignation was so very romantic! So utterly and wickedly what she had dreamed of that for once she could not think of anything to say. She, Amanda Richardson, was keeping a tryst with an earl! Randal read her like a book, and pulled her closer. "I have waited for this moment," he whispered.

"So have I. Oh, so have I!" she replied, finding her tongue at last.

"I have ridden up there to the pyramid every day."

"You . . . You are staying around here?"

"Three miles away, at a house called Bothenbury. I could not stay in London, knowing that you would arrive here."

"Does my uncle know this?"

Randal smiled. "Of course. Why do you ask?"

"Because he has allowed me to think you were in London."

"Ah. Well, I fear Sir Julian has set himself against our marriage. Unfortunately, he does not appear a big enough fellow to forget the past and look only to the future."

"I could not agree with you more," Amanda replied angrily.

Randal put his hand to her cheek. "But what does he matter?" he breathed. "My darling Amanda, I have loved you since I received your likeness."

"Oh, Randal . . ."

"How could I not love you? I cannot believe that my wife will be the most beautiful countess in all Europe."

She melted a little more. For the first time in her life, she was the one being toyed with, yet she did not know it. She looked at him and saw a blue-blooded hero who would give her the sort of social life and standing that she craved, the sort of life she deserved, the sort of life she would climb over all others to achieve. . . .

He smiled into her lovely blue eyes and slowly pressed her to the garden wall. "I'm going to steal a kiss, my darling," he whispered, then put his lips to hers.

She did not resist, and in a moment her arms were around him as she surrendered to a seduction that was infinitely more experienced than anything she had known before. She prided herself on always being in command, always capable of cruelty to others, always being able to use and then walk away without a care, but this man was her equal. She was playing with fire and was about to be burned.

Neither of them saw two sleek shadows moving along the top of the wall above them; neither of them knew anything at all until quite suddenly Randal had to pull away from Amanda's startled embrace in order to sneeze. He knew all the signs, and his head jerked up toward the two cats. He could have sworn they were smirking at him! With a string of four-letter words that widened Amanda's eyes to saucers, he scooped up a handful of small stones from the ground and hurled them. The feline faces disappeared as the stones flew past, then peered impudently down at him again.

Livid beyond belief, Randal grabbed more stones and flung them with all his might. "Take that, you biserable dabbed gribalkins!" he cried.

Amanda stared at him as if he had gone mad, and Ozzy and Cleo leaped serenely to safety inside the garden, then hightailed it gleefully toward the house.

# 21

*I*t was evening, and Tansy left her room to go down to her first dinner back in England. Everyone was to gather first in the library for a glass of sherry, that being Sir Julian's custom.

The way to the dining room took her around the landing above the atrium, and she paused at the balustrade. The face of the granite pharaoh seemed uncomfortably lifelike in the glow of the lighted girandoles on the wall behind her, and she almost expected the statue to stretch out a hand and pluck her from her vantage point. More fancy, she thought, cross for giving in to such imaginings, but it was difficult not to think like that in a house where Dorset seemed more distant than the Nile. Even her bedroom boasted a figure of the jackal-headed god Anubis, whose uncomfortable presence was hardly conducive to relaxed sleep!

Not that she had spent her time here so far in a state of nervous unease; on the contrary, Anubis or not, she had indeed slept for most of the afternoon and early evening. After the makeshift cots in the *Lucina*'s great cabin, on which she had slept fitfully at best, it was wonderful to have a proper bed again. And hers was quite splendid, its posts topped with lotus capitals, its golden hangings embroidered with chariot scenes. She had lain down upon the sumptuous coverlet when Dr. Chivenor at last departed after attending Martin, and the next thing she knew it was dark and almost time to dress for dinner! She hadn't realized how tired she was, but supposed it was understandable after all the turmoil since leaving Constantinople.

She began to walk on, around the landing toward the staircase, but then caught a glimpse of herself in a wall mirror and stopped again. She and Letty, the new maid her uncle had provided for her, had done their best to make her look presentable, but with no great success. Her hair seemed to have taken umbrage because of all the sea winds and salt air, and even though it was quite short it was so full of elf knots that Letty had labored long and hard to achieve some semblance of tidiness. It was in need of a good tonic, and the sooner an infusion of rosemary and chamomile was applied, the better!

Her clothes, however, were completely beyond redemption. Not because they had suffered from the sea, but because they were simply too inexpensive and nondescript. She had been wearing her one good evening gown when the *Gower* went aground, and the only other dress that was in any way suitable was the velvet she wore now. It was a sort of butter-cream color, with a square neck and long full sleeves that were gathered at the wrist. Unadorned, unbecoming, and uninspiring, it was the sort of garment that wouldn't warrant a second glance even were she to wear it in the midst of a column of nuns! So here she stood, her short dark hair resembling a bird's nest, and her gown looking as if it had been dipped in a churn. What chance did she possibly have of luring Martin's heart away from Amanda?

A mewing sound made her turn, and she smiled to see Ozzy and Cleo trotting toward her. The two cats had hit it off so famously that they were already inseparable, and as they pressed sensuously against Tansy's skirts in that way cats have, she was quite sure they were both smiling. Then they trotted on, making for Martin's closed door. Such things as doors did not present an obstacle to a determined cat, and Ozzy stretched up to the handle, but Tansy knew the doctor had left strict orders that Martin was not to be disturbed. The patient was to sleep as much as possible, and as comfortably as possible, which meant banishing all felines from his bed. So Tansy said "No," quietly but firmly, and wagged a stern finger at the two animals.

Cleo turned her back, her ears back slightly, and Ozzy gave a disgusted snort, but stopped what he was doing. Suddenly the handle jerked down, and the door opened so quickly that Tansy expected Martin himself to appear, but there was just the deserted doorway. The firelit room beyond was revealed, and the crimson-canopied bed where Martin lay asleep. Everything was red and gold, and the frescoed walls were alight with shadows of dancing flames. The cats tossed Tansy triumphant looks, then trotted in, jumped on the bed with him, and turned around and around in preparation to sleep.

Tansy was bewildered. How could the door have opened like that? She'd seen the handle pull down as if operated from the other side, and there had been no mistaking the click of the catch, yet Martin was in his bed. She could only suppose there was a slight draft, and that Ozzy had moved the handle sufficiently for the catch to give way. What other sensible answer was there? To consider other explanations would be to think of magic again, and that was something upon which she really did not wish to embark. She watched crossly as the cats lay down and curled up together, then peeped at her over their encircling tails. There were a number of unoccupied bedrooms for them to choose from, but no, they had to bother poor Martin, who was already stirring uncomfortably because of their weight. They would have to go!

Catching up her skirts, she hurried into the room to remove the guilty pair, but then paused to look down at Martin. The bronze cat lay on the bedclothes, which had been slightly tossed aside, revealing his body to the waist, and the gold chain and locket. He was lean, hard, and muscular, and his skin was smooth and tanned, for he was not the sort of officer to shrink from arduous tasks at sea. Dr. Chivenor had advised the continuation of the laudanum, which now acted with his fever, making him delirious. "I don't care who you are, sir, or what your rank!" he cried, and started up from the pillow as if to get out to deal with whoever it was to whom he spoke.

Quickly Tansy placed soothing hands upon his shoulders. "Martin? It's quite all right. There's no one here except me."

He allowed her to press him back to the pillows, then suddenly grabbed one of her wrists, his fingers surprisingly strong and viselike. "Speak like that again, damn you, and I will call you out . . . !"

"It's me, Tansy," she said again, putting her other hand to his forehead to push his damp, tousled hair back.

His eyes changed, as if his mind cleared a little. "Tansy?" he whispered.

"Yes."

For a moment he knew her, she could see it in his eyes. Then he pulled her hand to his lips and kissed it. "Forgive me . . ."

"There is nothing to forgive."

"There is."

"How are you feeling?" she asked.

"A little better, I fancy."

"I hope that is true," she said, and slid the bronze figurine into his fingers again. She had more faith in its healing warmth than in any amount of laudanum. Magic? Oh, yes, whether she liked it or not, there was magic here. . . .

He gave the ghost of a smile as the warmth spread gently through him again. "This, and a little more sleep will do wonders . . ." he whispered as he drifted away from her again.

Tears sprang to Tansy's eyes. She loved him so much that her whole being seemed composed of that single emotion. She wanted to put her mouth to his again, to breathe her love into him as well, as if it too could somehow assist his recovery. The need became too much, but just as her lips touched his, Amanda spoke from the open doorway behind her.

"Well, well, how sickly sweet, to be sure. And how very reprehensible."

The cats growled, and Tansy straightened with a guilty gasp. She stepped away from the bed, but it was a pointless gesture.

Exquisite in sequined silver satin, with a pink cashmere shawl trailing on the floor behind her, Amanda entered the room. She ignored the cats, being more intent upon poking fun at Tansy than giving the animals the wide berth she might otherwise have done. "Well, Coz, no doubt this is the only way you will ever enjoy his kisses," she said.

"I . . . I didn't know you were there."

"That much is obvious." Amanda's fan tapped in her pink-gloved palm. She was beautifully turned out, her golden hair shining and perfect, her ears and throat glittering with diamonds. Her new maid, a London girl called Daisy, had once waited upon a duchess, and was far more accomplished than Letty. As a result, Amanda's fashionable coiffure was all that Tansy's was not, and the contrast could not have been more pronounced—or more to Amanda's satisfaction.

In fact, everything was to Amanda's satisfaction. She was going to meet Randal again later on, and hopefully repeat the intimacies to which she had so wantonly surrendered earlier; at least, she had surrendered to them once the odd incident with the cats had ended and he had stopped speaking gibberish! She had been a little coy with him, resorting to blushes and protestations of maidenly modesty, but she had eventually permitted a resumption of the interrupted kisses. Not to the point of complete surrender, although she had been very tempted. His ancient lineage and impressive title were potent flames to such a moth as she, and maybe tonight, when temptation beckoned again, she would allow her lovely wings to fly far too close. . . .

She stood across the bed from Tansy and looked down at Martin, her sequins shimmering in the firelight. The cats hissed and spat, and got up with their backs arched, but she continued to ignore them. Her interest was drawn to the locket, and she bent to open it.

Tansy was shocked. "You shouldn't do that, Amanda!"

"Why not? He's hardly going to object, is he?" The locket clicked and opened. Inside there was a miniature of a woman in clothes that were fashionable in the 1770s. She was dainty and very lovely, with coal-black hair piled up on her head and tumbling in curls over her left shoulder. Her name was inscribed at the bottom of the painting; Marguerite Kenny.

Amanda's brows drew together. "Marguerite Kenny? Wasn't she an actress at Sadler's Wells?"

"I believe so."

"Why on earth would our brave first lieutenant wear her likeness around his neck?" Amanda mused.

"I really have no idea. Amanda, it's none of our business. Please close the locket again."

With a shrug, Amanda did as she said, but then straightened to look down at Martin again. "He is very handsome, is he not? No doubt you would like to win him, but he will not glance at you twice."

"I know that."

Amanda's lovely eyes fluttered. "I am the one he wants."

"Well, I suppose even he is not perfect," Tansy responded. It wasn't often that the Church Mouse bit back, but the moment called for it.

"Don't think you can best me, Tansy, for you will fail miserably." Amanda's eyes glittered like her diamonds. "I have decided to pass the time by making him confess his love for me."

"Even you would not be that cruel."

"Cruel? My dear, I will merely be doing that which you yourself would like to do. Do you deny it? Do you deny that you would like to hear the handsome lieutenant swear his undying love for you?"

Tansy didn't reply.

Amanda laughed. "He already thinks I am the one who sat by his bunk all the time. I told him it was me, and he believed it. Men always believe me, no matter how many lies I tell. I will soon have his avowal of undying devotion, you see if I don't. Then I shall toss it back at him and tell him I think he is most presumptuous for thinking he can aspire to me."

"You tread a very dangerous path, Amanda. Let us hope Lord Sanderby does not see through you until after the marriage, or you may not become a countess after all."

Amanda was amused. "My dear Tansy, Lord Sanderby is my willing slave already. He and I are admirably suited, have no fear of that."

"How can you be sure? You've never met him."

Amanda smiled enigmatically "I am certain of his lordship's undying devotion."

Tansy was puzzled, for it really was as if Amanda and Lord Sanderby had met. Yet that could not be. "Amanda, you may have exchanged letters with Lord Sanderby, but that does not mean you know him. I am sure that the man *I* perceive in those letters is vastly different from the one you perceive."

"Oh, I don't doubt it." Amanda laughed.

"Maybe in him you will meet your match," Tansy said quietly.

Amanda was scornful. "No man is a match for me."

"Take care, Amanda, for you will be playing with fire if you—"

Amanda interrupted cuttingly. "Don't advise me, Tansy, especially when it comes to handling men. I have been able to wrap them around my little finger since I was a child. Lord Sanderby is no different."

"You aren't doing all that well with Uncle Julian,

even though you have been exerting your charm for all it is worth."

Amanda was scornful. "He is a foolish old man who thinks only of antiquities and cats."

Tansy found Amanda's attitude thoroughly distasteful. To refer to Uncle Julian in such a derogatory and downright offensive way went against all her principles, especially when he had shown himself to be all that was kind and thoughtful. "It ill becomes you to speak of him like that, Amanda."

"And who, pray, are you to find fault with me?" Amanda was at her most arch and superior. "You are nothing, Tansy Richardson, a plain, dull nobody of a Church Mouse who will never amount to anything. You will die an old maid, for to be sure no man will ever want you."

"I would rather be me ten times over than be a *chienne* like you," Tansy said quietly.

Amanda's nostrils flared with outrage, and she began to come around the bed with a hand raised to strike her impudent cousin, but Ozzy growled his most dangerous growl, and then a door opened across the landing. It was Sir Julian leaving his private apartment, and both cousins could see him because of the open door. As he paused to absentmindedly tease the lace at the cuffs of his evening coat, Amanda immediately returned to her place across the bed and sat on a chair that was there; then she reached for Martin's hand.

She appeared angelic again, except that she pinched him hard to make him awaken. He opened his eyes just as Sir Julian noticed the little vignette and came toward the room. Calculating the approaching footsteps to the very inch, Amanda leaned tenderly over the patient. "How are you feeling, dear Lieutenant Ballard? Is there anything I can do for you?" she asked in her most winsome voice.

Martin gazed at her, then saw Tansy from the corner of his eye. His head turned toward her. "Tansy . . . ?" he whispered.

Amanda dug her fingernails into his hand again. "Look at me, Lieutenant," she said sharply, forgetting herself for a split second.

The cats saw Martin wince and heard his breath catch. It was too much for them, and as one they crept, bellies low, along the bed toward Amanda. Their tails lashed, their fur stood on end like the bristles of a chimney brush, and their growls and spitting were truly ferocious.

"Come away, my dear," Sir Julian advised quickly.

"Uncle?" she turned, able even now to pretend to be taken completely by surprise that he should be there.

Ozzy rose on his hind legs and waved his front paws at her, his formidable claws unsheathed. It may have been a slightly comical stance, but funny it definitely was not, for he was as much a fighting engine as any frigate, and his claws could inflict as much damage as a broadside. Cleo was less demonstrative, but supported him with some feline swearing that would have seen off the most ferocious Egyptian dog.

Sir Julian looked urgently at Amanda. "My dear, if you remain there, I will not be responsible for what happens. The cats do not like you, so I think it best if you remove yourself."

She got up at last, her eyes bright with studied tears. "I . . . I was only trying to comfort the lieutenant," she cried as she hurried to him.

"I know, my dear."

"I . . . I don't know why they don't like me," she said pathetically, moving so close to him that he was obliged to put his arms around her.

Sir Julian looked at Ozzy. "Ozymandias, that's quite enough from you. You're not supposed to be in here anyway. Off with you this instant. And you, Cleopatra."

Ozzy gave him a sulky look, but jumped down from the bed and left the room. Cleo followed. They were like two naughty children sent away in disgrace.

Sir Julian smiled at Tansy. "Come, my dear. We'll

all go downstairs now, hmm? The lieutenant must be left to his sleep."

"Yes, Uncle." She glanced down at Martin, who seemed to have sunk into sleep again; then she went to her uncle.

Sir Julian ushered Tansy out as well, and as the door closed behind them, Martin's eyes opened. He had not been asleep at all, and knew everything that had gone on around him over the past minutes, including Tansy's stolen kiss. Restored greatly by the figurine, he got up. He swayed a little, but after a moment felt steadier. . . . He went to the wardrobe where he knew his dress uniform hung with his other clothes. Tonight he would join the others for a while, and commence the business of fighting for something that had begun to matter very much to him—*someone* who had begun to matter very much to him.

But as he began the painstaking business of getting himself ready to go down to join the others for a short while, he did not notice that the gold chain around his neck had broken, or that the locket had fallen on the carpet beside the bed. Or that the figurine had disappeared from the bed.


Meanwhile, the cats had repaired to Tansy's room, where the hearth rug was particularly deep and warm. They sat side by side in a way that could only be described as triumphant. No guilty children they, for seeing Amanda off had been their intention, and they had succeeded. The rich sound of purring filled the room.

On the mantel above them stood the bronze cat. Its eyes shone in the flickering light, and had Tansy returned to the room at that moment, she would have been certain that the purring did not come from just the two cats on the hearth rug. . . .

# 22

Randal was having a bath at Bothenbury. The tub had been placed in front of the roaring fire in the bedroom, and Liza was applying a soapy sponge to her lover's chest as he leaned back against a soft white towel. He had been soaking for a considerable time now, and so far two fresh kettles of hot water had been required to keep him warm.

Liza wore a peach muslin wrap, and her unpinned hair hung in damp rattails over her shoulders as she worked with vigor, but then she halted as a maid knocked at the door.

"Begging your pardon, sir, madam, but his lordship's carriage will be ready in ten minutes."

Randal sat up with a jolt. "Is it that time already?"

Liza gave him a look. "Well, you *have* been lolling here like a whale this past hour," she pointed out.

Randal scrambled out of the bath and reached for the towel, which he flung at Liza. "Dry me," he said imperiously, standing there with the firelight shining on his wet body.

One sharp push into the flames, she thought, that was all it would take, and he'd be dry all right! But she resisted the urge and confined herself to simply obeying his orders. Well paid or not, she wished more and more that she had stayed at Mother Clancy's. Tending to this noble maggot's every need was a thankless task!

"Get me the clothes I wore this afternoon," he said.

"I'm not a maidservant, you know!"

"No, you're a whore whose services I've hired. Now get the clothes."

Her cheeks flushed with more than just the heat of the fire as she went to do as he commanded. "Where are you going?" she asked then, curiosity getting the better of her.

"To see my bride," he replied. "By the way, I shall not be needing you anymore. First thing in the morning I wish you to leave. I'll send you to Weymouth in the carriage, with enough money to purchase a ticket on a London stagecoach."

Liza didn't reply. So that was it. She was to be cast off without so much as a thank-you. Anger forged through her. If anyone had earned his ring on her finger these past weeks, it was Liza Lawrence. And what thanks did she get? None. He treated her worse than something he had trodden in, and now he was off to whisper sweet words to his future wife. It wasn't fair. It really wasn't fair. She contained the urge to rub him so hard with the towel that she made his skin raw, and as she helped him to dress, she began to think about how she could get back her own.

As soon as he set off in the carriage, she dashed to his room to go through his things with a fine-tooth comb. If there was anything worth taking, Liza Lawrence was going to lift it. Then she was going to skip back to London tonight and disappear. By the time Lord High-and-Mighty Sanderby got back from cooing and caressing with his bride, his whore would be long gone. And serve him right!

She went through his bedroom like a weevil through a biscuit, and, like a weevil, she was very thorough. The denizens of Mother Clancy's were adept at searching a gentleman's pockets, knowing that even the highest in the land might have a tear in the pocket lining through which interesting things might slip. Lord High-and-Mighty Sanderby proved to be no different; in fact, he proved to be astonishingly lax, for as well as several coins, she found a note that he had received, read, then pushed into the pocket and forgotten.

Liza cast her eyes swiftly over the scribbled writing.

*My lord. Regarding the matter you asked me to investigate on behalf of your friend. There is no longer any trace of the lady. The last I was able to firmly establish was that in December 1767, she consulted a prominent Mayfair doctor about a problem concerning the child she expected the following Valentine's Day. She gave a false name, but there is no doubt that she was the woman in question. Where she went or what happened to her remains a mystery, although you are already aware from another source that the child she bore was a boy. However, from the date of the appointment with the doctor, it is clear that the first wife was still living on the day your friend's father remarried, so the second marriage cannot possibly be legal. Nor, therefore, can your friend be legitimate.*

The note was signed by a man who was known to her, because he had called upon Randal a number of times in London. He was investigating something important that Randal pretended was on behalf of an anonymous "friend," but she had known all along that it really concerned Randal himself. She had often wondered what it was all about, and now it was suddenly only too clear. Lord High-and-Mighty Sanderby wasn't Lord Sanderby after all, because his father was bigamously married to his mother! The real Lord Sanderby was the boy born on or near St. Valentine's Day, 1768!

Liza smiled vengefully. What an idiot Randal was not to have destroyed outright a note containing such delicate information. She would show him what happened to uppity coves who thought they could kick

her aside like that. Blackmail wasn't her game, for
that would leave him enjoying all his privileges. No,
she had other plans entirely.

Pocketing the note, she prepared to leave
Bothenbury.

Everyone was enjoying a glass of sherry in the library, with as yet no idea that Martin intended to join
them. Apart from Amanda, they would all have been
most alarmed to know of his intention, for such an
exertion was not yet advisable for someone in his fragile state of health. Amanda, of course, would simply
resent the fuss that would ensue the moment he appeared, and would regard him as having stolen the
attention at her expense. As indeed she felt the conversation had already been stolen. On several occa-
sions she had done her utmost to make them all talk
about her marriage and grand future, but each time
she tried, she took a poor second place to such things
as sarcophagi, bas-reliefs, scarabs, papyri, and, of
course, the interminable hieroglyphs.

Bored to tears, she wandered around the library,
touching this and that. She was angry with Sir Julian
for failing to mention Randal's close proximity at Bothenbury, but could hardly reveal without prompting
questions as to *how* she knew! She paused in front of
one of the bookcases to look sourly at the volumes
within. What an excruciatingly dull collection! Names
leaped out at her, Herodotus, Pliny, Plutarch, and
Homer, to say nothing of titles such as *Pyramido-
graphia* and *Chronological Antiquities*. Ah, at least
there was one she could tolerate. *The Tales of One
Thousand and One Nights*. What on earth was a story-
book doing among all these other stuffy old tomes?
Ali Baba was one of her favorite pantomimes. She
had seen it when she was eight, and had paid great
attention, especially the part where the magic word
opened the cave and all the treasure was revealed.

Rather like the wonderful life that would open up to her when she said, "I will," and became the Countess of Sanderby. . . .

The cats were stretched on the floor in front of the fire, but suddenly they both awoke and got up to trot to the door, before which they waited expectantly. The handle turned, and Sir Julian and Hermione stopped talking and looked toward it in surprise, for all the servants would surely knock before entering.

Martin came in, and paused in a little embarrassment on seeing the astonishment that greeted him. He had managed to tog himself in his full dress uniform, but even though he looked so unwell and thin, and the clothes were no longer as fine a fit as they had once been, Tansy thought he was still heart-stoppingly attractive. The blue coat, with its blue standing collar, white lapels and cuffs, gold braid and gilt buttons, was somehow calculated to show any man to great advantage, especially a man like Martin, who was so very handsome in the first place.

Tansy gazed at him, conscious that his inner strength burned fiercely on. The brave lieutenant who had rescued them from Tel el-Osorkon was only resting and would soon be himself again. Her moments of inaction were short-lived, and she leaped to her feet to go to him. "Lieutenant, you really should not have left your bed!" she cried.

Sir Julian was in full agreement. "Hear, hear, young man. What in the deuce are you doing down here?"

Martin bowed to the room in general. "Forgive the intrusion, but I think I have languished in bed for too long. I need to push myself a little, and so have come to inflict my presence upon you for a short while. As soon as you go in to dinner, I will retreat to my lair, I promise."

Amanda suddenly appeared at his side. "Why, Lieutenant, how very dashing you look, to be sure," she breathed, treating him to the full force of her cornflower gaze.

He did not seem to hear, for he spoke to Tansy.

"May I impose upon you to assist me to a chair?" he asked.

"It is no imposition at all," she replied, and helped him into a comfortable armchair.

"Your bronze cat is indeed a magical thing," he said quietly as she bent over him. For a moment his hand rested on hers, his fingers warm and firm, their touch far from accidental; then she straightened. Their eyes met, and for the single beat of her heart she felt alone with him. They might have been far away from Chelworth, just the two of them. . . .

Sir Julian was anxious to return the conversation to more important matters. He went to his desk, and opened the drawer to take out the two pieces of papyrus—or rather, to take out the two papyri that were now one whole sheet, for they had fused together as if they had never been ripped at all. He gaped at the single sheet for a moment, then cleared his throat and spoke to Hermione. "Mrs. Entwhistle, as a fellow antiquarian—"

"Oh, you honor me too much, I fancy," she answered quickly, quite clearly a little flustered.

He smiled. "Dear lady, in my opinion you know more about Ancient Egypt than many of the gentlemen at the Society of Antiquaries."

Amanda heaved a theatrical sigh.

No one took any notice of her, and Sir Julian pushed the papyrus across the desk. Ozzy and Cleo jumped up onto the desk and sat with their tails tidily wrapped around their paws as they surveyed the papyrus. From their pricked ears and brightly watching eyes, it was as if they understood all about such things. Or so it seemed to Tansy.

Not knowing quite what to think of the mysterious way the separate pieces had become joined, Sir Julian stood back for Hermione to examine the picture. The chaperone's face changed, and her startled glance leaped toward Tansy. "My dear, I . . . I think you should come to look too!"

Puzzled, Tansy joined them, and was amazed to

once again gaze upon the scene that graced both the
wall at Tel el-Osorkon and the scroll on the *canja.*
She picked up the papyrus. "Uncle, may I please show
it to the lieutenant?"

"Why, yes, of course."

She hastened to Martin's chair and placed it on his
lap. He stared at it, and then up at her. "How
incredible . . ."

"To have seen this particular illustration twice is
remarkable enough, but *three* times . . . ?"

"But was the cat always there on this scene?" he
murmured.

The pensive softness in his tone seemed to stroke
her. He only spoke of a painted figure on an ancient
papyrus, but Tansy looked past the words to the caress
that seemed woven into his voice. She knew she was
being ridiculous, but she had no control over her
heart. Just to stand close to him like this was to need
to touch him. Before she knew it, she had put her
hand on his shoulder. Before she knew it again, his
fingers rested fleetingly over hers. It was over in a
moment, a gesture that was unseen by everyone else
but that meant everything in the world to the two
people involved. Their glances met, and she saw the
caress warming his eyes as well. She wasn't imagining
it. She wasn't.

"Seen what three times?" Sir Julian demanded.
"Will someone tell me what's going on?"

Martin looked apologetically at him. "Forgive me,
sir. All I can tell you about this picture is that there
is another version of it among the antiquities we com-
mandeered in Egypt. When I first saw it, I was quite
sure there was no cat in the scene, but when I looked
a second time, there it was."

Tansy added her contribution. "And I first saw the
scene on the wall at the temple where we took refuge.
When we left, I looked back at it, and was quite convinced the cat had vanished."

Hermione looked at her in surprise, for this was the
first she had heard of it. Sir Julian was equally sur-

prised, and yet, perhaps not. He gave Tansy and Martin a slightly rueful smile. "Well, to be truthful with you, I too have experienced something odd. You see, I am ashamed to admit that I, er, borrowed a papyrus from the British Museum, because it reminded me so of a similar papyrus here at Chelworth. It proved to be so similar as to be another piece of the *same* papyrus."

Tansy and Martin gazed at him, then Tansy asked, "Which one is this? Yours, or the one from the museum?"

"Ah, well that is the strange thing. What you have there is *both* fragments. They have, well, joined themselves together somehow." He spread his hands, not knowing quite what to say next.

There was utter silence; then Amanda gave a scornful sigh. "Oh, how very silly! Such things simply do not happen."

Sir Julian shifted uncomfortably, for truth to tell he felt a little foolish for having confided such a matter. Amanda was right; two pieces of ancient papyrus *couldn't* fuse into one. Yet the single papyrus now before them was proof positive that the impossible had become very possible indeed. And taken together with vanishing and materializing cats . . . Oh, he didn't know what to think.

Hermione was quite prepared to believe it all, having developed a healthy respect for the mysteries of the past. She was disappointed not to have a tale of her own to add. "Well, I fear I have nothing out of the ordinary to report. Mayhap more than a leaning to the psychic is required, mayhap a belief in it."

Amanda's irritation grew. "For goodness' sake, how ridiculous you all sound. None of the things you say can possibly have happened, so I think you are all letting your imaginations run away with you."

Sir Julian shrugged. "Maybe you are right. Who can say?"

*I can,* Tansy thought, for she was in no doubt that these strange things were happening. If only she knew *why!*

Sir Julian stroked his chin. "It is all most mystifying. So there is another version of the scene among the antiquities, eh?"

"Yes," Tansy said.

Hermione shivered. "Dear me, I daresay I'm being foolish, but although I may not be psychic, I nevertheless feel something untoward is going on."

Sir Julian smiled at her. "I tell you, dear lady, I believe Egypt was once a civilization more advanced than Greece or Rome, which it undoubtedly preceded by many centuries. I do not find it hard to imagine they had powers then that we have forgotten now. After all, we in England have stories of fairies and giants, but can we be sure they are simply stories? Who is to say that such things did not once exist? Maybe our fairy tales have some basis in fact, and merely *seem* fanciful to us in this modern age."

Amanda was more irritated than ever. "Soon you will be telling me that Ali Baba is centuries old, when we *all* know he was created for the pantomimes at Astley's!"

Everyone endeavored not to look at one another, but no one corrected her about Ali Baba's far more ancient antecedents. An invention for Astley's he most certainly was not! The wind stirred outside, and a draft drew down the chimney, making the flames flare for a moment. The brighter light glanced around the room, and Hermione happened to be looking at the statue of Isis that stood beside the mantel. It was the first time she had really noticed it, and now she straightened with great interest. "Good heavens, it's one of those!" she said.

"One of what?" Sir Julian turned. "Isis, do you mean?"

"Yes. My late husband showed me . . ." She caught up the skirts of her gray velour gown and went closer to the statue. Before Sir Julian realized what she was doing, she reached up to its headdress and pressed down on the scarab that was carved there. A little flap swung down, revealing a cavity behind, in which lay some folded sheets of paper.

Amanda hurried to join her. "Oh, something really exciting at last! Is it a map to buried treasure?" she cried, and she grabbed the papers to see what they were. It was unforgivably rude, but Amanda was never one to observe the niceties of good manners.

Sir Julian spoke sharply. "No! Please be so good as to replace it immediately, Amanda!"

"But it's only an old letter from—"

"Enough! It may only be an old letter, madam, but it's *my* old letter! A private matter that is no business of yours, so put it back this instant!"

She flinched at his anger, and hastily shoved it back into the statue. An embarrassed hush fell on the room as Hermione, mortified at having exposed the secret in the first place, quickly closed the flap, turned the scarab, and stepped away from the statue as if she feared it would point an accusing finger at her.

Sir Julian overcame his anger, then summoned an apologetic smile. "I must ask you all to forgive me, but the letter happens to be precious to me."

Amanda tossed her head and went back to the bookcase she had been examining before. Hermione was still too embarrassed to meet anyone's eyes, and she quickly went to take a seat on an empty sofa opposite Tansy, who smiled encouragingly at her.

Sir Julian put the papyrus away and came to join them, being careful to sit with Hermione, by way of showing her he was not upset with her. She stole a shy glance at him, found his upon her already, and looked quickly away again. But the awkwardness did not last long, for they both had too much in common and far too much to talk about.

Amanda sighed loudly as she sauntered to the next bookcase. Her sequined gown glittered in the combination of candles and firelight, and Tansy's attention was drawn to her. There was definitely something different about her tonight, something reminiscent of an

occasion in their childhood when Amanda had been
the first to find out that Tansy's mother was ill and
would not get better. Tansy could hear her childish,
taunting voice even now. *I know something you don't
know. I know something you don't know.* . . . Amanda
had that look about her again tonight.

Martin watched Amanda too, and he shared Tansy's
suspicions. Something was afoot, and he did not think
it boded well for anyone. His hand crept up to rest
over Tansy's once more, and this time her fingers
curled into his, warm, gentle, and more beloved to
him than he had quite realized.

# 23

The handclasp between Tansy and Martin did not escape Amanda's eagle eye. Scarcely able to credit that he could show such favor toward the Church Mouse, Amanda was immediately stirred with a malignant urge to spoil things if she could. So she went to the decanter of sherry, poured a glass, and took it to Martin, approaching him in such a way that Tansy was forced to release his hand and step aside. Amanda promptly inserted herself neatly in the resulting gap, then turned her back on Tansy as she pressed the glass upon Martin. "I think it most splendid of you to come down like this, Lieutenant, and I for one do not wish you to scurry away again when we go in to dine."

He summoned a slight laugh. "I do not think I am about to scurry anywhere, Miss Richardson. A painful shuffle is about all I can manage at the moment."

"Well, however you move from A to B, sir, I must beg you to stay down here with us. I look to you to rescue me again from the horrors of Ancient Egypt, for I vow that so far tonight the conversation here has more resembled the market chatter in Cairo or Alexandria than a country house in England!"

Sir Julian raised an eyebrow at her. "Come now, Amanda, I do not think we have been *that* bad."

Tansy went to sit down on a nearby chair, where she was able to feast her eyes on Martin. She drank in the soft shadows cast by his dark lashes, and admired the curve of his lips, lips she had now kissed twice. Her heart almost turned over with love. *Please don't let me be misunderstanding this now. Please don't let it be a lonely fantasy. . . .*

Amanda was replying to Sir Julian. "Oh, yes, your conversation has indeed been that bad," she said, fussing over Martin like a nurse with a small child. "I am not in the least bit interested in old pieces of stone or bits of horrid papyrus, yet that is all you and Mrs. Entwhistle have talked about. I think I will scream if you continue in the same vein when we go in to dinner."

Sir Julian held up his hands in mock submission. "Very well, Amanda, we promise not to utter the word *Egypt* at the table."

"I trust instead that you will tell us all about London. Didn't you say earlier that you'd been there recently?"

"Er, yes, I believe I did." Sir Julian didn't see the trap yawning before him.

"Did you encounter Lord Sanderby while you were there? Oh, you must have done, for how could you not? Do tell me all about him, Uncle." Amanda was curious to know what he would say. After all, he had been most sparing with the facts so far!

Sir Julian did not wish to speak of Randal Fenworth, but Amanda pressed again until at last he decided to be frank. "My dear, you already know that I do not like Sanderby in the least, so I think it would be wiser if we left the subject alone, don't you? I wish to enjoy my dinner, not suffer indigestion because of him."

There was an awkward silence; then Amanda's chin came up resentfully. "I don't think that is very amusing, Uncle!"

"Nor is it meant to be. I'm sorry, my dear, but since you insist upon speaking of Lord Sanderby, you leave me no option but to be frank with you. In my opinion he is a scoundrel of the first water, and I can hardly bring myself to be civil about him, let alone discuss him amicably over dinner. You are my niece, so I feel a responsibility toward you, which is why I have to advise you—again—to withdraw from this match while you can.''

The others remained awkwardly silent, for there was really nothing any of them could say or do. Hermione kept her eyes downcast, and Martin studied the wall opposite. Tansy just fidgeted. Amanda, however, was ready to argue. "Why do you *really* offer such advice, Uncle? Can't you bear to think I will enjoy a greater status in society than you?"

Martin squirmed, wishing he'd remained in his room after all. Tansy and Hermione were shocked by what Amanda said. "Amanda!" they both cried together.

She regretted nothing. "Oh, keep out of it, for you two are nobodies anyway!" She didn't take her eyes from Sir Julian. "My Lord Sanderby didn't fall out with you over your horrid Egyptian things, his father did, so why are you so venomous about him? I demand you tell me!"

"You will demand *nothing,* miss!" Sir Julian replied sharply.

Amanda didn't even flinch. "I don't care what you think about the earl. I'm going to marry him anyway! And if you think I will have anything to do with you afterward, you are very much mistaken! When I am Countess of Sanderby, I will be far too grand a lady to bother with a silly old antiquarian who is the laughingstock of London!"

A nerve twitched at Sir Julian's temple. "I will forgive you for this outburst because I do not doubt that you are very tired after your demanding voyage, but if you speak to me like this again, I will expel you from Chelworth and leave you to manage as best you will," he said quietly.

Amanda stared at him. Her expression was still truculent, and for a moment it seemed she would continue to defy and insult him, but to everyone's relief she fell silent. Hermione found her tongue and changed the subject; then Martin injected a note of humor into the proceedings, and the atmosphere lightened percepti-

bly. The brief altercation was forgotten—but not by
Amanda, who never forgot an insult, real or imagined.

The new topic Hermione raised was cats, which, of
course, was something else in which Amanda was
completely disinterested. As Sir Julian, Tansy, and the
chaperone discussed the merits of their favorite creatures, Amanda leaned down close to Martin. "Aren't
they all too boring for words?"

He cleared his throat slightly and didn't reply, so
she tried a different tack. "It truly is delightful to have
you here like this," she whispered, giving him the full
benefit of her most alluring expression as she set about
driving the Church Mouse completely from his mind.

"I have never seen myself as delightful company,
so I think you are far too kind, Miss Richardson,"
Martin replied.

"Amanda, please," she corrected. "After all, I sat
with you every day on the voyage, and you called me
by my first name then."

"Did I? I don't recall."

"You are trying to spare my blushes, I know. But
the truth is that I feel far more for you than I should;
indeed, I am in danger of forgetting which man I am
soon to marry." She was confident of playing him like
a fish.

Martin looked up at her and spoke in a low voice
only she could hear. "Miss Richardson, what I did
when at death's door I cannot really comment on, but
now that I am on the way to recovery, I can assure
you that I have no desire whatsoever to address you
by your first name," he said. "In fact, I have no desire
for you at all, having overheard far more of your
shrewish tongue than you think. I find it very hard
indeed to believe that you would *ever* forget that you
are to marry Lord Sanderby, because gaining a title is
clearly the be-all and end-all of your shallow existence.
So pray do not try to charm me, for it will not work.
I cannot be impressed by a woman I consider to be
despicable in every way. Your cousin puts you com-

pletely in the shade, and I would rather spent one minute with her than a thousand with you."

Amanda recoiled as if he had stuck her with a pin, not only because it was the first time a man on whom she had set her sights had rejected her, but because he had been aware of some of the things she'd said to Tansy. Conflicting emotions battled on her face so that she almost grimaced with the effort of controlling them. Jealousy swung through her like an unstoppable pendulum. How dared he prefer Tansy! How dared Tansy win him! With a superhuman effort, she gathered in her rage and turned suddenly to Sir Julian. "I . . . I fear I feel a little unwell. Another headache . . ."

"Oh, my dear, is there anything I can do?" Hermione inquired.

Amanda ignored her. "I think I will go to my room to lie down."

Sir Julian was concerned. "But what of your dinner?"

"I'm not hungry."

"Amanda, if this is due to the disagreement we had a few minutes ago . . ."

"No, of course not."

It was impossible not to feel thankful when the door closed behind her, for her blend of quarrelsome temper and strutting vanity was too much to stomach. Sir Julian and Tansy remained convinced that the sudden headache was due to the sharp things the former had said, but Hermione and Martin knew otherwise. The chaperone had observed the whispered exchange with Martin and wondered greatly what he had said. Something had not only displeased the future countess, but shocked her too, for her cheeks had gone the sort of a deep, dull red that denotes humiliation as well as outrage. Had the handsome lieutenant snubbed her? Oh, how Hermione Entwhistle hoped so!

Martin was not in the least repentant because he considered the rebuke to have been richly deserved.

In fact, the poisonous little vixen warranted more punishment by far for some of the things she had said and done.

The thirst for revenge poured through Amanda's veins as she flounced across the black-and-white-tiled floor of the atrium. She had never, *never* been spoken to like that before, and if it was the last thing she did, she would wipe the smile from Lieutenant Martin Ballard's face! She would see to it that his name was reviled throughout society!

The anger and disbelief that engulfed her were so overwhelming that she needed to lash out at something. But there was nothing at hand, except the beautiful ferns around the pharaoh. With a snarl that was very unlovely indeed, she seized the fronds of one and wrenched with all her might. The fern rocked in its terra-cotta container, then slowly toppled over, cracking and spilling earth and black water all over the pristine tiles. And over Amanda's immaculate gown. Dirty splashes stained the exquisite silver satin, and she became more enraged than ever.

With a choked cry, she kicked out at the terra-cotta. It was not a wise act when wearing slippers that were made of the same silver satin as the spoiled gown. As her toes were painfully stubbed, she resorted to one or two of the disgraceful new words she had heard Randal say by the postern. Only then did she realize Tansy's wide-eyed maid, Letty, was watching her antics from the entrance to the kitchen. It was a little late to assume some dignity, but somehow Amanda achieved it. "Well, don't just stand there, girl, clean it!" she snapped. Then, nose in the air, she ascended the staircase in a manner she hoped was regal.

As she reached the top, she hesitated. Martin's closed door seemed so inviting. She glanced back down. The atrium was deserted, the maid having hurried away to get things to clean the mess. Would there ever be a better opportunity to search the dear lieu-

tenant's room and do some mischief? Hardly had the
thought entered her head than she acted upon it, slipping into the firelit chamber to search everything. Two
furry shadows slunk in behind her, moving low around
the edges of the room and slipping beneath the bed.
Then they peeped out from beneath the trailing coverlet, watching every move she made.

Most of Martin's things were in his locked sea chest,
the key to which was nowhere to be seen, and after
a few unsuccessful attempts to get in, Amanda soon
gave up. Outside the wind had risen a little more, and
occasionally the flames flared in the hearth as a draft
sucked down the chimney.

She would not have found the locket if she hadn't
trodden on it. Her eyes glittered as she bent to pick
it up, her questing fingers within easy reach of a feline
armory that remained strangely inactive. She opened
the locket to look again at the little portrait of Marguerite Kenny. She held it to the firelight, and only
then noticed the inscription on the other half of the
locket. *To my beloved son, Martin, on his first birthday, 1769.* So dear Mama was a low actress, was she?
No doubt the good lieutenant was very careful to keep
*that* a secret from his fellow officers!

She closed the locket with a click, and slipped it
into the bodice of her gown. It must be precious to
Martin, or he wouldn't wear it all the time, so with
luck its loss would cause him considerable anguish.
Stealing it was small revenge for the things he had
said, but it would do to be going on with . . .

Hearing something down in the atrium, she hurried
back to the door, then halted as Tansy's voice carried
up to the landing. Then Martin answered, and
Amanda tiptoed to the balustrade to peep down.
Tansy was assisting him toward the staircase, because
he was returning to his room, and they paused for a
moment where two footmen were now assisting Letty
with the damaged fern. Amanda drew back out of
view and ran to her own room.

Ozzy and Cleo emerged from beneath Martin's bed

and trotted down to the ground floor. They had business to attend to, and so took no notice of Tansy as she spoke to them. They crossed the hall to the kitchens, then found an open window in the scullery. Within moments they were on their way toward the postern.

Back in the house, Tansy helped Martin climb the stairs. The effort he'd put into dressing in his uniform and then coming down to the library had really begun to tell now, and halfway up he had to pause to rest awhile. "Dear God above, this is ridiculous!" he breathed. "I am weaker than a kitten!"

"You had no business leaving your bed."

"Right now I have to agree." He smiled at her.

Warmth suffused her cheeks. "Lieutenant . . ."

"My name is Martin," he interrupted quietly.

She was full of confusion, which she tried to conceal by glancing back toward the ferns. "I . . . I think we had better continue before we attract attention," she said, making to take his arm again, but he resisted.

"Only if you call me Martin," he said.

She avoided his eyes. "Very well . . . Martin."

He allowed her to help him once again, but as they reached his door and she made to leave him, he prevented her. "Tansy?"

"Yes?"

"I want you to know that I think you are perfection."

Her heart, indeed her whole body, was in danger of melting. "Perfection? Oh, I hardly—"

He put a finger to her lips. "Don't say anything. Just know that—"

Sir Julian's voice rang up from the atrium below. "Tansy? Do come down, for dinner is served at *last!*"

Heart thundering, she hurried back downstairs.

# 24

$S$hortly afterward, having changed out of her ruined evening gown, Amanda left her room to keep her second assignation of the day with Randal. Beneath her fur-lined cloak she now wore rose silk, and her maid had repinned her hair, so once again she looked all that she should. Excitement bubbled through her as she hurried across the black-and-white tiles of the atrium. Sir Julian, Tansy, and Mrs. Entwhistle were still in the dining room, so all was quiet as she entered the deserted billiard room then went out into the gardens.

The night air was cold and fresh, with the tang of salt on the stiff breeze that now swept in from the sea. Clouds scudded swiftly inland, obscuring the stars, and the daffodils and other spring flowers shuddered as she gathered her cloak to hurry up toward the postern. Her progress was observed from the top of the wall, where Ozzy and Cleo were waiting a suitable distance from the postern—out of *furshot,* so to speak—for on this occasion they were not interested in upsetting Randal in any way. They edged a little nearer as Amanda opened the postern, but did not go too close.

Randal was waiting, and she ran into his arms, lifting her lips to his with no thought of her reputation. The call of common sense was very faint indeed, for she regarded his ring as all but on her finger. She was confident she had cast her spell over him, made him a slave to his passions, convinced him she was the most desirable, most exquisite, most irresistible bride in the whole world, but in Randal Fenworth she had met her match. He had no conscience as he sighed, whispered his undying subjugation, soothed and excited her, called her his countess, and did all the things she had dreamed he'd do. Her vanity was flattered as never before, and the shock of Martin's rebuff almost ceased to matter. Almost, but not quite, for she would never forgive and forget what he had said.

But at last Randal deemed the moment ripe to introduce a little cold light of day into her dizzy darkness. "You know, your uncle would probably have me hung, drawn, and quartered if he found us like this, don't you?" he whispered, his lips brushing her hair, her forehead, the tip of her little nose. . . .

"Oh, don't let's think about him . . ." she breathed, trying to kiss him again.

But he drew back. "No, Amanda, it must be said. You see, there is something you don't know."

"Oh?" She paid attention unwillingly.

"Sir Julian is set against me because of his quarrel with my late father. And also because"—Randal allowed his voice to falter—"because he had an affair with my mother."

Amanda stared.

"I have always made clear my support for my wronged father," Randal added, his voice choking with emotion.

"I . . . I heard there had been an affair of some sort, but I didn't know who was involved. I certainly didn't hear your mother's name mentioned!"

"As if a liaison with my mother were not bad enough, Sir Julian disliked my father to the point of threatening to prove to the world that I am not the rightful Earl of Sanderby." Randal turned away, as if so overcome with the injustice of the situation that he could not bear to meet her startled eyes.

Amanda's mouth opened and closed; then a new

wariness began to creep in. What was this? Was she
about to be denied her title after all?

"I *am* the rightful earl, I hasten to add," Randal
went on quickly, sensing her reaction from her silence,
"but there was a time when my mother believed my
father already had a wife when he married her. She
wrote of this to Sir Julian, telling him that my father's
first wife had a son who was the real earl. Sir Julian
saw fit to keep the letter. Now, in order to prevent
me from marrying you, he is threatening to make it
public. An irksome court case is bound to result, even
though I can prove my case." He turned then, his
usually cool features a study of tortured emotion.

Amanda was shaken. A court case? What of her
dazzling future? "Tell me you jest . . ." she began.

"I fear I am in earnest. Litigation is certain." He
watched her. "Of course, if it were not for the
letter . . ." he murmured.

"Are you quite sure it exists?" she asked, although
she knew about the secret letter.

"Oh, yes. I have Sir Julian's word on it. Well, not
his word, exactly, more a slip of his tongue. It's somewhere here at Chelworth, and if we were to find and
destroy it—"

"We?" The single word was sharp and guarded.

"Well, it's in your interest as much as mine to
thwart him."

She drew away. "If there is any doubt at all about
your right to your title, I'm afraid . . ." She let her
voice trail away.

"That one letter may be an embarrassment to me,
Amanda, but I rather fancy that all those you wrote
to me from Constantinople could be just as embar-
rassing to you. If I were to make them public, you
may be certain no other titled husband would come
your way. So I fear you are saddled with me."

She gazed at him. "That is blackmail, sir."

He put his fingertips lovingly to her chin. "No, my
darling. I simply love you too much already to ever

part with you. Besides, all we have to do is destroy my mother's letter to Sir Julian, and all will be well again. You will be my countess and will enjoy all the status, privilege, and respect that accompanies such a fine title."

She knew that she had no choice but to go along with him, for the last thing she wanted was for her foolish letters to go on public view. She turned away from him. "As it happens, I think I already know where my uncle keeps the letter you require."

His interest leaped. "You do? Where?"

She told him about the secret compartment in the statue of Isis, and Sir Julian's reaction when the letter had been taken out. "I did not have a chance to read it, but I did see the address of the sender. It was sixteen-B Grosvenor Square."

"My town house in London. It belonged to my father before me." Randal's fists clenched furiously. "I searched that damned library from floor to ceiling, but found nothing. I didn't think of the statue!"

"It's a very clever hiding place. If Mrs. Entwhistle hadn't come across such a thing before, I wouldn't know now."

"Do you think you can open the compartment again?"

She shook her head. "Oh, no. I'm not going to do it! I'm not going to risk being caught in anything. If you want to destroy the letter, you must do it yourself. It's something to do with the beetle thing in the statue's headdress."

"The scarab?"

Amanda nodded. "Yes, I think that's what they're called. It has to be pushed down somehow; then a flap opens. The letter is in a cavity behind it." She eyed him suddenly. "You wouldn't lie to me about this, would you? I mean, your mother *was* wrong about bigamy having been committed?"

"She was a very emotional woman and misunderstood something that was perfectly commonplace. My father had a mistress before his marriage, but he cast her aside as soon as he took his bride. My mother got it into her head that he was actually married to this other woman, who had a son by him. My illegitimate half brother."

"And is this, er, commonplace situation applicable in your case as well?" she inquired.

Randal was caught off guard. "What do you mean?"

"Do you have a mistress?"

"No, I do not have a mistress," he said.

Amanda turned away again, shivering as the sea breeze gusted along the wall, carrying the noise of surf from the bay. "Why have you told me all this?"

"I want no secrets between us."

She was unsure. Her mind kept harping back to the so-called mistress his father was supposed to have kept. "Your father's mistress, who was she?"

"Why do you want to know?"

She looked at him. "Because it matters to me."

"Very well. Her name was Marguerite Kenny."

Amanda was thunderstruck. "The actress?"

"Yes. What is it? Why are you—?"

The scales were falling from her eyes, and as the truth began to gleam before her, so the balance was tipped. No longer was she taken in by his every clever word; instead she saw right through him. "Did you know there is an injured naval lieutenant here at Chelworth?" she asked.

"Yes, but what has he to do with it?"

Amanda's eyebrow twitched. "You tell me, sir. You tell me. His name is Martin Ballard, and in a locket around his neck he wears a likeness of Marguerite Kenny. The locket is inscribed 'To my beloved son, Martin, on his first birthday, 1769.' That makes him just over a year older than you, does it not? So, is he your illegitimate half-brother by your father's mistress? Or—much more likely, I fancy—is he the only too legitimate son of your father's first wife, and therefore the rightful earl?" She paused. "Well, my lord? Have you nothing to say?"

Randal was so shaken that he had to lean a hand

on the wall. He bowed his head and closed his eyes, trying to keep a firm hold on his wildly scattered thoughts. His damned half brother was *here*? He drew a long, shuddering breath, only too aware that he had to try to keep a hold upon Amanda. After a moment he looked up at her. "Marguerite Kenny was my father's mistress, not his wife."

"I don't believe you. Your mother's fears were well-grounded, and that is why you are so keen to enlist my aid in this. You are afraid you will be disinherited, so you need a rich wife to support you. Is that not so?"

He began to see how he had underestimated her. "No, it isn't. Amanda, my mother was the lawful Countess of Sanderby."

Amanda was never more sure of herself, for even in the darkness the lies were large in his eyes. "You would not be all that concerned about the letter if it contained untruths. Oh, fate has played a very shabby trick, has it not? Depositing your long-lost sibling here, in the very heart of matters."

Shabby trick? It was downright diabolical! "What do you intend to do?" he asked flatly, for there was nothing to be gained by tiptoeing around things. She had him in her palm, and there was nothing he could do about it. If the letter was made public, he was ruined, and if she did not marry him, he was finished completely.

Amanda said nothing for a moment. Her dismay to realize she was not after all contracted to marry the true Earl of Sanderby was tempered by her exultation at possessing the ultimate means of punishing Martin Ballard. She had the power to make him Earl of Sanderby, or leave him in obscurity. Well, she knew she stood no chance of becoming Lady Sanderby if *he* were the earl, so it pleased her to do the latter. She smiled at Randal. "Do? Why we are bound together, Randal."

"So, our marriage is to proceed?"

"Neither of us has any choice. But I will not help you find and destroy the letter. That you do alone."

A little later, as she hurried back to the house through the dark, windswept gardens, she did not see the bronze figurine lying on the path. She trod on it once again, but managed not to scream as she tumbled on the path, ruining a second gown in the process. Her eyes grew large as she saw what had tripped her. No, it couldn't be! But it was. Strange things *were* happening to her after all, and she didn't like it one little bit! A primitive alarm swept over her, and she hurled the figurine away, just as she had at Tel el-Osorkon. There was no hollow clatter this time, just the rustle of one of the topiary sphinxes as the bronze cat fell into its leafy depths.

Then Amanda glimpsed two feline shadows slipping stealthily across the trembling grass between the sphinxes, and her alarm increased. Scrambling to her feet, she hobbled to the house as quickly as she could.

# 25

*L*iza had walked from Bothenbury to Weymouth, and although it was only a few miles, her feet were sore, it not being her custom to ever wear sensible shoes. No one at Mother Clancy's wore *sensible* anything! She was cold, windswept, and tired, and not a little uneasy that Randal might find out what she'd done, guess her destination, and pursue her.

She made her way through the dark streets to a busy coaching inn by the harbor, where inquiries at the ticket office soon elicited the information she needed. The Wareham stagecoach left at daybreak, and it would take her right past the lane that led down to the beach at Chelworth. In the meantime she'd have a fine dinner and then take the best room in the place—all at Lord High-and-Mighty's expense, of course. She purchased the ticket, then went into the inn, where she gave a false name, and paid handsomely for everyone's silence regarding the presence of a guest fitting her description. If Randal did happen to come, he would be met with blank expressions and shrugged shoulders.

Dinner was over at Chelworth and everyone adjourned to the library. But as they crossed the atrium, Sir Julian detained Tansy, permitting Hermione to go on ahead.

"Tansy, my dear, I feel a little guilty about my contretemps with Amanda earlier. I fear I may have offended you by speaking so harshly to her. If so, I crave your forgiveness. It is just that I fear she would strain the patience of a saint."

"I was not offended, Uncle, nor is there is anything to forgive. Amanda is not an easy person to get along with."

"How diplomatic you are, for that is not how *I* would describe her. If she were mine, she would long since have been over my knee for a sound spanking. Franklyn was ever too soft."

*He wasn't with me,* Tansy thought, glancing away. Amanda's father may have been lenient to a fault with his own child, but his penniless niece was never allowed any latitude.

Sir Julian watched her face. "You've had a difficult time of it, haven't you, my dear?"

"It would ill become me to complain, Uncle, for there are thousands who are far worse off."

He smiled a little. "And no doubt you are fearful of what the future may hold for you?"

She lowered her eyes quickly. "I do not deny it."

"Then be at ease, for Chelworth is your home now, and will remain so for as long as you wish."

Tansy looked up with swift gratitude. "Do you really mean it, Uncle?"

"Certainly I do. How could I not welcome with open arms a young woman who so adores cats that she brought one with her all the way from Egypt? Ozzy would never forgive me if I ejected you." Sir Julian chuckled. "Now then, I think we should join Mrs. Entwhistle?"

"Yes, of course." Tansy smiled. "Hermione is a very interesting lady, Uncle. When I first knew her I thought she only ever thought about crochet, but I could not have been more wrong."

"Crochet? By gad, what a waste of a good woman!" he declared stoutly; then he cleared his throat. "Er, I notice that you address her by her first name. . . ."

"I like her, Uncle. I like her very much."

He was quick to reassure. "Oh, do not think I was about to criticize, my dear. On the contrary, I was about to say how pleased I am."

"Pleased?"

"Yes, for I too approve of her, and if you and she are close, well, that makes it easier for me to know her, does it not?"

Tansy stared at him. "Uncle Julian, am I to understand . . . ?"

"That I like the lady? Yes, my dear, I rather think I do. It is a long time since I found someone with whom I can feel so utterly and completely relaxed. She is not only a delightful and charming person, but she actually understands what I am talking about. When I mention Egypt, that is."

Tansy smiled. "She shares your interests, Uncle."

"Yes." He returned the smile. It was indeed a long time since he had so enjoyed female company—not since Felice, in fact.

Tansy now had tactful second thoughts about accompanying him to the library, so she excused herself, feeling quite sure he and Hermione would both rather be alone together. Oh, how she hoped they would become a couple, for there could not be a more perfect wife than Hermione Entwhistle for a bachelor antiquarian who lived and breathed Ancient Egypt!

But as Tansy ascended the staircase, her cream velvet gown very pale and ghostly in the glow of the few candles still alight, she knew she had another ulterior motive for not joining them in the library—if she didn't join them, she might be able to see Martin instead. If he was awake. She knew a chaste young lady should not wish to be alone with a gentleman in his bedroom, and that it was one thing to be Martin's devoted nurse when he'd been so ill, but quite another to go there now that he was recovering. She also knew that with so much unsaid between them, her motives erred on the side of impropriety. As perhaps they had done from the first time she saw him. Would Sir Julian still think so highly of her if he knew what was going on in her mind? He clearly considered her a model niece, but he was comparing her with Amanda. Tansy Richardson was not the sweet, demure little thing he believed, especially where First Lieutenant Martin Ballard of His Majesty's frigate *Lucina* was concerned!

Reaching the top of the stairs, she paused, glancing toward Amanda's room. Should she go to see if her cousin was all right? She didn't want to; indeed, she had been more than pleased that the future countess had remained in her room since flouncing off so ridiculously before dinner. No, perhaps this was one sleeping dog better left lying, Tansy thought cravenly, for the last thing she felt like now was another dose of Amanda's cutting sarcasm or airs and graces.

She looked instead toward Martin's door, and to her surprise it was slightly ajar, revealing the dancing firelight within. To her further surprise, she saw her bronze cat figurine lying on the threshold. How did it come to be there? Curious, she went to pick it up. There was a little mud on it. Now *that* was quite impossible, for she had polished it with a soft duster.

Martin's voice spoke from within the room. "Tansy?"

She went in and saw that he wasn't in the bed, but seated on the floor in front of the fire, with Ozzy and Cleo beside him. He was leaning back against a heavy armchair that looked like a pharaoh's throne, and was still in his uniform, the gold braiding of which gleamed in the firelight. The bandage lay discarded on a table, and she saw the graze left by the French shot, still red and angry against the drawn pallor of his face. He smiled at her. "I thought you would never come."

"You . . . You have been waiting for me?"

"Of course." He held out his hand.

Still holding the figurine, she went to him, but then hesitated about taking his hand, for to do so would change the atmosphere between them forever. There would be no going back. But then he stretched forward and caught her fingers, drawing her down beside him. She sank down so naturally into his arms that she might have been fashioned to fit into them. And it then seemed so natural to kiss him that she no longer hesitated about anything. Their lips came warmly together—no, not just warmly, but passionately.

She felt his fingers curling into her hair, delighted in the sweetness of his kiss and the pressure of his body against hers. There was no laudanum to affect him now, no fever to disguise what was real and what was not, just the candor of open desire. Nor was there any pretence, no nod in the direction of what was right or wrong, just the abandonment of all caution to the winds. The figurine slipped from her fingers into the creamy velvet folds of her gown, where it glinted in the firelight.

At last he drew away, cradled her close, and rested his cheek against her dark curls. "I do believe I love you, Tansy Richardson," he whispered.

"I know I love you, Martin Ballard. I have known it since Tel el-Osorkon."

"You have?" He put a finger to her chin and tilted her face to look up at him. Flames were reflected in his eyes as the wind outside blustered around the eaves, and the fire glowed more brightly.

"Yes, but I thought you preferred Amanda."

"Definitely not. I do not like your cousin in the least."

"But—"

"Tansy, I was drawn to you from the beginning. I thought she was very lovely, fascinatingly so, considering the real Amanda behind the loveliness, but you I find beautiful in a different way . . . a way that is beyond words."

"I know that isn't true," she murmured, wishing it was.

He kissed her forehead. "Beauty isn't all on the outside, Tansy. Your loveliness comes from within, and it makes you glow."

"Oh, you know the right things to say, sir," she

breathed, moving against his lips and then stretching up to kiss him again.

His arms tightened around her, and she was conscious of her heart pounding. Her body ached for more than just kisses. She loved him so much, craved him so much, that she hardly knew herself. Their lips moved richly together, and his warmth and masculinity seemed to invade her. A wild recklessness swept her along, leaving demureness far, far behind.

She kissed his mouth, his eyelids, his temple, his wound; she untied his neck cloth in order to kiss the little pulse at his throat. . . . She wanted to kiss the locket because it would be warm from his body. But the locket wasn't there, just the broken chain. The realization sent desire into retreat. "Oh, Martin, your locket—!"

"What of it?"

"It's gone!"

His hand went swiftly to his throat. Sure enough, there was only the severed chain. Tansy began to get up. "It can't be far away, for you've only been from here to the library and back again."

"I'm sure it will come to light." He put a hand on her arm to make her stay. "Don't go," he said softly.

She relaxed into his embrace again. "What is in the locket?" she asked, not liking to ask him outright about Marguerite Kenny.

He gave a low laugh. "Tansy Richardson, you know perfectly well what is in the locket, because you and Amanda took a peek before going down to the library."

Tansy's cheeks flamed. "You . . . knew?"

"Yes. I'm afraid I was guilty of subterfuge." He smiled. "I was most disappointed when Amanda interrupted, for you were about to steal a kiss."

Tansy couldn't look at him. "I behaved most outrageously."

"I didn't think so. It was an agreeably sensuous moment."

She smiled a little. "Yes, it was," she agreed, remembering.

"What followed was very enlightening too. It certainly confirmed my low opinion of your cousin."

Tansy felt guilty about the locket. "I'm sorry she looked in it. I should have stopped her from prying."

"It would take more than your disapproval to stop Amanda from doing anything."

"True." Tansy looked up at him. "Why do you carry Marguerite Kenny's portrait around your neck?"

"She's my mother."

"Your mother?" Tansy sat up to look properly at him. "Truly?"

"Truly. Didn't you see the inscription? Actually, forget I asked that, for neither of you saw the inscription or you would have said."

Tansy's brows drew together. "Did she like living in Minorca? I . . . I mean, that was why your parents went there, wasn't it?"

He was silent or a moment. "There was nothing wrong with her health, Tansy. She and the man I call my stepfather moved there in order to avoid her husband, my real father."

Tansy's lips parted in surprise.

"And before you ask," he went on, "I don't know who he was. I was never told, and from what I have heard of the way he treated her, I do not ever wish to know about him. It shames me to know I have the blood of such a scoundrel flowing in my veins, and I am more than proud to carry my stepfather's name, even though he was never legally married to my mother."

"Have you no curiosity at all about your real father?"

"No. He and my mother were very much in love at first, but married clandestinely because he was well-born and she was only an actress, and he feared she would not be accepted in society. But unfortunately their love foundered when he became addicted to gambling, and incurred huge debts he had no hope of settling. That was when he decided he wished to forget the wife he had begun to regard as an encumbrance, and marry a richer bride instead."

"Oh, Martin . . ."

"He threw my mother out, with threats of violence if she ever breathed a word of their marriage; then he coolly underwent a bigamous match with a gullible heiress whose fortune rescued him entirely. By then my mother had discovered she was expecting me, so she feared not only for herself, but for me as well. She had met Richard Ballard, my stepfather, whom she told the complete truth about her circumstances. He loved her too much to let anything stand in the way of happiness, so he took her off to Minorca, and they spent the rest of their lives there, well away from the danger imposed by my damned father."

"And that is truly all you know about your real father?"

"Yes. Oh, and the fact that he and his second wife had a son, my half brother, who is obviously illegitimate in law, but has nevertheless inherited everything."

"Don't you have any desire to claim what is rightfully yours?"

He hesitated, then gave a dry laugh. "I don't really know, and that is the truth. I despise my father so much that part of me wants nothing to do with anything that was his. Another part of me thinks it is only right that I should inherit."

"There are no documents? A marriage record? His name on the record of your birth?"

"None that I am aware of. My mother was very afraid of my father, Tansy, and took nothing with her when he threw her out, unless you count me, of course." He smiled at her again.

"But somewhere in England you have a half brother?"

"Yes, and he, poor fellow, believes himself to be

born on the right side of the blanket. Little does he
know." He looked at her in the firelight. "Do you
think any less of me for hearing this, Tansy?"

"Less of you? Oh, no! Besides, who am I to think
less of anyone? I am a poor Church Mouse of a thing,
that is all."

"But you are a very lovable Church Mouse of a
thing," he said softly. "I'm glad you know my background now, Tansy, for I want us to be open with
each other. Always."

Her heart seemed to skip a beat, for the way he
spoke made it seem he envisaged them together for a
long time to come.

"Now I have found you, I do not intend to let you
go," he whispered, and pulled her close once more.
His lips found hers, and all else was forgotten as they
gave themselves to more kisses.

The wind sighed down the chimney, and the flames
leaped, sending sparks fleeing up toward the darkness
of the night. Ozzy and Cleo were still sitting content-
edly side by side before the hearth. They looked at
each other, then touched noses, for all the world as if
they too were kissing.

And all the while the figurine shimmered mysteriously in the folds of Tansy's skirt. Then suddenly it
disappeared.

# 26

Sir Julian and Hermione did not quit the library for their beds until the small hours, obliging Randal to kick his heels in the cold wind at the edge of the woods as he waited for James's signal from the billiard room to tell him the coast was clear. He was impatient to get on with things and more than a little anxious to dispose of the letter now that the real heir had turned up so inconveniently. Down in the bay the waves crashed on the beach, and the lights of a vessel glimmered out to sea. The wind soughed through the trees behind him, and the taste of salt was on his lips as he stared resolutely toward the house, willing the signal to appear. But still there was nothing, yet he was certain that the candles had been extinguished in the library several minutes ago. What in God's own name was delaying that fool of a footman?

At that moment, James was in the billiard room struggling to light the signal lantern. Try as he would, the wick simply would not take flame. He cursed beneath his breath as he wrestled with it, and was unaware of two pairs of feline eyes peeping at him around the open door, making certain he was preoccupied.

Then the cats drew back and trotted into the deserted library, which was now only illuminated by firelight. Once there, they acted swiftly, with Cleo waiting impatiently by the hearth as Ozzy jumped onto Sir Julian's desk, where the bronze figurine now stood among the clutter of papers and other objects. The tomcat mewed and rubbed his whiskers against it, then began to push papers aside with his paw until at last he found what he had noticed earlier in the evening. It was a long letter from a rather eccentric gentleman in Scotland, who believed that Plato's lost land of Atlantis was actually beneath the Sahara Desert, and that it had been inundated with waves of sand, not water. To the tomcat it was simply a folded sheet of paper of the desired size and appearance.

He patted it across the desk until it fell to the carpet, where Cleo took it in her mouth, then leaped up on to the mantel, which only she was small enough to stand on with any comfort. She edged carefully along until she was as close to the statue of Isis as could be managed; then with a dainty but determined paw, she patted and pushed the scarab until at last she succeeded in opening the secret compartment. She delved in the cavity with claws extended until she managed to hook the precious letter and draw it carefully out. Allowing it to fall to Ozzy below, she then set about putting the Scottish gentleman's missive in its place.

It was a feat of quite astonishing dexterity, ending with a quite undignified scramble over Isis's head, but at last the little tabby succeeded, and just managed to close the flap of the compartment before she lost her footing and fell, almost on top of Ozzy. But the deed was done, and without further ado the two furry schemers ran out of the library again, Ozzy carrying the letter in his mouth, for all the world like King Osorkon's retriever cat. They had just disappeared among the ferns around the pharaoh in the atrium when James at last succeeded with the lantern in the billiard room. The cats' eyes shone as they watched through the open door as the footman went out onto the terrace to signal to Randal.

Tansy and Martin, meanwhile, had fallen asleep in each other's arms in front of the fire. He still leaned back against the chair, and she was cradled close in his arms, her knees drawn up as if she would curl around him. The fire had burned a little lower, but still glowed in the draft from the wind in the chimney. The sound of something falling awakened her suddenly, and she sat up, for a moment fearing discovery in such a very improper situation.

But the room was quiet. She was tempted to close her eyes again and snuggle back into Martin's embrace, but then she saw the bronze figurine lying in the hearth. She must have moved, and in doing so dropped it, she decided, carefully unlinking herself from Martin's arms and managing to get up without disturbing him. He needed all the sleep he could get if he was to recover fully, she thought, pausing to touch his hair. She could still hardly believe that he felt the same for her as she did for him. She, Tansy Richardson, the Church Mouse to end all Church Mice, had won the heart of a handsome naval lieutenant who was everything any woman could desire!

Taking the figurine, she placed it on the mantel, then went softly to the door to see all was clear before she went out. A night candle burned down in the atrium, casting a very faint light up to the landing. Shadows swayed with the solitary flame, and she was about to hurry to her own room when she heard something downstairs. What was it? A stifled cough? Curious, she lingered at the balustrade, looking down to see who was there. She was sure she heard footsteps in the billiard room. And whispers!

As she watched, two men walked into view. They were cautious, furtive even, looking this way and that before crossing the atrium to the library. One she recognized as the footman called James; the other she did not know, except to see that he was very well dressed. A gentleman? Surely not if he was creeping around the house when everyone had gone to bed! As they disappeared from view, she caught up her skirts to hurry downstairs. It did not occur to her to awaken Martin, or raise the alarm in any way, just to see what the men were up to.

At the bottom she halted. A candle had now been

lighted in the library, and by the shadows on the wall she could see the gentleman next to the statue of Isis. He was trying to open the secret compartment! Slowly she crossed the atrium, and suddenly became aware of Ozzy and Cleo blocking her way. The cats sat directly in front of her, clearly trying to prevent her from continuing, but she moved quickly around them and reached the door just as the gentleman operated the scarab.

In a trice his gloved fingers had closed over the letter, and he'd begun to rip it into shreds. Tansy was rooted with shock, unable to do anything except watch as he calmly tossed the torn pieces of the letter onto the fire.

Suddenly James saw her in the doorway. "Sir!"

Randal turned sharply, and at last her lips parted to scream, but before a sound escaped her, she was struck hard from behind. Pain lanced jaggedly through her, then blackness lurched in from all sides, and she knew no more as she slumped senseless to the floor. The last thing she was aware of was the bronze cat on her uncle's desk; it seemed to be glowing. . . .

Amanda dropped the candlestick with which she'd struck the blow, then looked down at Tansy. "You aren't going to spoil things, Coz," she breathed.

James's face had drained of all color. "Have you killed her?" he whispered.

"Don't be such a fool," she replied.

Randal didn't share her certainty, and he hurried over to crouch by Tansy and make certain she was still breathing. "Now what?" he demanded, looking up at Amanda. "She saw me, and while she may not yet know yet who I am, she will damned soon."

"Don't panic," Amanda replied in a level tone. "You and James will have to remove her. I don't care where you take her or what you do with her, just make certain she can't do any more harm. Leave everything here to me."

Randal straightened, his blue eyes reluctantly admiring. "You're a cool one," he breathed.

"One of us has to be," she answered. She had made her choice, and she would protect her own interests with every breath she had. No one was going to prevent her from becoming Countess of Sanderby. *No one!* But then her glance fell upon the desk and the bronze cat. She stared at it. She'd thrown it into one of the topiary sphinxes in the garden, yet here it was!

Randal followed her gaze. "What's wrong?"

"That bronze figurine . . ."

"What about it?" he asked.

For a moment she considered telling him, but then thought better of it. "Look, the longer we dither here, the more chance there is of Tansy coming around. So get on with it. I want her out of here before she comes around. Just be waiting for me at dawn at that place by the woods you mentioned before."

"Waiting for you?" Randal repeated.

"You have a tame clergyman at Wareham, and I am the bride. That is all you need for a swift marriage, is it not?"

"What of the special license?" he pointed out swiftly, misliking the speed with which she was cornering him.

"You have already explained about that. A special license will be forthcoming, and everything upon it will be exactly as it should be. Is that not so?"

"Yes, but—"

"But nothing. Humor me, Randal, for I'm sure my fortune is worth it . . . to say nothing of my silence." The threat hung deliberately in the air, for it wouldn't do for him to feel too safe now the letter had been destroyed. She had to remind him that she still had it in her power to tell Martin the truth, even if she could not prove it.

Randal regarded her in the firelight. "Have a care, Amanda—"

"No, *you* have a care!" she breathed. "*Noli tangere ignem,* remember? Just be warned that you will indeed play with fire if you try to cross me."

He stared at her, beginning to realize more and

more that she was his match in every way. It wasn't a feeling he relished, but there was no longer anything he could do about it. The die was cast.

From the atrium there suddenly came the loud sound of yowling cats, as Ozzy and Cleo set up a warning racket that resounded through the whole house. Almost immediately Sir Julian's voice was heard from the floor above.

Amanda spoke quickly to Randal. "So just be waiting for me at dawn."

"I will be there." He beckoned to James to help him with Tansy's limp body, and Amanda hurried to open the French windows. They carried Tansy out onto the windblown terrace, and Amanda closed the doors softly behind them. Then she hurried to the bookcase and took out *The Tales of One Thousand and One Nights*.

She was about to hurry out into the atrium, where she could hear Martin and Hermione as well as Sir Julian, when her attention was pulled to the desk. The bronze cat had gone. Her cornflower eyes widened fearfully, but there was no time to think any more about it because someone was coming downstairs now. She hurried out toward the atrium, but got no further than the library doorway because Ozzy and Cleo were barring the way. Hissing and spitting, their tails lashing furiously, they crouched as if about to pounce. Startled to see her, Sir Julian and Martin halted on the stairs, while Hermione peered nervously over the balcony.

Ozzy and Cleo redoubled their noise, and Amanda drew back a little, bursting into artful tears. "Oh, Uncle! They're frightening me!"

Sir Julian spoke sharply to his tomcat. "Ozymandias! Be quiet this instant!"

Ozzy's ears went back, but his racket subsided. Cleo followed his lead, but they both continued to crouch threateningly.

Amanda whimpered pathetically. "Make them go away, Uncle," she begged in a small voice.

He waved an arm at the cats. "Off with you!" he snapped.

Ozzy considered defying him, but only for a moment. With a resentful growl he turned and slunk away toward the kitchens. Cleo watched him go, then looked a last time at Amanda, before following the tomcat.

Amanda immediately ran to Sir Julian, who had not stopped to pull on his dressing gown over his nightgown. His nightcap was awry, and his feet were bare, for he had not had time to don his Turkish slippers either. She flung herself into his arms. "Oh, Uncle! I didn't do anything, truly I didn't. I . . . I couldn't sleep, so I came down to get this book! That's all, but the cats made such a noise and wouldn't let me out of the library again."

He stared at the volume she waved before him. "Oh, my dear . . ."

"I think they thought I was a thief." Amanda sniffed and bit her lip. "I'm not. Truly I'm not."

"No, of course you aren't, my dear," Sir Julian replied. "It's clearly a fuss about nothing, so we'll all go back to bed." With his arm around her shaking shoulders, he ushered her past Martin and back up the staircase.

Amanda could not resist glancing back at Martin. Their gazes met, his suspicious, hers alight with triumph. Then she looked ahead once more, and on reaching the landing almost ran into Hermione's arms.

Martin went slowly up the stairs behind everyone. Where was Tansy? He remembered falling asleep with her in his arms, and guessed she had returned to her own room without disturbing him, but he wished she had awoken now and come out with everyone else. For a moment he almost went to knock at her door, but then thought better of it. She deserved her first good sleep since leaving Constantinople.

So he returned to his own room.

\*      \*      \*

Tansy regained consciousness slowly and painfully. She was in complete darkness, and the air was icily cold. Where was she? For a moment she could not think what had happened, but then realized she was lying on a stone floor with her wrists and ankles tied. She tried to twist her hands free, but to no avail. Her head was pounding, and she recalled seeing a strange gentleman stealing and destroying Uncle Julian's letter; then someone had struck her from behind. Who was it? Who had done this to her?

There wasn't a sound, except perhaps . . . Yes, she could hear the wind playing around the eaves. At least, she presumed it was the eaves. Was anyone near? "Hello?" she called. Her voice echoed eerily. *Hello? Hello? Hello?* "Can anyone hear me?" *Hear me? Hear me? Hear me?* Fear began to steal over her. Was she just going to be left here like this to die?

# 27

*I*t was dawn when Martin awoke. As he lay there in the warm bed, thinking of Tansy, he was aware of how much stronger he felt now. He had improved in leaps and bounds ever since he held the bronze cat.

The gray light of early morning filled the room, and as he sat up he saw from the window that the sea was bleak and wintry. A fierce wind blew across the bay, and the leaden waves were flecked with white. The eastern sky was stained bloodred, promising worse weather to come. But the weather vanished from his thoughts as he suddenly realized he could see out. The curtains had been drawn when he'd returned to the room after the disturbance with Amanda, yet now they had been flung open. Another strange thing was that Tansy's bronze cat stood in the middle of the sill. Who had been in the room? Tansy herself?

Pushing the bedding aside, he got up to go to the window. He was naked, and the fire had burned low in the hearth, so the cool air on his skin made him shiver slightly. But as he picked up the figurine he was again aware of the welcome warmth of the bronze passing through him—no, the welcome *magic* of the bronze passing through him.

There was a movement on the terrace below, and he drew self-consciously back as a cloaked woman hurried to the steps that led down to the open heath. Her hood was raised over her head, and the cloak flapped in the wind. There was something familiar about her. Who was she? A maid keeping an assignation with her sweetheart? Yes, who else could she be? He watched as she ran down the grassy clearings through the bracken, and as she eventually disappeared into the wooded combe, he replaced the figurine on the sill and turned to put on his dressing gown. He had a fancy for a morning cup of strong tea, which the navy had taught him to appreciate, and as he knew the servants would be up and about by now he decided to hie himself to the kitchens.

But as he emerged from his room, he heard Ozzy mewing and saw both cats by Tansy's closed door. Cleo was scratching urgently at the paintwork, and Ozzy was stretching up to the doorknob, which resisted his best efforts. Why hadn't Tansy admitted them? She loved cats far too much to exclude them, and surely she could not sleep on when they were making such a fuss at the door. The first finger of true unease began to trace down his spine. There had been no sign of Tansy last night when Amanda went down to the library, and now there was still no sign of her. Was she all right?

He hastened to the door and knocked loudly. "Tansy?" The cats waited expectantly, their ears pricked. There wasn't a sound from within. "Tansy? Are you awake?" Still there was only silence. Cleo mewed, a plaintive sound that sent the uneasy finger in motion again. Ignoring the niceties of etiquette, Martin flung open the door. The cats rushed into the darkened room as he strode to the windows to fling back the curtains; then he looked at the bed. It was just as Letty had left it the night before, the bedclothes turned neatly back, Tansy's nightgown and wrap lying in readiness. Ozzy and Cleo jumped onto the bed and paced restlessly, mewing all the while. They were trying to tell him what had happened.

Martin obviously could not understand what they were saying, but he realized instinctively that Tansy had been missing since before Amanda's exploits during the night. But where was she? What had become of her? He ran an agitated hand through his hair, trying to clear his mind and marshal his thoughts, but then there came the sound of female voices out on the landing. One belonged to Hermione and was striving to be calm; the other belonged to Amanda's maid, Daisy, and was tearful and upset.

"Just take a deep breath, Daisy," Hermione was saying. "That's better. Now then, tell me what is wrong."

"It . . . It's Miss Amanda!" Daisy cried.

Martin hurried out, and Sir Julian's door opened across the way. The older man's head appeared, the tassel of his nightcap falling over his nose. "What in the devil is going on out here?" he demanded.

Hermione continued to speak to the maid. "Do go on dear. What about Miss Amanda?"

"She's gone!" Daisy wailed, dissolving into more tears.

"Gone? What do you mean, dear?"

"Gone! Run away! Eloped!"

Hermione went pale. "Daisy, if this is some sort of jest . . ."

"It's the truth, madam! I wouldn't lie about it. She told me last night, but I didn't believe it. Then, when I took her morning tea just now, she'd gone. Her small valise has gone too. Oh, please don't dismiss me, for it isn't my fault. I truly believed she was teasing me!"

Sir Julian came hastily around the landing. "Did I hear you say eloped?"

"Yes, Sir Julian." Daisy managed to bob a curtsy.

"But she hasn't had time to even *meet* the scoundrel!"

Hermione raised an eyebrow. "Clearly she has, sir. Clearly she has."

Martin struggled to absorb this new development. The cloaked woman! "I don't think she has been gone more than a few minutes, sir. I saw a woman in a cloak crossing the terrace, then going down the hill to the woods. There seemed something familiar about her, and I thought she must be one of the maids here, but now that I think again, I realize it was Amanda. I saw her wear that cloak on the *Lucina*."

"Down toward the woods, you say? There's a lane down there that leads from the turnpike road!" Sir Julian cried. "I'll have Sanderby's gizzard for this! So help me I will! I'll send some men down there immediately, although I imagine they are well away by now." He strode to the staircase to shout for a footman, but Martin's next words halted him.

"Sir Julian, I think you should know that Tansy is missing too."

Liza was on the morning stagecoach from Weymouth to Wareham, crammed uncomfortably between a fat, red-cloaked countrywoman with a screaming baby and an equally large farmer who smelled like a cow byre. She craned her neck for the signpost to Chelworth, and it was with some relief that she saw it at last. She stretched across the farmer to lower the window glass and shout to the coachman to stop.

He reined in, and she climbed swiftly down into the cold wind. The dry keys of an ash tree rustled and shook overhead as she stepped back for the stagecoach to drive on. On a hill about half a mile to the south, seeming almost to pierce the low clouds, was the pyramid she knew belonged to Chelworth. She glanced up at the racing clouds and wondered if perhaps her thirst for revenge upon Lord High-and-Mighty was quite worth all this. But then she remembered that the alternative was to leave him enjoying the title and inheritance, to which he had no right, and her resolve hardened. Holding her cloak around her to keep out as much cold as she could, she set off down the lane as it wound downhill toward the sea.

Soon she came to a narrow path on the right. It led to the pyramid and was little more than a fox or badger track that wound through the windswept gorse and dead bracken. Just then she heard a carriage approaching at breakneck speed. There was something

about the sound that made her fear to stay in sight;
so she dashed a little way along the path and hid behind a clump of yellow-flowering gorse. She was immediately glad she had, for as the carriage came into
view around the corner, she saw it was Randal's.

Keeping her head down, she watched the vehicle
rattle closer. The blinds were down, which made her
curious, but as it passed, the blind snapped up and
she saw the two occupants. Furthest away was Lord
High-and-Mighty himself, but the nearest person was
a young lady with golden hair and the loveliest—if
sulkiest—profile Liza had ever seen. Liza didn't doubt
that the young lady was Miss Amanda Richardson, for
she exactly fitted the description Randal had delighted
in boasting of.

The carriage swept on by, and soon its racket was
lost in the gusting of the wind. Liza crept out of hiding
and returned to the lane. Now why would his lordship
be driving like the very devil with his bride beside
him? An elopement seemed the most obvious answer.

Liza pulled a face after the now vanished carriage.
"You'll regret it, Miss Richardson," she murmured.
"The fine fellow you're running off with is only an
earl's by-blow, and *that* won't get you into Almack's!"


Tansy lay in the relentless darkness. She had hoped
there would be a window so the coming of daylight
would reveal her surroundings, but nothing had
changed. Once or twice she thought she heard seagulls
screaming outside, but she wasn't sure. She had no
idea how far away from Chelworth she had been
brought, or how long she had been lying here abandoned. All she could be really certain of was the endless moaning of the wind.

# 28

The men Sir Julian dispatched to the combe had soon returned with word that the birds had definitely been there, but had now flown. Marks left by a carriage were clear in the muddy lane, but all that had been found was a lady's scarf made of cat fur. It clearly did not belong to Amanda, who would not have countenanced such an item, but the real owner was a mystery. For the time being it was left on a small console table in the atrium, where it was given a very wide berth indeed by Ozzy and Cleo, whose coats stood on end each time they passed.

The next resort for Sir Julian was to send more riders across country to Bothenbury, in the faint hope that Randal had taken his bride there, but of course there was no one in residence. It was ascertained that Lord Sanderby's belongings were still at the house, but his person was definitely not. Nor was that of the redheaded female with whom he had been consorting, according to his disapproving cook, who did not hold with such loose conduct.

Sir Julian blamed himself for what had happened, believing he had failed in his responsibilities toward both his nieces. But Amanda's disappearance was nevertheless not reported to the authorities. It was clear she had not been abducted; therefore to make a noise about her flight could only have a most detrimental effect upon her character. So he decided that this was a time to let sleeping dogs lie, in the hope that all would be well in the end. Although how anything could be "well" when Randal Fenworth was involved, he could not really imagine.

Tansy's disappearance was another matter, however, and was most certainly reported to every quarter that Sir Julian could think of. She could not possibly have gone of her own volition, nor had she accompanied Amanda, so what had become of her could only be conjectured. The possibilities were legion—and alarming.

No one was more distraught about Tansy than Martin, who did not remain idle. In the vain hope that she might be with Amanda after all, he accompanied the men to Bothenbury, managing the rigorous ride because he took the cat figurine with him, tucked inside the coat of his naval uniform. The fierce wind howled across the Dorset hills, and occasionally there was stinging rain in the air, but nothing seemed to touch him because of the figurine's comforting, invigorating warmth. However, nothing could protect him from the chill that engulfed his heart now that Tansy was missing. He had known he loved her before; now he knew how far and how deep that love ran. She meant the whole world to him, and no stone would be left unturned until he found her.

It was as he and Sir Julian's men were riding back from Bothenbury, along the ridge above Chelworth, that something made Martin rein in a few hundred yards from the pyramid. The others continued over the breast of the slope and down toward the house, but he remained behind. The wind blustered across the heights, and seagulls wheeled and screamed excitedly overhead. Far out to sea, a shaft of sunlight briefly pierced the racing clouds and flashed brightly on the otherwise dismal gray of the water. He could see the waves thundering ashore in the bay, where only yesterday the stillness of the fog had made the surface as smooth as a millpond. It was hard to believe the *Lucina* had been so becalmed down there—or, indeed, that it had only been yesterday.

Where was Tansy? Was she all right? How he wished he knew the answers. If any harm had befallen her at someone's hands, he would not rest until—The thoughts broke off as a small sound caught his attention. He turned in the saddle, glancing around the swaying gorse and bracken, but there seemed nothing there. Then he saw Ozzy and Cleo bounding toward him and knew he had heard their excited mewing. The cats halted a few yards in front of him, then trotted back the way they had come. When he made no move to follow, they paused and looked around reproachfully. Their mewing became more imperative, and at last he realized they were trying to lead him somewhere. He moved the horse after them, and they dashed ahead, taking him swiftly toward the pyramid.

They led him to the entrance and began meowing loudly. As he dismounted he was sure he heard a woman's muffled voice. "Help me! Oh, please help me!"

"Tansy?" he cried, and ran down the steps to try the door. The lock had recently been broken, for the wood was freshly splintered, so the door opened easily. Daylight shone upon the room beyond, where for a moment—just a fleeting moment—he thought he saw the painting from Tel el-Osorkon on the wall opposite the entrance. But the impression was so fleeting as to have been imagined, for the wall was bare.

Tansy lay on the stone floor, bound with ropes and her tearstained face pale as she stared fearfully at his silhouette against the daylight. Then she realized who he was and began to weep. He hurried to her, and the purring cats rubbed around them both as he cut her free with the small knife he carried in his pocket. Then he removed his coat to wrap around her and gathered her into his arms. "Oh, Tansy, my darling . . ."

"How did . . . did you find me?" she sobbed.

"Ozzy and Cleo led me to you."

"They did?" She blinked her tears away as she stroked the two delighted animals. "Where am I, Martin? Where is this horrid place?"

"The pyramid on the hill above Chelworth."

"So near? I . . . I thought I must be miles away."
She glanced around, able to see for the first time because of the open door. Her attention caught upon the wall, and her lips parted. "Oh, I . . ."

"Yes?"

"I thought I saw . . ." She couldn't finish the sentence, for it seemed she was seeing things all the time!

"You thought you saw the painting from Tel el-Osorkon?" Martin finished for her.

"Yes. How did you know?"

He smiled a little. "Perhaps because I thought I saw it too. Just for a split second."

"Yes, that's how I saw it too." She snuggled into his coat, which was warm from his body. It smelled of him too, a fresh, slightly spiced smell, maybe from the sandalwood-lined sea chest in which it was sometimes kept onboard ship. "Oh, Martin, I was so terrified lying in here all alone."

"I know, my darling. I know," he said softly, his lips against her forehead.

"How long have I been here? I have no idea of time . . ."

"Well, it must have happened sometime last night. It's midmorning now."

"So, it's not all that long. I feel as if I've been here for days. I was afraid I would be here forever," she added, then winced as pain jabbed her head again. She probed her hair with careful fingertips and gasped as she felt the lump resulting from the blow.

"What's wrong?" he asked swiftly.

"I . . . I was hit from behind."

"Who was it?"

"I don't know," she whispered, fresh tears welling to her eyes. "I left your room to go back to my own, and I heard something downstairs. I looked over into the atrium and saw one of the footmen, James, I think he's called, going to the library. A man I didn't know was with him. I followed them, and . . ."

"Oh, Tansy, why didn't you awaken me? Or just raise the alarm?"

"I don't know," she confessed, only too aware now of how very foolish she had been. "Anyway, I watched from the library door as the strange man—a gentleman by his clothes—opened the secret compartment in the statue of Isis. He destroyed Uncle Julian's letter. That's all I remember. There was a sharp pain at the back of my head, and everything went black. The next thing I recall was waking up here. I didn't know how long I had been here, or even if it was night or day. Everything is completely black when the door is closed. All I could hear was the wind, and sometimes the seagulls." She tried to rub the feeling back into her arms and legs, which were sore and stiff from being bound for hours.

Martin tried to help her, massaging her ankles as gently but firmly as he could. Then he thought of the bronze cat, and quickly took it from the pocket of his coat. "Here, hold this. It will help you more than anything else."

She took it, and immediately she felt its heat stream into her hand. It flooded up her arm and into her body, swiftly reaching everywhere, and the feeling of well-being that accompanied it was quite extraordinary. She gave an incredulous laugh. "Why, it's amazing!"

"I know. I believe that if one is unwell, or injured in some way, it acts as a restorative. Don't ask me why or how. Just accept that it is so."

"Magic?" she whispered with a small smile.

"Definitely," he replied, and kissed her forehead.

The cats reached up on their hind legs to pat the figurine, and their rich purring became even louder. The pyramid seemed to be filled with the sound.

Martin straightened and reached down to help her to her feet. Then he insisted she put on his naval coat properly. "Let's get you back to the house." He hesitated. "But first, there's something I should tell you. Amanda has run off with Sanderby." He explained what Daisy had said.

Tansy stared at him. "Run off? But she hasn't even met him yet, so . . ." The words faltered as she remembered thinking that Amanda spoke as if she and Lord Sanderby had indeed met.

"What were you going to say?" he pressed.

She told him, then went on. "Daisy is absolutely sure Amanda has gone with Lord Sanderby?"

"Yes. It seems a carriage was waiting in the woods, and there can surely be no doubt that it was the earl's. Sir Julian has sent out search parties, but there's no sign of either Amanda or Sanderby. They're long gone by now, and it's my guess she'll be married before the day is out." Martin smoothed his hair back. "Her reasons are plain enough, for by hook or by crook she means to be a countess; but Sanderby's reasons are more curious. Where elopements and heiresses are concerned, as a rule one thinks only of adventurers or fortune seekers. Sanderby is neither."

Tansy went to the doorway and breathed deeply of the morning air. Ozzy and Cleo accompanied her and rubbed sensuously around her skirts. Tansy bent to touch them, but she was thinking about Amanda. "You are right about by hook or by crook, so I suppose I'm not really surprised Amanda has done something like this. And I agree that Lord Sanderby's motives are a mystery. But out of everything that went on last night, I'm most intrigued by the destruction of Sir Julian's letter. What on earth could it have contained that the strange gentleman was so desperate to be rid of it?" A thought occurred. "You don't suppose the intruder was Lord Sanderby, do you? I mean, I don't know what he looks like, but this man was definitely too well dressed to be a common thief."

"Anything is possible, Tansy, and Sanderby clearly isn't a gentleman, to have eloped with Amanda. The honorable thing would have been to wait for all the formalities."

"I do not know Lord Sanderby's character, but I do

know Amanda's. If the runaway bride were anyone else, I would credit the elopement as the result of blind love."

Martin went to her and slipped his arms around her waist from behind. "I know what blind love is, Tansy," he whispered, closing his eyes as he rested his cheek against her hair. The dark curls fluttered in the wind, touching his face gently. It was a sensuous and unbelievably intimate sensation. "When I did not know what had happened to you, or whether you were all right, I went through such agonies that I knew how desperately I have come to love you."

She turned into his arms, lifting her parted lips to meet his. He pulled her against him, bewitched by the sheer ecstasy of holding her again. He knew he could never let her go, never risk being without her. He broke from the kiss to take her face in his hands. "Marry me, Tansy," he urged. "I wish I could claim to be a rich man, but I am not. I cannot promise you a fine country estate, London seasons, or a life that will even vaguely approach the privilege that Amanda will enjoy, but I do offer myself, body and soul. Please give me the answer I crave. Say you will be my wife."

"I will. Oh, I will," she breathed, her heart almost bursting with happiness as she reached up to kiss him again.

They clung together, almost forgetting everything else, but then there came the sound of hooves and they drew apart to watch as some more of Sir Julian's men returned to Chelworth, this time from Weymouth. The riders noticed Martin's horse by the pyramid and began to rein in. They would have come over to investigate had not Martin gone out to wave to them that all was well.

Then he returned to Tansy and took her hand. "Come. We had better go back to the house, to let everyone know that you are all right." He lifted her sideways onto the horse, then mounted behind her. With a steadying arm around her waist, he urged the horse away down the hill.

Ozzy and Cleo lingered in the doorway of the pyramid. They stared toward the wall where Randal had seen the King Osorkon painting. It was just a blank wall, but the cats knew it was not always blank, nor was it necessarily always the same scene that appeared upon it.

# 29

When Tansy and Martin arrived back at the house, they went directly to the kitchens, it being Martin's intention to deal with James, but no one knew where that young man had gone, for he had already taken to his toes, as the saying went. Knowing that Tansy had seen him the night before, and realizing that she might well be discovered in the pyramid, the footman had deemed it a wise precaution to leave Chelworth, never to return. Even as Martin demanded to know his whereabouts, the ne'er-do-well had reached Weymouth, from where he planned to take passage on the first available vessel.

Tansy was greeted with great delight by the servants, and a maid scurried to the library to tell Sir Julian and Hermione she had returned. Sir Julian and Hermione were just hastening across the atrium as Tansy and Martin left the kitchens. Hermione gave a glad cry and rushed to embrace her former charge. "Oh, my dearest, dearest girl! How *glad* I am to see you safe and, I trust, sound? Where have you been? What happened?"

"Yes, I'm safe, and sound enough, if a little shaken. I've been imprisoned up at the pyramid, and I have no idea at all who did it to me, except that James the footman was involved."

Sir Julian's jaw dropped, and he hastened over as well. "The pyramid? James? But—"

Hermione shook her head at him. "Not now, sir.

Questions can be asked in due course. For the moment all that matters is that she is back with us." She looked at Tansy again. "We've been utterly wretched with worry, my dear," she said, glimpsing the clasped hands beneath the cover of Martin's naval coat. She was pleased, for if ever there were two young people whom she liked and thought belonged together, it was these two.

Sir Julian went to kiss Tansy warmly on the cheek. "How relieved I am that at least one of my nieces has been given back to me!" he declared, then turned to gesture to the maid who'd brought the glad tidings. "Tea and hot buttered toast in the library, as quick as you can."

"Yes, Sir Julian." The maid gave a swift curtsy and ran back to the kitchens.

Hermione ushered Tansy into the library, and Martin walked with Sir Julian, explaining how the cats had led him to Tansy's prison. But it wasn't until the tea and hot buttered toast had been brought that Tansy actually related what she'd seen during the night, commencing, of course, with how she'd seen James the footman leading the stranger across the atrium.

Sir Julian's face changed. "So I had *two* vipers in the bosom of my staff? First Joseph and now James. He's gone, d'you say?"

Martin nodded. "My first thought on returning was to take him by the throat, but he's made himself scarce. I doubt we'll see him again."

"James saw me in the doorway," Tansy explained, "so he knew I'd seen him."

"But what were they doing in here?" Sir Julian asked. "And who was the gentleman?"

"They came to destroy the letter you had in the statue," Martin said, "and from all accounts they succeeded."

Sir Julian went pale and stepped quickly to look in the secret compartment. Sure enough, it was empty. He closed his eyes, thoughts running one after another through his head. Even if he still had the letter, would he want to expose anything now? Such an action would not only ruin Randal, but Amanda as well, and much as he disliked Franklyn's daughter, could he bring himself to make the wicked past a thing of public discussion at her expense? She was, and always would be, his own brother's child. Nothing could ever change that.

Hermione went anxiously to him. "Julian? Are you feeling unwell, my dear?"

Tansy and Martin exchanged glances at the easy way she addressed him by his first name.

Sir Julian shook his head. "I'm quite all right, Hermione. Just a little shaken by all this." Shaken? The word seemed hardly adequate for the way he felt right now. After all the years of keeping Felice's secret, suddenly he had to face the fact that it was no longer in his power to do anything. Oh, he could trumpet the truth across the country, but who would believe a bitter old man who had such a very well-known ax to grind where the name Sanderby was concerned? He would become more of a laughingstock than he was now; indeed, he would be reviled! And all for nothing, because without proof of any kind at all, Randal Fenworth would remain firm and cozy in his ill-gotten gains. So Sir Julian knew it was out his hands now. The only thing on God's own earth that would prompt him to confront the ridicule, would be the sudden appearance of Marguerite Kenny's son—the real Earl of Sanderby. . . .

Ozzy and Cleo were seated in front of the library fire, and they watched Sir Julian's face in such a way that Tansy felt they knew what he was thinking. Then they got up to go to Martin, around whose legs they wove like two furry shuttles. But other than Tansy, who didn't understand what they were trying to say, no one else noticed, and as Sir Julian didn't say what he knew, no one even guessed who was right there in the library with them.

Tansy looked from the cats to her uncle. "I'm so

sorry about the letter, Uncle Julian, but there was nothing I could have done. The moment the gentleman found the letter, he ripped it into pieces and threw them on the fire."

Sir Julian tried to pull himself together. "But how did he know about the secret place? Answer me that." He paused. "Can you describe him, my dear?"

Tansy did as he asked, and his eyes cleared. "Randal Fenworth!"

Hermione looked at him curiously. "But why on earth would Lord Sanderby wish to enter the house in the dead of night to destroy your letter?"

"Well you might ask," Sir Julian replied wryly.

"And how did he know where to look for it?" Martin added.

"I don't think we need go further than Amanda for the answer to that," Sir Julian replied, his thoughts running on. Was the scheming little minx in full possession of the facts? How far would she go in order to become a countess? The answer was starkly obvious—any length. Any length at all . . .

Hermione sighed. "I suppose Amanda *is* the obvious source. After all, no one else here has had any contact with Lord Sanderby since I so foolishly revealed the hiding place. Except that reprobate James, of course, but he wasn't present when I opened the secret compartment."

Sir Julian went to draw her palm to his lips. "Don't blame yourself, Hermione, for you weren't to know."

"I think there is rather a lot I—we—don't know, Julian. To begin with, you still haven't said why the letter would be of importance to Lord Sanderby. Or is it something you prefer not to discuss?"

"Well, I—" Sir Julian broke off in astonishment as there came from the atrium such a torrent of bad language from a raised female voice, that Tansy and Hermione went quite pink with embarrassment. Sir Julian was incensed. "What in the name of perdition is going on out there?" he breathed as he strode out to investigate. The others followed, and found two footmen struggling with a redheaded woman whose supply of expletives seemed quite endless.

"What is the meaning of this?" demanded Sir Julian, in a tone that brought instant silence.

Liza shook herself free and confronted him. "Are you Sir Julian Richardson?"

"I am. And who, pray, are you?"

"Liza Lawrence. I'm Lord Sanderby's—"

"Inamorata? Yes, your name is now known to me," Sir Julian interrupted, for the cook at Bothenbury hadn't minced her words to his men about Randal's *belle de nuit*.

"Well, I don't know being an inamerera, but I was his whore, right enough," Liza admitted candidly. Then her glance happened upon the console table. "My best Russian chattie!" she cried, and pounced upon it. "Oh, I have missed this!"

Ozzy and Cleo, observing from the library door, eyed her with complete disgust.

Sir Julian was taken aback. "The scarf is yours?"

"Oh, yes," Liza confirmed, as she wrapped it around her throat and patted it neatly into place. It was a little damp, but not much, and it didn't seem to have come to any harm for being benighted in the woods.

"What were you doing in my woods?" Sir Julian asked her.

"Eh? Oh, Lord High-and-Mighty Sanderby used to bring me along when he came here. He'd wait down in the woods for a signal, then come up to be let in the house. He was searching for something."

"I know that too," Sir Julian replied heavily, thinking that the damned mongrel had eventually found it!

"Look, I don't know much about all this," Liza went on, "but I do know sufficient. And I don't half want to get my own back on the miserable excuse for a gentleman who hauled me all the way down here to the sticks, used me, then chucked me aside like an old stocking!"

"So you are here on an errand of revenge?"

"I am."

Sir Julian exhaled slowly. "I fear you are too late."

"Too late?" Liza looked at him. "Oh, you mean because he and your niece have run off to Wareham?"

Martin stepped forward. "Wareham?" he repeated.

"That's right. Their carriage passed me in the lane. They've gone off to Wareham, where his lordship has bribed a vicar to do the honors. St. Winifred's church, I think."

Martin held her gaze. "Are you quite sure about this?"

"Yes, of course I am. Lord High-and-Mighty used to brag to me about how clever he was. When he decided to throw me out, he'd have done well to remember how much he'd blabbed. She'll be his bride before nightfall, unless someone goes to stop it. You'll know his carriage if you see it, for it has a torch badge on its door."

"I know his badge well enough," Sir Julian said, then ordered the footmen to have his own vehicle made ready as quickly as possible.

But as the men hastened away, Martin intervened. "Do you intend to go after her, sir?"

"Yes, for it is my duty."

"With all due respect, sir, I think it would be better if I went instead."

"You? But, Lieutenant, you are hardly a well man." Sir Julian became puzzled. "Although, I admit you do seem to have undergone a remarkable recovery."

Martin smiled. "Put it down to Egyptian magic, sir. Oh, it is quite a story, and I will explain when I return, hopefully having rescued your other niece."

Tansy took off Martin's coat and returned it to him; then she caught up her skirts to hurry to the staircase. "I'm going to go with you, Martin!"

Hermione was appalled. "You? My dear, you have just undergone another ordeal, so I think *I* should be the one to go. Besides, there is propriety to consider!"

"Oh, but—"

Sir Julian was adamant. "No, Tansy, my dear. I will

not hear of it. To have one niece rushing around the countryside alone in a carriage with a gentleman is bad enough, but to have *two* . . . You stay here. And you too, Hermione, for I do not trust Sanderby one inch further than I could throw him. He has no scruples, and would as soon strike a woman as a man. I will see that some of my men accompany the lieutenant."

Martin shook his head. "It is better if I go alone, sir. It will attract attention if I take men with me. The chance of scandal may yet be avoided if I can quietly persuade Amanda to come back with me."

Hermione's lips twitched. Quietly persuade that uppity miss to come back? Chance would indeed be a fine thing!

Sir Julian thought the same, but gave in nevertheless. "As you wish, Lieutenant. And thank you for this. Thank you from the bottom of my heart. Indeed, it seems to me that I am continually in your debt where my nieces are concerned."

Tansy had remained where she was while this went on, but now she continued up the staircase anyway. "I'll just go to my room to change into a day dress," she called back over her shoulder, but as she rushed to her wardrobe, it was her warmest cloak she took out. Moments later, after scribbling a swift note of explanation, she slipped stealthily onto the landing again, still carrying the comforting bronze figurine. The atrium was deserted, everyone having adjourned to the library, including Liza. No one was there to see as Tansy slipped outside into the continuing wind, and hurried along the drive to a convenient clump of bushes. But as she parted the swaying branches to watch the house, she became aware of not being alone. Ozzy and Cleo were with her, their ears back in discomfort as the wind blew their fur the wrong way. Tansy knew without being told that they expected to accompany her in the carriage. How she knew it she could not have said, but the knowledge was there.

Within a minute or so Lysons brought the carriage to the door, and Martin hurried out to climb in. But as the vehicle set off toward her, she stepped into its path, obliging Lysons to haul upon the brakes. "Are you mad, Miss Tansy!" he cried, knowing how close he had come to running her down.

Martin lowered the glass and looked impatiently out. "What's happened?"

Tansy ran to the carriage, Ozzy and Cleo at her heels. "It's me, Martin. I'm coming with you, whether Uncle Julian likes it or not."

"Tansy—"

"If you do not let me in, Martin Ballard, I shall tell Uncle Julian of the liberties you took at the pyramid."

Martin saw the steely glint in her eyes and gave in. Opening the door, he reached down to pull her swiftly inside. He made no move to prevent the cats from leaping in as well; then he slammed the door, and Lysons urged the team on.

# 30

As Martin and Tansy drove off at speed for Wareham, Sir Julian, Hermione, and Liza were in the library at Chelworth. Liza was eating a piece of toast that Sir Julian had offered her. "I do hope your lieutenant gets there in time," she said, then winked at Hermione. "A proper tasty morsel he is, eh? Just about the tastiest naval officer I've ever clapped eyes on."

Hermione shifted. "Well, I . . . er, suppose he is handsome, yes," she replied.

Sir Julian regarded Liza. "Since you have imparted some important information concerning my niece's whereabouts, you will not go unrewarded."

"I don't want anything," Liza answered. "Besides, I haven't finished yet. I've brought you this." She searched inside her cloak and drew out the note she'd found in Randal's pocket lining. "I think you'll find it very interesting. It's from a man who was working for Lord High-and-Mighty, investigating about someone's first wife. His lordship pretended it was on behalf of some friend or other, who was worried about his legitimacy, but it was really Lord High-and-Mighty himself who was worried. And rightly so, if you read what the note says."

Sir Julian almost grabbed the note, but when he'd finished he was unsure of whether to be hopeful or not. Liza watched his face. "What's the matter? It's clear enough, isn't it? Lord High-and-Mighty's father was still married when he took his second wife. Bigamy they call it, don't they?"

Hermione's jaw dropped. "Bigamy?" she repeated. "Lord Sanderby's father committed *bigamy?*"

"Yes, my dear, he most certainly did," Sir Julian answered, then returned his attention to Liza. "Miss, er . . ."

"Lawrence."

"Ah, yes, Miss Lawrence. I fear that although I know this note tells the truth about Lord Sanderby, in the absence of any names . . ."

"You mean, it isn't any use after all?" Liza's face fell almost comically. "And I was so hoping that I'd get my own back. . . ."

"Never mind, my dear. You did your utmost."

Hermione was unable to bear the suspense a moment longer. "Will someone *please* tell me what all this is about?"

"Yes, yes, my dear. I promise you shall know all in a moment. First I must attend to this young woman." Sir Julian went to his deck, took out the leather purse he kept there, and gave it to Liza.

Her eyes widened. "The whole purse?" she gasped.

"Certainly, for I think you have earned it. Where are you bound now?"

"Well, London. Back to Mother Clancy's bawdy house. Begging your pardon, madam," Liza added quickly, glancing at Hermione.

Sir Julian beckoned to her and went to the door to address the footman who waited by the statue. "See that Miss Lawrence is given a proper meal in the kitchens; then have the pony and trap made ready to take her to Weymouth. An inside ticket is to be purchased for her on the next stagecoach to London."

"Yes, sir." The footman led Liza away.

Sir Julian immediately returned to Hermione and handed her the copied pages. "The late Lord Sanderby did indeed commit an act of bigamy some thirty or so years ago, with the result that Randal Fenworth has no right whatsoever to his title or fortune."

"Good heavens!" Hermione gasped.

"The time has come for me to unburden myself to someone, and with your permission, my dear, I would like that someone to be you."

"Of course, Julian, and you may be sure that not a word will pass my lips."

"I know that, my dear." Sir Julian began to tell her the whole story of his heartbreaking love affair with Randal's wronged mother.

Amanda had played with fire once too often and was already Randal's wife. In the little Norman church of St. Winifred's, on the edge of Wareham, the false Lord Sanderby slipped the ring on his bride's finger. It wasn't a proper wedding band, just his heavy signet ring, but it was on the correct finger. The vows had been taken, the final words uttered, and she was Countess of Sanderby at last! Well, almost, for there remained the consummation. The irregularities that accompanied the ceremony were not of any real consequence, for the entry was in the register, and the clergyman was clearly genuine. The special license would be later rather than sooner, but a rider had already been sent to Lambeth Palace for the necessary paperwork to be done. Within a day or so the records of the marriage would be as solid and safe as if it had taken place in St. George's, Hanover Square, in front of all Mayfair!

Amanda would have preferred a grand wedding at London's most fashionable church, but having the thing over and done with made her feel secure. She was Countess of Sanderby at last, and with the letter gone forever, Martin Ballard stood no chance whatsoever of discovering the truth. Nor could Uncle Julian do anything. She and Randal had succeeded in suppressing the disagreeable facts from the past, and they could now look forward to a good future together. Oh, she was going to be one of the finest ladies in London, with wonderful clothes, a sheaf of invitations propped behind the candlestick on the mantel, and a list of admirers flocking to her door. She would take London by storm, and she would have nothing more to do with her uncle, or with Tansy. They were beneath her now.

Emerging from the church porch, Amanda laughed as the wind caught her skirts and flapped them wildly. She was still happy and laughing as Randal escorted her across the churchyard toward the lych-gate. St. Winifred's stood between the vicarage and a comfortable coaching inn called the Black Bear. They had already secured the best suite of rooms, and Randal wasted no time about conducting his bride upstairs to the great four-poster marriage bed.

If Amanda had been hoping for a romantic wooing, with many kisses and fair words to enhance her mood, she was gravely disappointed. Once the door closed behind them, Randal almost pushed her onto the bed in order to set about his husbandly duty. Not a single kiss was bestowed upon her lips, nor a single caress stroked her skin; there was just the swift business of coupling. Very swift, as it happens, for Randal was prone to rush things the first time, whether or not he wanted to. As Liza could have told his bride, the first was over in a blink, and the second in three. Four was unheard of! Amanda, whose adventures in Constantinople had been a little too adventurous, resulting in her not being quite the innocent little virgin her new lord believed, consoled herself with the thought of all the lovers she would have in the near future.

Thus the runaway marriage was made secure, and all chance removed of any third party putting it asunder.

Lysons was a Dorset man and knew Wareham very well. He certainly knew St. Winifred's, and reined the sweating team to a halt outside the Black Bear, where a glance through into the yard immediately revealed Randal's carriage, with its telltale badge.

Martin flung open the door and climbed down, but as he turned to assist Tansy out as well, Ozzy and Cleo jumped out and disappeared into the yard. Martin watched them go, then looked at Tansy, whose hand he still held.

"I would rather you waited out here," he said quietly.

"No."

"Tansy—"

"No!"

With a sigh, he gave in. "Very well, but you are to keep behind me. Is that clear?"

"Yes." She gazed at him. "I do believe you are being masterful, sir," she murmured, unable to help the coquettish note that crept into her voice.

"And you, miss, are playing—"

"With fire?" she supplied.

"Yes." He took her face in his hands and kissed her roughly on the lips; then he looked deep into her eyes. "The time is not far off when I will show you what that fire can really do, Tansy Richardson. In fact, I intend to singe your adorable wings."

"Oh, I do trust so," she whispered.

"Make no mistake of it. However, for the moment we are here on another errand entirely. Have a care now, Tansy, for what I've heard of Sanderby does not fill me with admiration." Taking her hand, he led her through into the inn yard.

They were soon informed where they would find Lord Sanderby and went upstairs to the suite, which was at the front of the building, overlooking the road. Two small shadows were at their heels, one ginger, one tabby, and both waited intently as Martin paused before putting his hand on the door latch, lifting it, and walking straight in.

Amanda and Randal were now in the bed, as naked as the day they were born, a fact that was only too obvious as they sat up sharply. Amanda pulled the bedclothes over her charms, but then her alarm turned to a smirk as she saw who had entered. She raised her left hand and waggled the fingers. "You're too late. I am already Lady Sanderby, so if dear Uncle Julian has sent you to drag me back to Chelworth, he is going to be sadly disappointed."

Randal's gaze was fixed upon Martin, in whom he saw more of his father than in himself. This had to be Marguerite Kenny's son—his only too legitimate half brother! Martin sensed nothing. That they were siblings did not even cross his mind.

Tansy's gaze was equally fixed upon Randal, whom she recognized immediately as the gentleman who'd destroyed Sir Julian's letter.

Ozzy and Cleo jumped onto the bed, and Amanda recoiled in disgust. "Ugh! You've brought these vile creatures with you!" Cleo spat at her, by way of returning the insult, and Amanda pulled the bedclothes up to her chin as she edged further away against the pillows. Ozzy, however, could not have cared less about Amanda, for his attention was upon his favorite prey, Randal Fenworth. With a low growl, the tomcat advanced toward his goal, and Randal hastily grabbed the bed coverlet and hauled it around himself as he jumped out of the bed. "Dab it all. Get theb out of here!" he cried, edging away until he pressed against the adjacent windowsill.

Martin looked at him in astonishment. No one had mentioned that Sanderby had a speech impediment! Tansy was thinking the same, but endeavored not to show it as she spoke instead to Amanda. "Amanda, I think you should come back to Chelworth."

"And be insulted, ignored, and generally maltreated? No, I think not."

"But, Uncle Franklyn will not like it that you—"

"Leave my father out of this, if you please," Amanda snapped. "Look, why don't you both just go? I am Randal's wife now, and that is how I intend to stay. As you can see, there is nothing anyone can do about it." She indicated the crumpled bed, all the while keeping a wary eye on Cleo, who was staring unblinkingly at her.

Randal looked hatefully at Martin. "You heard by wife. She beans to stay with be, and I have certainly done enough to bake the barriage safe!" Ozzy disliked his tone, and he gave a long, low, wavering growl that seemed to contain as many expletives as were at Liza's disposal. Randal's glance slid toward his pillow, beneath which he had hidden a loaded pistol. It was no ordinary pistol, but possessed a magazine and was capable of firing nine shots in succession.

Martin sensed the other's loathing but had no way of knowing the cause, so he endeavored to remain reasonable. "My lord, I accept that the situation has reached the point of no return, but if you and your bride will just return to Chelworth to convince Sir Julian of your union . . . He has been appointed your wife's guardian, and so is bound to require proof that the marriage is genuine."

Had he deliberated for a year upon which words would provoke Randal the most, Martin could not have chosen to more effect. Each syllable touched a raw nerve, and with a savage cry, Randal dove for the pillow, in the process dropping the coverlet that spared his blushes. Tansy and Amanda both screamed as he grabbed the pistol, cocked it, and swung it toward Martin, who retreated hastily.

"Sweet Jesu, Sanderby!"

"Farewell, by fine lord!" Randal breathed, and began to squeeze the trigger.

Ozzy leaped, and struck Randal with such force that he lost his balance and tottered backward. The pistol went off, the shot thudding into the ceiling; then Cleo leaped for Randal as well. With a cry he stumbled heavily back against the window, which gave way beneath his weight. For a terrible moment Randal seemed to hang in the air; then, amid a shower of glass and wood, he plunged out of the window and down into a large, exceedingly full rainwater butt.

Icy water cascaded everywhere, and then the butt, which was rather old, began to split. Randal Fenworth and the rest of the dirty water were spilled upon the cobbles, where startled onlookers stared in amusement at his lack of a stitch of clothing. Ozzy and Cleo stood on the windowsill above, looking very pleased with themselves as the dismayed landlord hastened to relieve Randal of the pistol, which was still clutched in his hand.

Tansy and Martin were stunned by what had happened, and so initially was Amanda, but the latter recovered apace. Her hard voice rang into the silent room. "There's nothing either of you will ever be able to do! You've been outwitted, and that is the end of it!"

Tansy whirled to confront her. "You are welcome to your marriage to that . . . that murdering excuse for a man! You and he should, I trust, be very happy together. When he is released from jail, that is!"

"Jail?"

"Well, he did just try to shoot Martin, or did that escape your attention?"

Amanda's cornflower eyes were bright and venomous. "He thought Martin was about to shoot him. I shall vouch for that. So it will be our word against yours."

"Except that Martin does not have a pistol," Tansy hurled back.

Martin exhaled slowly. "I'm afraid that isn't true, Tansy. I may not have drawn it, but I do have one. Look, all in all, I think we should just leave this as it is."

"Leave it? But—"

Amanda's scathing tones cut in. "Oh, just do as your little lieutenant tells you, Church Mouse, for to be sure he has a soupçon more sense than you do. Mind you, that is about all he does have, for he is hardly the rich suitor you'd really like, is he?" She began to laugh, peal upon peal of triumphant laughter that was only silenced when Cleo returned purposefully to the bed and dealt her a very sound scratch to the cheek, then jumped neatly out of reach of Amanda's furious fingers.

Martin pulled Tansy toward the door. "The new Lady Sanderby isn't worth bothering with," he said. "I definitely think we should leave them to get on with it. If I press charges against Sanderby, the resultant scandal may touch upon you as well."

Amanda hurled a pillow at them. "You may be sure it will, for *I* will see to it!" she screamed.

Martin raised an eyebrow at Tansy. "I'm afraid you and I are far too lowly to associate with such *grand* and refined persons, Tansy."

"How *dare* you!" cried Amanda, almost forgetting herself enough to climb out of the bed, but remembering just in time that she too was without a stitch of clothing.

Martin opened the door. "Come, Tansy, let us leave this, er, person to her own devices. She has made her bed, and now she must lie in it." He almost bundled Tansy from the room, and once again the two cats accompanied them.

They drove away from the Black Bear, leaving Randal trying to extricate himself from the landlord's clutches, that indignant fellow being in no mood to put up with guests who went around firing pistols willy-nilly, no matter how nobly born they said they were. And there was the small matter of paying for the shattered window. A *cat* did it? No, *two* cats? Well, if he was expected to believe that, he might as well be expected to fly up to the roof of St. Winifred's as well! No guest at the Black Bear, lord or not, was going to leave without paying up for all damage done!

Tansy sat with Martin in the carriage, needing his warmth and closeness after what had just happened. Her heart was still beating swiftly, and now that they were safe, she felt like crying with relief. She was more glad of his arm around her than he could have begun to imagine, and as she rested her head on his shoulder, she had to close her eyes to stop the tears from having their way. Ozzy and Cleo occupied the seat opposite, looking so prim and proper that it was hard to believe they had just knocked the Earl of Sanderby out of a window into a butt of none-too-clean rainwater.

Martin smiled. "Look at them. One would think butter could not melt in their mouths."

Tansy opened her eyes and smiled too. "They shall have a dish of cream each when we return to Chelworth."

Martin chuckled. "How like your uncle you are," he murmured.

"I shall take that as a compliment."

"And so it is."

She was silent for a moment, then craned her neck to look up into his eyes. "Martin, what do you think he meant?"

"Who?"

"Amanda's unlovely new husband. He said 'Farewell my fine lord' when he aimed the pistol at you."

"Did he? To be honest, Tansy, I haven't a clue what he said. I was more concerned with what he was doing."

She turned to the front again. "Well, that's definitely what he said. Don't you think it rather strange?"

"Does it matter?"

"No, I suppose not."

# 31

Sir Julian and Hermione listened in horror as Martin related the events at the Black Bear. They were all four seated in the library, their faces lit by the dancing fire as the stormy March afternoon faded into darkness once more. When Martin finished, Sir Julian got up wearily and went to the fireplace. Resting a hand on the mantel, he gazed into the flames.

"It would seem Amanda is quite beyond redemption," he said heavily.

Tansy felt the need to comfort him if she could. "She is still the Countess of Sanderby, Uncle, so I do not think she is exactly ruined."

Sir Julian glanced at Hermione, who quickly lowered her eyes.

Tansy was still thinking of her cousin. "I did not think that even Amanda could be so vile, but the things she said at the inn were quite unforgivable."

Sir Julian nodded. "Your cousin is a spoiled, utterly selfish, entirely disagreeable young wench, and thus the perfect bride for a man of Randal Fenworth's caliber." Again he looked at Hermione, this time with a query in his eyes. Should he tell Tansy and Martin everything? Was there any point now that the letter had been destroyed, and with it all hope of proving anything?

Before Hermione had a chance to reply, the library door swung open, and Ozzy and Cleo came in, the latter holding the letter in her mouth. Everyone thought of King Osorkon's retriever cat, for that was indeed how she seemed, even to her tabby fur. She trotted to Martin and laid the letter on the carpet at his feet. Not realizing what the folded sheets of paper were, he gave a slight laugh and bent to pick them up. "What's this?" he murmured.

Sir Julian thought the papers looked only too familiar. "Good God, I believe that's my letter, the one from the statue of Isis! But it can't be, for Tansy saw it destroyed!"

Martin glanced at the papers. "It is indeed a letter addressed to you, sir. From a lady by the name of Felice."

Sir Julian was thunderstruck. "It's impossible!" He hastened across the room to grab the papers. "By all the saints, it *is* the letter! Hermione, it's safe after all! I have Fenworth in my palm again!"

Tansy was bewildered. "But . . . I definitely saw Lord Sanderby rip it up and throw it on the fire. I didn't imagine it."

Sir Julian went to pat her shoulder quickly. "I'm sure you saw exactly that, my dear, but clearly it wasn't my letter that he destroyed, for here it is. Although how the cats have it, I can't begin to imagine."

Martin looked at him. "The letter is clearly of some importance to you, Sir Julian."

"It is, my boy. It is. Mind you, I still do not know what to do with it for the best." Sir Julian met Hermione's eyes again. Again she looked away, for she shared his uncertainty. The impulse to ruin Randal was strong and justified, and Amanda certainly did not deserve consideration; but the new Lady Sanderby was still Sir Julian's niece, and the whereabouts of the real heir remained a mystery.

Cleo had watched the letter's progress from Martin to Sir Julian, and her ears went back disapprovingly. Calmly she followed Sir Julian and reached up to pat his leg.

"Eh? What is it?" he inquired, instinctively bending to stroke her head, but to his surprise she took the

letter from his hand and carried it back to Martin, this
time jumping up to deposit it in his lap. Sir Julian
smiled. "I shall take that as a sign that the letter's
contents should be made known to you all. Read it
aloud, my boy."

"Me? But—"

"No, no. You read it. That is what Cleo wants, and
I have no objection." Sir Julian went to the desk,
where not long before a footman had placed the tray
upon which stood the glasses and decanter of sherry
that preceded dinner at Chelworth. No one had
changed for the evening, or indeed intended to. Tonight was not that sort of night.

"As you wish, sir." Martin unfolded the sheets. "It's
dated Tuesday, June eleven, 1775, and was written at
sixteen-B Grosvenor Square, London." He cleared his
throat, and continued.

*"My dearest, most darling beloved Julian. What I am
about to tell you must never be told to another. On
that I expect your promise upon your honor. I only tell
you this darkest of dark secrets because I feel I owe it
to you.*

*"There is no easy way for either of us. I must simply
say that it is now quite impossible for me to leave Sanderby and come to you. Oh, my heart breaks as I pen
these words, for you are the most precious thing in my
life. Well, almost the most precious thing, for I must,
as a mother, put my child first. Randal is so small and
defenseless, and if I were to defy Sanderby and go to
you, Randal's future would be completely destroyed.*

*"Maybe you have gathered from the above that
Sanderby knows about us; indeed, it seems he has
known for some time. He chose to inform me at the
theater last night, after I had written to you on the
handbill and sent it by the box keeper. He waited until
the handbill had been given into your hand, which he
saw well enough from our box opposite; then he informed me of his awareness. He also told me something
that has brought my entire world in ruins about my
ears. You see, my darling, I am not really Lady Sand-*

*erby at all. He tells me that our marriage was an act of bigamy on his part, because he was already married to the actress, Marguerite Kenny . . ."*

Tansy sat forward with a gasp. "Oh, Martin!"

Martin met her startled eyes for a moment, then read the last two sentences to himself again. The Lord Sanderby of 1775 had been married to Marguerite Kenny? The implications were not lost upon him.

Hermione looked at them both in alarm. "What is it? Is something wrong?"

Martin cleared his throat. "I, er . . . don't know. You see, Marguerite Kenny was my mother."

Sir Julian put the decanter down with a clatter. "*Your* mother?" he repeated.

"Yes, sir."

Hermione flapped a hand at the letter. "Read on, Lieutenant! Read on!" She already knew most of the facts from Sir Julian, but certainly not all.

Martin did as she asked. *"I was left in no doubt at all that I had never been the object of Sanderby's affections; rather, it was my fortune that lured him. He informed me that Marguerite was the great love of his life, but that he had been very foolish to go so far as to marry her. An earl cannot present an actress wife at court, or indeed take her to the grandest of houses, because she would not be acceptable. And even though he still considers her to be the most beautiful and divine creature that ever walked the earth, he cast her aside when his gambling debts grew so enormous that he needed an heiress to keep him out of jail. So Marguerite was hounded from his door, with all manner of threats should she be foolish enough to lay claim to her title, and I became, as I thought, the Countess of Sanderby. It was when I was carrying Randal that Sanderby learned Marguerite had borne him a son. He moved heaven and earth to find her, but she had disappeared, the boy with her. I know nothing of this child, except that he was born on St. Valentine's Day."*

Martin's mouth ran dry. St. Valentine's Day was *his* birthday. . . . If this letter was genuine, and the information it contained accurate, there could not possibly be any doubt that he was the boy to whom the writer referred—any doubt that he, not Randal Fenworth, was the rightful Earl of Sanderby.

Hermione watched the expressions on his face. "It's your birthday too, isn't it, Lieutenant?" she said quietly.

"Yes, I fear it is."

Sir Julian stared at him as if he had suddenly sprouted horns and a tail. "You are the missing heir?" he whispered. "Dear God in heaven, how is it possible that you should come here? To the one house in the realm where the truth about your true heritage could be learned?"

Tansy nodded at Martin. "Finish reading it, Martin."

Somehow he managed to continue. *"In due course I was brought to bed of Randal, who was treated as the rightful heir to his father's title and fortune. I truly believed he was, because I did not know I was never married. But I know now, Julian, and Sanderby tells me that if I leave him for you, he will make this horrid tale public. It will mean ruin for me, and illegitimacy for Randal. The former I could endure, my darling, but not the latter. If I stay with Sanderby, Randal will in due course inherit all that is his father's. I know that he is not entitled to it, because Marguerite's son is the real heir, but she has hidden herself so well that no one knows where she is, or even if she and her son are still alive. If I thought they were, and that they could be found, I would behave honorably, but in the absence of any proof of their continued existence, it is my dearest child I must protect. And the price I have to pay to secure his future is that I must give you up.*

*"Oh, my darling, If there were any other way I would take it, but not where my boy is concerned. Silent tongue and still, as the old saying goes. I will hold you to keep my secret for as long as you live, and I know I can rest easy that you will do as I ask.*

*"I will never stop loving you, Julian, nor will I ever stop despising Sanderby. But my boy I adore beyond all reason. He is my lodestar, and for him I will sacrifice everything. And if you love me, my darling, you will sacrifice all for him as well.*

*"Be strong for me. Adieu. Felice."*

Numb, Martin carefully folded the letter. Surely he was asleep and dreaming, and would soon awaken. But he knew he was awake, and the facts were only too plain. He had always known that he wasn't Martin Ballard, but until now he had not known he was really Martin Fenworth. Nor could he possibly have imagined he was the legitimate heir to a title.

Tansy swallowed. "Well, at least we now know what Lord Sanderby meant when he called you lord." She looked at Sir Julian. "And it is now equally plain from some of the things Amanda said, that she knew the truth as well. She is fully aware that Martin is the real earl, and she is prepared to hold her tongue simply so that she could call herself a countess!"

Hermione sighed. "I fear that Amanda has no scruples, my dear."

Tansy watched Cleo, who was seated on the floor in front of Martin, gazing up at him as if she knew exactly what the letter was and what it contained. Maybe she did. King Osorkon's faithful cat had known too. The story from Ancient Egypt had been repeated here today. Cleo had been the retriever cat; Martin was Osorkon, the true heir denied his rights by his wicked brother.

Sir Julian continued to gaze at Martin, now seeing him with completely new eyes. "Felice always said that if Marguerite Kenny's son was found, she would admit the truth, but you and your mother seemed to vanish from the face of the earth. Where were you, boy? How was it that all inquiries and searches led nowhere?"

"We lived in Minorca, sir."

"Good God. Small wonder no one found you." Sir

Julian studied him. "You are very like your sire. I make no bones about loathing Esmond Fenworth, but I concede that he was a handsome devil."

Martin smiled. "I loathe him too, sir, even though I have never met him. Throughout her life my mother declined to name him because she feared what he would do, but she did tell me how he treated her. Ballard is the name of the man with whom she lived, a kind and honorable man whose name I have been proud to carry. I regarded him as my legal stepfather, even though he was unable to marry my mother because of her previous contract. But no one in Minorca knew that."

Sir Julian toyed with the stopper of the decanter. "I gave my word to Felice that I would keep the secret. Whatever my opinion of Randal, he is still her son, her flesh and blood. And Amanda, heaven help her, was utterly set upon marrying him. I saw no possible advantage in exposing the truth. What good would it have done? True, it would have denied Randal the privilege he has so illegally enjoyed, but that is the only advantage I could see. Would it have made Amanda happy? No, for nothing on this earth could do that! Would it have punished Randal's miserable sire? No. Would it have harmed Felice's memory? Yes. Would it have made me feel better? Possibly, but that would have been a very selfish approach. So I have always put Felice first, always honored her wishes, and remained staunchly loyal to her memory. But if she were here now, she would be the first to insist that the correct thing must be done. Lieutenant, your father's title and wealth should be yours, not Randal's, and so I gladly give you the letter, which is the only firsthand proof in existence. I have searched everywhere for proof of that first marriage, but Esmond was very thorough. His second son was not, however, and this very day his disaffected mistress brought us a note she found in his coat pocket. Unfortunately, interesting though the note is, it gives no names, and so it cannot be of use, even though I *know* it concerns Esmond Fenworth's bigamous activities. When Esmond set about expunging all trace of what he'd done, he left nothing to chance. Even the clergyman who must have officiated seems to have vanished off the face of the earth. I'm surprised Esmond wrote an incriminating diary, but he died quite suddenly, and no doubt he would have been rid of it first if he'd realized he was soon to meet his Maker. Randal clearly saw the danger of keeping it, and destroyed it as soon as he realized its importance. Would that some use could be made of the note his *belle de nuit* found, but I fear not."

Hermione looked up suddenly. "Unless we can find the fellow who wrote it. Maybe Liza knows who he is."

"Now there's a thought," Sir Julian murmured, more hope quickening through him.

"Felice's letter is important evidence," Hermione went on, "and maybe Liza's note, even as it is, will serve to back up what the letter says. In court, that is."

"In court?" Martin hadn't even begun to think of what would happen now.

"Why, yes. My boy, you *have* to take what is yours. You owe it to your mother and to any children you might have. Would you wish to deny your own son the heritage he is due? Would you want him to be set aside in favor of two people as disgraceful and undeserving as Randal Fenworth and my niece Amanda? I tell you this, sir, if you are prepared to do that, you will sink so far in my estimation that I shall regret ever learning your identity."

Martin met Sir Julian's eyes, and then turned to Tansy. "I must speak with you," he said, and got up to seize her hand.

"Me? Oh, but—"

"Now," he said, and almost pulled her from the room.

Sir Julian looked blankly after them. "What is all *that* about?"

Hermione gave him a long-suffering look. "Julian, my dear, you really can be very blind at times."

"Eh? You mean, Tansy and the lieutenant are . . . ?"

"In love? Yes, that's exactly what I mean."

# 32

Out in the candlelit atrium, Martin turned Tansy to face him. The wind could be heard moaning around the dome far above, and the pharaoh rose eerily beside them. A draft crept through the house, making the candles sway. "Tansy, I want to know what you want."

"My wishes should not influence you in this, Martin. It's your decision . . . your birthright."

"And you are going to be my wife," he reminded her. "Do you wish to be Countess of Sanderby?"

She stared at him. "I . . . I hadn't thought . . ."

"No, I didn't think you had." He caught her close to kiss her forehead.

But she pulled away. "Perhaps it would be more to the point to ask if you still want to marry a Church Mouse? I bring you nothing at all, Martin, yet as Lord Sanderby you could attract a bride like—"

"Like Amanda?" he interposed dryly. "Do you honestly think I want such a wife? Tansy, I asked you to marry me because I love you. It doesn't matter that you have no fortune, just that you are you. So the question remains. Do you want to be Lady Sanderby?"

She stepped away, trying to assemble her thoughts.

He gazed at her in the candlelight. "I want what is mine, Tansy, but I don't want it without you."

She turned. "Whatever you decide, I will be at your side," she promised.

His eyes cleared, and he went to her, crushing her into his arms and kissing her passionately on the lips. Then he met her eyes again. "My darling Church Mouse, you shall have everything my title can provide, but most of all, you'll have a lord who worships the very ground upon which you tread," he whispered.

Their lips met again, but this time with a tenderness that spread warmly through their veins like the magic of the bronze cat. There was magic all around them, a tingling in the air that seemed to bring brief images of all the things that had brought them together. Tel el-Osorkon and the Nile, Tusun, the wall painting, the escape on the *canja,* the *Lucina,* Chelworth itself . . . But above all, the cats. Ozzy and Cleo rubbed around their legs, and the wonderful sound of purring seemed to throb through the entire house.

It was a sound that made Tansy draw from the kiss to smile down at the two animals. "Martin, I can't help thinking about the story of King Osorkon."

"I have thought of it as well."

"What happened here today is exactly the same, except that it took place in modern England. You are Osorkon, and Cleo is the retriever cat who saved you from your evil brother."

"It seems so farfetched, and yet who can doubt that strange things have occurred since we met?"

"Will they continue to occur, I wonder?"

"Only time will tell."

It was breakfast at 16B Grosvenor Square, and the May sunshine was pouring in through the east-facing window. A bowl of lilacs stood in the hearth of the elegant pink marble fireplace, on the mantel of which was carved the Fenworth motto, *Noli tangere ignem, Do not stir up fire.* It was advice to which it was far too late for either Amanda or Randal to pay wise heed.

Amanda was sorting through the latest invitations that had been delivered to Lord Sanderby and his new bride. She was wearing a sapphire blue morning wrap that frothed with lace and ribbons, and her lovely golden hair was pinned up in the intricate style that her new Parisian maid managed so effortlessly. Everything about her was exquisitely beautiful and fashionable, but the fixed expression in her cornflower eyes was anything but beautiful as she paused to gaze coldly at Randal across the breakfast table. "*What* did you just say?" she demanded icily.

Randal's face had lost all color, and the letter he was reading fell from his fingers. "The game's up, Amanda."

"Up?" As yet she knew nothing about the moves in progress to strip Randal of his title in favor of Martin. Randal had been very careful indeed to keep her in the dark about such a discomforting development, not because he feared to lose her and therefore her fortune. That was all fully signed and sealed now, with entries in place where they should be, and a license so well absorbed into the records that no one on earth could have disproved it. No, Randal's reason for saying nothing to Amanda was simply that he was terrified of her temper. Liza Lawrence might have been the one with red hair, but it was Amanda who had the vile temper.

Randal's eyes slid to the motto on the mantel. They had both played with fire and were about to be burned. The moment had arrived to make a clean breast of things. He dreaded her reaction, but he couldn't put off the evil moment any longer. Their world was about to fall about their scheming ears, and she had to be told. He cleared his throat. "Well, I'm afraid it's like this, Amanda. Thanks to that damned old fool Richardson, Martin Ballard has come forward to claim his rights, and according to my lawyers, his case is bound to be proved." There, it was done at last.

Amanda became so still she seemed to have ceased to breathe. But then she spoke in a soft and trembling voice that gave due warning of the fury that had begun to rise within her. "Proved?" she breathed. "But how can it be *proved*?"

"It seems, among other things, that the papers I burned at Chelworth were not the vital letter." Randal got up and went to the sideboard to pour himself a large glass of brandy, which he drank in a single gulp. He felt a strange tickle start in his nose and looked around swiftly. A cat? Where?

Amanda rose, trembling, to her feet. "How can this be? You swore to me that—!"

"I know what I swore."

"You just said among other things? Among what other things? There is more?"

"Yes, I rather fear there is. They have found the clergyman who originally barried by father to Barguerite Kenny!" Randal's eyes watered profusely, and he searched desperately in his dressing gown pocket for a handkerchief. Goddamn it all, there wasn't even a cat in the house! So how . . . ?

"For heaven's sake, Randal! Get on with telling me what's happened!" cried Amanda.

"I . . . I believed the buffoon was long dead, but it seebs he is now a herbit on an island off the coast of Scotland." Randal sneezed violently. "Barguerite Kenny once bentioned his nabe to her dear son, who had the presence of bind to suddenly rebebber it. Richardson's creatures went to the island and obtained a witnessed statebent that by father did indeed barry Barguerite Kenny! Due to this and the evidence of the letter, the courts are also prepared to take into account a dabbed note I'd forgotten. The scoundrel I ebployed to investigate it all has agreed to give evidence against be." He wiped his streaming eyes and tried to resist the second sneeze that was tickling his nose.

"What forgotten note? What 'fellow' you employed?" Amanda breathed ominously.

He poured and drank another glass of brandy, then faced her. He explained about the agent he'd sent here, there, and everywhere, searching for Marguerite Kenny, and then finished with, "I ab afraid I was a little rebiss and forgot the fellow's note. It was in by pocket, and Liza—" He broke off abruptly, for now was definitely *not* the time to acquaint Amanda with Liza's existence as well.

But Amanda had already pounced upon the name. "Liza? Who is Liza?"

"Oh, nobody. A baid at Bothenbury."

"Don't lie to me! You had a whore there, didn't you! You were whispering in my ear, seducing me with your kisses, and all the time you had a trollop warming your bed!" Amanda screamed, and hurled her plate of scrambled eggs, bacon, and sausages at him.

He ducked, and the scrambled egg spattered his family motto instead. "Abanda, dearest, I—!"

"So after all our plotting, I'm not Countess of Sanderby after all?" Amanda's cup of coffee followed the plate. Again she missed her target, but found another instead. Not the mantel this time, but the cook's fat tortoiseshell cat, Tiddles, the existence of which had not been guessed by the master and mistress of the house. The unfortunate feline had a minute or so earlier slunk in to sun herself on the sill behind the gold-fringed green velvet curtains. It was the first time she had managed to get into the main part of the house, and she was thoroughly enjoying the east-facing window. Now, however, being suddenly drenched in hot coffee and pelted with porcelain, she erupted from her cozy place with a yowl like something from hell itself, and fled from the room.

Hardly able to credit that one of his greatest aversions had managed to get in the room, Randal recoiled as she passed.

Amanda screamed again at her husband. "Well? *Is* that what you're telling me?"

"Abanda, dearest—!"

"OH, STOP SPEAKING LIKE SOMETHING OUT OF BEDLAM!" she shrieked, so livid and beside herself that every word was uttered at the top of her lungs. If anyone looked and sounded like a denizen of Bedlam, it was she.

"I CAN'T HELP IT!" Randal bawled back. "Look, Abanda, I didn't bean things to get to this pitch! I truly, honestly—"

"Truly? Honestly? You don't know the meaning of the words!" she cried.

"But, dearest, we aren't exactly destitute. I bay no longer have a title, but we have your fortune. . . ."

Amanda froze. A nerve fluttered at her temple, and her fingers closed over the corner of the tablecloth.

Randal backed away nervously. "There's bore I have to tell you. . . ."

"More?" she repeated softly.

"Tansy and my half brother are to be barried next bonth at St. George's, Hanover Square. Virtually the whole of society is to be there, even the Prince of Wales."

With a strangulated banshee wail that was heard the length and breadth of the gracious Mayfair square, Amanda seized the tablecloth and wrenched it ferociously from the table. Everything crashed to the floor, and Randal made a very hasty exit, only to fall over the hapless Tiddles in the hall. He went sprawling, and the cat shot up a curtain to the pelmet, from where it looked balefully down at him, just as certain other furry faces had once looked over a garden wall in Dorset.

The sea had never been more blue as Tansy and Martin rode along the hilltop behind Chelworth. He wore a pine green riding coat and white corduroy breeches, and she was in a gold velvet riding habit that became her dark coloring very well indeed. There was gold on her finger too, the wedding ring that Martin had placed there at the lavish Mayfair ceremony attended by the grandest society in the land.

Ozzy and Cleo bounded ahead of the horses. At least, Ozzy bounded, for Cleo was obliged to be a little more sedate due to being in what the genteel termed *an interesting condition.* No one doubted that the kittens would be a mixture of ginger and tabby.

London was still abuzz with the Sanderby scandal. Amanda had left Randal, and the last anyone heard she was on her way to join her father in Australia. No one knew what had become of Randal, for he had been much pressed by duns as soon as word got out that he was no longer Earl of Sanderby. He had disappeared one night, and rumor was that he too had left the country. Canada had been mentioned; indeed, there was a whisper, a very sly one indeed, that he had somehow taken passage on no less a vessel than the *Lucina,* posing as a keeper of the regimental goat. But it was just a whisper.

The pyramid soared against the sky, and Tansy and Martin reined in beside the entrance. The cats lay on the grass, Cleo quite thankfully, for she found so much exercise quite a trial. Not that anything would have persuaded her to stay behind in the house when there was an outing to be had. "It will look very regal here indeed when Uncle Julian's new sphinxes are built," Tansy said, gazing at the pyramid.

Martin nodded. "An unforgettable landmark," he said, shading his eyes to look out to sea, where a frigate very like the *Lucina* was beating eastward for Portsmouth.

"Do you miss the navy?" Tansy asked anxiously.

He shook his head. "Not enough to rejoin, if that is your fear. Besides, I have estates to run now, and retainers for whom I am responsible. I can't do that if I'm sailing around the Mediterranean."

"When are we leaving for Sanderby Park?" Sanderby Park was in Westmorland, and it seemed very far away.

"Next week. It is all arranged." He reached across to put his hand on hers. "If you do not like it there, we will not live there."

She summoned a smile. "I'm sure I will be happy wherever we are."

"I adore you, Lady Sanderby."

"And I adore you, my lord."

Martin glanced down the hillside toward the house.

"I wonder if Sir Julian and his new fiancée have progressed in their battle with the hieroglyphs?"

"I do hope so, for they have both become quite unbearable about it."

Sir Julian and Hermione, who were to celebrate nuptials of their own in the fall, spent every possible hour studying the inscriptions on the slab of black basalt, and when they were not poring over that, they were absorbed by the mysteriously joined papyrus instead. They talked of little else, and if the conversation at dinner shifted at all, it was merely to other aspects of Ancient Egypt. There was no doubt indeed that they would regard it as a calamity of the highest order if someone else solved the mystery first.

Tansy smiled again. "Shall we try to prevent them mentioning Egypt at dinner tonight? Just to be a little wicked? I love to see them squirm because there is only the one thing on their minds and they haven't the time or patience to discuss anything else."

"You are a minx, Lady Sanderby."

"True."

They were about to ride on home when a metallic sound made them both look down the steps to the entrance to the pyramid. Ozzy and Cleo got up swiftly and uttered little mews. Their ears were pricked, and their bodies quivered with interest.

"What was that?" Martin asked.

"I don't know. It sounded like . . ." Tansy shook her head. "It can't be, because I know I left it on the mantel in our room."

"The figurine?"

"Yes."

"Oh, Tansy, since when has where it was left had any bearing on things? I think we should investigate."

He dismounted, and then reached up to help Tansy down as well. Hand in hand they went down the steps, preceded by Ozzy and Cleo, who were impatient for them to open the door, but it opened anyway, as if someone inside were about to welcome them all.

Tansy's steps faltered a little nervously.
"Martin . . ?"

"Come on, I have a feeling that everything is all
right," he said, and led her into the room where she
had been held prisoner a few months earlier.

The bright May sunlight flooded in from behind
them and fell directly on the wall opposite. Once again
there was a painting there, but not of King Osorkon
and his cat. Instead they found themselves looking at
Tel el-Osorkon as it had once been, with the statue
of Bastet crowning the hill.

Tansy's fingers curled tightly in Martin's, and she
knew she was holding her breath but couldn't help
herself. Something rolled across the floor. It was the
bronze cat, and it came to rest between Ozzy and
Cleo, who were crouching in front of the painting,
their bellies to the floor, their heads lowered.

"What's going to happen?" Tansy whispered,
shrinking closer to Martin, who pulled her to him.

"I don't know," he replied; then they both took
involuntary steps backward as the painted statue of
Bastet came to life. The goddess stepped down from
her throne, and from the wall itself, an elegant, graceful, cat-headed woman in the robes of Ancient Egypt,
with kittens playing about her feet. She bent to take
the figurine from the floor, then turned to place it at
the very spot where Amanda had first trodden on it.
Then she looked down at Cleo and beckoned. Cleo's
ears pressed lower, and she didn't move. She was the
picture of wretchedness.

"Oh, no!" Tansy cried then, suddenly understanding
that the goddess was summoning her attendant back
to Tel el-Osorkon. "Please don't take her! She's happy
here with us, and with Ozzy!"

Bastet straightened, her amazing feline eyes looking
directly at Tansy, whose heart was thumping so much
that she was sure it could be heard. Time seemed to
hang, and then Bastet turned back toward the wall.
Accompanied by her throng of kittens, she returned

to Tel el-Osorkon and became part of the painting once more. Then the whole scene faded, until there was just the plain wall again. Ozzy and Cleo did not wait for the goddess to change her mind, but scuttled out of the pyramid as fast as their paws could carry them.

Still filled with wonder, Tansy turned to look at Martin. "Did that really happen?" she whispered.

"If it didn't, we shared the hallucination," he said.

"I wonder if anyone else will ever step on the bronze cat?"

He slipped his arms around her waist. "I think there is a definite chance, but as to whether another heir will ever be restored to the inheritance denied him by his wicked brother, well, that is another story. Although, there is Tusun, of course . . ."

"Yes! His uncle stole everything. Oh, I do hope Tusun goes to Tel el-Osorkon again. Martin, we must make sure that he does. When the war is over, we must return to Egypt, find Tusun, and tell him everything. If Bastet has replaced the bronze figurine, we must make Tusun tread upon it, and maybe it will all start again. Can we do that? Please say we can."

"Of course we can," he promised.

She linked her arms around his neck to kiss him, and the wonderful warmth that was conjured between them had no need of the bronze cat's magic.

# EXPLORE THE WORLD OF
# SIGNET REGENCY ROMANCE

## EMMA JENSEN

"One of my favorites, the best of a new generation of
Regency writers." —Barbara Metzger

## LAURA MATTHEWS

## BARBARA METZGER

"One of the genre's wittiest pens." —*Romantic Times*

To order call: 1-800-788-6262